# ~HAUNTED~

A Bridgeton Park Cemetery Book

BY OPHELIA JULIEN

Published by Ophelia Julien

* * *



*Original Cover Art by Carmen Elliott*



ISBN: 1-480158-10-0

*To Teresa Basile who first gave me voice, and to Char Biesenberger who couldn't wait another fourteen years but nearly needed to.*

The author wishes to thank:. Jay Eageny, former sergeant of the Glendale Heights, IL Police Department; Dr. William Ernoehazy, FAC,Emergency Medicine; the helpful staff at Sunny Ridge Adoption Agency; super-editors Peggy Tibbetts and Hanley Kanar; amazing advisors Norm Cowie, Terri Reid (thank you for the bonus words, Terri!), and Michelle Sussman with a shout-out to Deb Deutsch for facilitating. All structural, grammatical and proofing errors are the author's. And thanks to my own group of personal cheerleaders -you know who you are! Couldn't do this without you!

***Fifteen years earlier…***

*The four-year-old girl looked up and saw Uncle Tee stepping through the front door and coming toward her, her mother a little behind him. She knew Uncle Tee and she liked him. Sometimes he brought pizza, and sometimes he brought her a toy or a box of animal crackers.*

*"I have something to show you," he said. His voice was always soft and gentle and he made her feel safe. She was never afraid of him. "I have a question for you," he added.*

*She put down her crayon and looked at him.*

*He placed a picture on the small table where she sat drawing. It was a big, color picture of a schoolgirl, not much older than she herself was, but old enough to wear the royal blue jumper from the school two blocks away, and to have rainbow barrettes in her hair. She had happy blue eyes, and a missing front tooth. The little girl didn't know the girl in the picture, but she felt the tug as soon as she looked at the face smiling up at her.*

*Uncle Tee cleared his throat. "Her name is Kelly," he said. "What do you think?"*

*She touched the picture gently, running one small, pudgy finger along the girl's cheek. An answering darkness came to her. A darkness and a quiet. "Dead," she said.*

*Uncle Tee's face became sad and he looked down at his shoes for a moment. But he nodded and patted her hand once or twice. "Thank you," he said.*

*"Get out of here." Mom was mad, really mad. The girl could tell by the way her mother talked, using her loud and "hurting"*

*voice. The voice that hurt the girl's ears and stomach and made her want to cry. "Get out and don't come back."*

*"I won't," he answered, his voice soft as always. He turned back to the girl. "Good-bye," he said. "Be a good girl for your mom."*

*She looked at him and wanted to smile but there was so much sadness on his face, and her mother was so mad, that she thought she must have done something very bad. She started to cry.*

*"You're upsetting her! Just go," her mother ordered.*

*Uncle Tee never came back.*

# ~ CHAPTER ONE ~

No one knew exactly who started the Thursday night ghost stories, or when. They had been a staff tradition at The Poet's Corner Bookstore since Cassie Valentine had started working there in the spring, and now in the dark afternoons of early autumn, the stories were more appropriate than ever. The days were getting shorter and at times there was just the slightest bite in the evening wind, hinting at colder days and nights ahead. Sometimes, as she was pulling the outside bookrack back into the store, preparing to close up for the night, she could catch just a whiff of smoke from someone's fireplace a block or so away.

Dark coming earlier made her sad, made her think of autumn just a year ago and the last time she had seen Daniel's living smile, and then her memories leap-frogged even further back to when her own life held a rainbow of possibilities and the future could still look both bright and exciting. Back to when she had first met him, and her schedule meant classes during the day and Daniel's warm strength and affection in the evenings and on the weekends. The memories hurt and she pushed them away, focused on getting a good grip on the slippery metal corners of the outside bookrack.

Tonight the wind was blowing in strong gusts, scattering sprinklings of leaves across the sidewalk, snatching at the long locks of Cassie's hair and whipping them into her face as she wrestled the metal rack back through the front door of the shop.

Nick Borja came to help her, and then she had his black ponytail blowing into her face as well.

"You're not helping," she said, half-joking, half complaining.

Nick ignored her and shouldered the door wider, tugging the case backward with her until it was in its overnight position just in front of the display window. "Ingrate," he said with a grin. The smile made his eyes crinkle. "Think Steve's got the room set up already?"

They both looked toward the back where Steve Crawford, the owner of the bookstore and their boss, was shelving stray children's books. Fredo Donardo, store manager and Steve's second-in-command, was shutting up the receiving room. May Parrish and Mark Hemmler, two regular customers who came into the store to visit as often as they came in to make purchases were also included in the ghost story sessions and were standing at the coffee nook talking quietly.

They looked at each other and shrugged. "I'll go set up the tea and the hot chocolate," he said.

"Don't eat all the cookies!" Cassie called after him. She went back to the cash register and began tidying up the counter space, re-hanging bookmarks that had slipped off their pegs, sorting through the inevitable pile-up of discarded receipts, book-order slips, and the scraps of paper filled with Nick's sketches. Those she put aside in case he came looking for them later.

She was startled when the door opened again and a gust of wind scattered all her neatly piled papers onto the floor. Annoyed, she bent to scoop them back up, rose, and then stopped abruptly as she realized with a small shock who it was that had just walked into the shop.

*Michael Penfield.* The name sprang into her mind without conscious effort, even though she hadn't seen him in at least four years, maybe five. At that time, both of them on the brink of starting high school, he had been only slightly taller than she was and she hadn't needed to look up to meet the mischievous brown eyes, or smile back at his own infectious grin. But that had been years ago.

The young man who entered the shop now was well over six foot tall, with strong shoulders and powerful-looking hands. His hair, a brown mop with stray curls falling across his forehead, was the same. But the expression on his face was one she didn't recognize at all.

He looked serious, way too serious for the Michael she remembered. Even grim. There was a scar that started at his left eye and traced its way down the side of his face, tugging at the outer corner of his lip before slipping down his jaw to his neck and disappearing into his collar. He had a backpack slung over his shoulder but despite his casual stance, one hand hanging onto the pack, the other tucked into the front pocket of his jeans, Cassie noted an undercurrent of tension in his posture.

He looked at her and though she saw a flicker of recognition in his eyes, it was gone the next moment and all thoughts she had had of running around the counter and giving him a welcoming hug went with it. He frowned at her slightly. "Cassie Valentine?" he asked.

"Michael Penfield," she replied and couldn't help smiling, but it faded when he didn't return the greeting. "What are you doing here?"

"I work here, now. You, too?"

"Since last spring. How did you–"

"Mike! Glad you could make it!" Steve came forward and reached out his hand. Michael shook it reluctantly. "Come on in and get comfortable. I think you're really going to like ghost story night here." Steve whisked the young man off in the direction of the break room and Cassie stared after them in disbelief.

Nick joined her at the register. "Ah, I see our new hire is

here for the festivities."

"You knew?" Cassie looked at him.

"Well, yeah. Steve hired him yesterday while I was here. You weren't," he added pointedly.

"Why didn't you tell me?"

"I did. I said at lunch today that a new guy was coming in. You were too busy reading to do more than grunt."

Cassie reflected back and realized Nick was right. *A new guy* was exactly what he had said. But the phrase, even as she shrugged it off, had conjured up another Fredo or even another Steve. Somehow, she hadn't been expecting someone the same age as she and Nick. She certainly hadn't been expecting Michael.

She followed Nick into the break room where the others had already taken their seats. Steve never sat at the head of the table, preferring the chair closest to the back wall. "Closest to the microwave," he said. Steve thrived on tea and hot chocolate.

Fredo was just settling his large frame into the chair at the head of the table; the seat was always his just for practical purposes. It was the roomiest accommodation available. Fredo was a big man, not overly tall, but stocky, with black hair going to gray in patches around his head. Nick teased him mercilessly about that and would duck away, laughing, from the playful but stinging *whack!* Fredo would land on him if he could.

May Parrish, the store's unofficial grandmother and a loyal customer, sat adjacent to Fredo, a fragrant cup of tea in front of her. She had a small plate for cookies as well. May was the only who bothered with that sort of nicety. Nick, who sat on her left, simply cadged cookies in two's and three's from the plate as it went around and held them in his hand as he ate.

Michael had parked himself uneasily on one of Steve's sides, his backpack on the floor beside him. He took an oatmeal cookie from the plate and had a mug of hot chocolate in front of him.

He looked out of place and uncomfortable, just this side of miserable, and Cassie felt a fleeting wisp of pity for him. Steve must have told Michael that the new hire traditionally told the story for that evening.

Mark Hemmler, the other regular customer, sat on Steve's other side at the far end of the table, blowing on a cup of coffee as he and Steve argued about the novel that occupied the number one spot on the *New York Time*'s bestseller list.

Cassie took the chair on the corner as she always did, partly because she was usually the last to sit down, and partly because she was the smallest person there and didn't mind sitting at the corner.

Steve smiled at her as she settled down. "We're all here," he said. "Got a good one for us Mike?"

"You know I don't believe in this nonsense," Mark began.

"You always say that, and yet you always stay," Steve said. The exchange was the official opening of the evening round. "Tell us a juicy one, Michael. There's a storm coming. I want to lie awake in bed tonight, listening to rain and thunder, and worrying that the creaking on my stairs is actually footsteps."

Michael cleared his throat uneasily. "This is the first one that comes to mind," he said. His voice was quiet, quieter than Cassie had ever heard him speak, and she wondered again at the change in him since they last saw each other. She looked at him curiously and he met her glance and looked away immediately. "It's short and maybe not all that scary, but it's true."

"True. That's the operative word," Steve said. He took a chocolate chip cookie and bit into it. "Have at."

Michael was silent a moment, gathering his thoughts. "This happened years ago," he said finally. "When I was a kid. My family and I used to go to a cabin on a lake every summer for two weeks. There were boats and wave runners, and you could fish, or water ski, or just swim off the dock, whatever you wanted. And every year, the same people came back at the same time, so we all hung around together for those two weeks and got to know each other. Especially the kids."

Cassie felt a prickle of uneasiness. She and her mother had been two of those people who went back to that lake at the same time every summer, and it was there that she had become acquainted with Michael. She tried to catch his eye again, but he refused to look at her.

He took a sip of hot chocolate before continuing.

*The lake was up in Wisconsin, close to a bunch of small towns, a fairly rural area. There was an old cemetery not far from the dock and all the cabins dating back to the time when the region was farmland. It was no longer in use. The graves had dates from the 1800's; some of them as far back as 1840. With its overgrowth of grass and weeds, abundance of grasshoppers and lightning bugs at night, and the wide open spaces despite the scattering of tilted and tumbledown tombstones, the cemetery was a place that children visiting the lake could not leave alone.*

*Michael knew, even as a boy, that prowling around the graves in the dark was stupid. Both poison oak and poison ivy grew in abundance. At dusk, mosquitoes rose in clouds, whining and biting as the children slapped them away. But every summer, a whole gang of them would wind up at the cemetery at least once, and always after dark. There was a group of five or six that always went: Michael and his brother, Benny; a pair of cousins who had a cabin down the road from the Penfields; and one girl. There was always one girl who went on that annual outing.*

Fredo interrupted. "Was she okay or a priss?"

"Okay," Michael said without any hesitation. "She could play softball with the best of us and was better at climbing trees than I was. She didn't even mind bugs or snakes."

Cassie felt her face growing warm and hoped no one else had noticed. She took a sip of chocolate to hide her discomfort.

*The last summer before the Penfields stopped going to the lake, the children made their customary trek to the graveyard. The night was darker than usual, storm clouds rolling in from the west, eating away at the stars that were just beginning to appear. In a short time, the moon would also vanish. But the children grabbed flashlights to stave off the night and ran off along the dusty road. As usual, the boys began a rough and tumble game that was somewhere between catch and dodge ball, but the girl wandered off by herself to read the gravestones.*

*Michael thought reading gravestones was about as entertaining as writing essays, but he eventually dropped out of the game and came to see what had caught her attention. Playing catch in the dark was idiotic.*

"Boys are stupid," Cassie interjected suddenly. She wanted to laugh out loud as she remembered those evenings in the cemetery. For one brief second, Michael looked at her and she saw the familiar sparkle of humor in his brown eyes. She had made the same comment to him frequently enough all those summers in Wisconsin.

"Hey!" Nick said. "Let the man speak."

Michael continued.

*The girl was standing at a monument for a family named Johanssen, and when he came up to her she pointed out the names and dates listed at the bottom. "Look," she said. "This whole family died in 1847. I wonder if it was small pox or something like that since everyone in the family died so close together. The father passed away first. Do you think they found each other after death?" she asked. "On the other side?"*

*That was too weird a topic for Michael to consider so he just shrugged in response.*

*She got weirder. "I come to this grave because it feels safe," she said. "Like the dad is still here. Sometimes I feel like he watches us while we're playing."*

*Michael felt a chill run up the length of his spine, the hairs on the back of his neck rising with a nasty tingle. He shrugged again, trying to stop the feeling, and called for everyone to start heading back. It was getting darker and the rain was definitely coming.*

*The other children went back to their cabins, but the girl followed Michael and Benny to the Penfield cottage where they sat around the table eating ice cream bars and playing cards.*

Michael paused, and Cassie found herself holding her breath. She remembered the whole evening well enough, playing cards with the brothers, being annoyed that it was so hot that the ice cream and chocolate shell began to melt off the stick and drip onto the table. She even remembered that wistful conversation with Michael, perhaps thinking about her own father at the time.

But she hadn't known there was a ghost story from that night. She looked at Michael's face as he stared down at the table, his voice growing softer and softer as he continued the story.

*While the other two played cards, Michael was startled to see that there was a man standing behind the girl's chair. The other two did not seem to notice, but Michael saw the man clearly. And the man saw Michael. He smiled and nodded at the boy.*

*"Hey, what did you say was the name of that family in the cemetery? The one where they all died around the same time?"*

*"Johanssen," she answered. "Why?"*

*"What do you suppose the dad looked like?"*

*She answered promptly, not at all surprised that Michael would ask for a description. "Like a farmer. And he had a dark beard that was almost long enough to touch his collar. He had nice eyes. Friendly eyes."*

*She closed her own as if trying to remember every detail. "He probably wore a blue shirt with patches on it, with a pipe sticking out one of the pockets, and for some reason, I think he has a scar across the back of his hand. A big one, like something huge cut him there." She shrugged. "I don't know why. I just picture him like that."*

Michael swallowed and hesitated. "And the person she described was the person I could see behind her chair," he said. "The beard, the patched shirt with a pipe in the pocket, even the huge scar across the back of his hand. He disappeared while I was looking at him."

There was silence around the table and then Cassie shivered. "It's a true story?" she asked.

"You know it," Michael replied, voice even. This time he didn't look away from her.

Cassie blinked and turned away first. She picked up her mug of chocolate and drained the last of it, not sure what to make of Michael's tale. Until recently, she had never thought of herself as being a character in a ghost story, especially with the strong skepticism her mother voiced at home.

"That was a good story," Steve said at last, interrupting Cassie's introspection. "I liked it. Not horribly scary, but just enough detail to be true. Welcome aboard, Michael. Well told."

Michael dipped his head in acknowledgement and began eating his cookie.

Nick, who had apparently been working through something in his head, said, "So what you're saying is that this girl described a dead farmer *you* were seeing?"

"Yes."

"And that this dead farmer followed you from the cemetery to the cabin?"

"That'd be what I was saying."

"Yikes! I can see haunted houses and cemeteries. But one following you around? And someone else describing him for you? Dude, that's disturbing."

Michael nodded. "Yeah, it is. And you want to hear something else? When the girl left our cabin to go back to her own, I saw him turn up again and follow her down the road. He watched until she went inside and closed the door, then he faded away like before."

"Shut *up*," Nick said. "That's *just disturbing*."

Cassie found it equally disturbing, especially since she had no idea the event had ever happened. She was about to rise from the table, meaning to rinse out her mug and then take her leave. Her mind was spinning with the story, Michael's abrupt appearance, and the inevitable thoughts of Daniel, and she wanted to go home. But then May Parrish leaned forward to say something. Cassie sat back in her chair.

The old woman capped the evening for them. "Talking about them, reading about them, it attracts them, you know."

"What, ghosts?" That was Mark Hemmler, being his usual skeptical self.

May nodded at him, her eyes both serious and serene behind her glasses. "Oh, yes. Of course. Talk about them, read or write about them, and they'll come to you. Like it or not, they'll all come to you."

There was another moment of silence, broken at last by Nick. "Hey, Steve. Happy sleeping tonight."

# ~ CHAPTER TWO ~

Eloise was waiting for Cassie when she arrived at home, sitting on the top step of the front porch, arms clasped around her knees. Eloise Janks had been Cassie's closest friend through high school. They had found each other in second period math, freshman year.

Eloise looked like an escapee from a yard sale gone horribly wrong. When short striped sweaters had been the fashion, she had worn hers with bright red plaid skirts, white crew socks, and black high-top Keds. She had rolled her jeans to mid-calf for years, and when the shorter pants length became the trend, had switched to ankle-length skirts and saddle shoes obtained off the Internet.

She frequently wore a head scarf and usually sported a temporary tattoo because she liked the idea of getting one but had not yet found an image she wished to make permanent. Today's choice was a dragon that was crawling up the side of her neck and partway onto her face.

"I got it wrong," she admitted to Cassie, who had complimented the tattoo when she was close enough to see. "If you get too close you'll notice his wing is crooked and it looks like his neck is broken." Cassie couldn't find the flaws even after inspection under the porch light. To round out the effect, Eloise had painted her long nails dark green with gold tips.

"It's getting cold out here," Cassie said. "And it's starting to smell like rain. Why didn't you just go in? You have a key."

Eloise shivered and looked around herself. "I hate your house. You know that."

They pushed through the front door after Cassie unlocked it and Eloise made a beeline for all the light switches.

"Hey, calm down! My mom will have a fit at the electric bill." Cassie turned off half the lights Eloise had flipped on. "So if you hate my house so much, what are you doing here?"

"Nick called and said the new guy came into the bookstore tonight and told a story."

"Yeah, so?"

"Nick also said that he sensed something between you two."

Cassie rolled her eyes at her friend and headed for the kitchen, Eloise trailing her. Nick had once been Cassie's date before they decided they liked each other much better as buddies. He had eventually wound up with Eloise, and the two of them together were bigger gossips than any six old women Cassie could think of.

Cassie wasn't ready to discuss the confusion she felt at seeing Michael after so many years, or the fact that the story he told had been about her, so she went for the superficial. "So Nick sensed something? What exactly does that mean?"

"I have no idea. That's why I'm here."

"I'm having soup. Want some?"

"Sure. And grilled cheese."

"This isn't *Denny's*. But okay, grilled cheese." She opened the can of soup and put it in a microwave dish to heat. She would make the sandwiches first. "So what else did Nick say?"

"Just that the story this guy -Michael? Is that his name?"

"Michael Penfield."

"Nick said the story Michael told was moderately scary. A girl who could describe a ghost she wasn't even seeing? And the idea of being followed around by a dead person." She shivered again. "I really hate your house."

"Why? Do you think there are dead people following you around in here?"

"Shut up. Don't say that." Eloise got plates and bowls from the cupboard along with soup spoons, and put them on the table with a stack of paper napkins.

Cassie stopped clattering around with the butter and the bread and looked at her friend. "You do, don't you? Think there are dead people following you around in here?"

"You said it, not me."

"But do you?" Cassie persisted.

"I don't know." She blinked once or twice. "But you're changing the subject. What about Michael?"

"What about him?"

"Come on. Nick's almost always right about you when it comes to hunches. Wasn't he right about the job at the bookstore?"

"Well…"

"So give already. Tell me about Michael."

Cassie finished making the first sandwich and started on the second, hitting the button on the microwave to warm up the soup at the same time. "Michael Penfield. Actually, Nick was right about one thing–"

"I knew it!"

Cassie ignored her. "Michael and I know each other from a long time ago, when we were little kids. Our families used to vacation up at the same lake in Wisconsin so we saw each other every summer."

"For real? How old were you?"

"Maybe six or seven, around that age when we first met. We were there for a bunch of summers in a row. I think the last time I went up I was twelve. Same age as Michael." She stopped a moment before flipping the sandwich on the griddle. "Funny thing, though. Right after eighth grade, I ran into him at the mall. He was shopping with his family and he told me that they were going to move here from Ohio. He got my phone number, but he never called. I figured they didn't move here after all."

"Really? And now he's working at the bookstore with you?"

"Yeah. He's changed a lot since that last time."

"Well, it's been five years since we were in eighth grade."

"No, I don't just mean that he grew up. And boy, did he. He got really tall and big. You know, buff chest and shoulders, and really strong-looking hands."

"Ooooh. That sounds like a good thing."

"Well, he's good-looking, but he always was. Even when we were kids. I used to have a big crush on him, but I never would have admitted it. No, but something happened to him since then. He's really quiet, now, almost reserved. I think telling that story tonight was kind of hard for him, but you know Steve and his traditions." After a moment she added, "Plus he's got this scar on his face."

As expected, Eloise was fascinated. "Scar? Where?"

"It starts up by his left eye and goes all the way down his face, even down his neck. His collar hides the rest of it, but I wouldn't be surprised if the scar reaches down to his shoulder."

"I gotta see this guy."

Cassie smiled. "But he's different. Michael was always goofy. You know, the loud and really funny type. But not now. He barely acknowledged me when we first saw each other, even though I know he recognized me."

And then there was the story. She didn't tell Eloise the details, and apparently for all his *sensing*, Nick didn't realize that the girl in the story had been Cassie. She wondered why Michael had chosen to tell that particular ghost story, or that he even agreed to tell one at all. And she wondered about her own apparent ability to describe someone she had never seen. But that thought she filed away for later.

They ate in silence for a while and as usual, when Eloise was finished nibbling at her food, she began crumbling the remaining crust from her sandwich into bits, scattering the crumbs around the plate. *Nervous eater and half-lunatic*, Nick had once described her.

Cassie smiled at the thought and wiped her mouth with her napkin. "So do you want to hang around and watch a movie or something?"

"No. I gotta get out of here. You know how this place is after dark."

"Yeah, *I* do, seeing as how I live here. What exactly are *you* talking about?" Cassie knew very well what Eloise was talking about –the creak and movement of furniture in empty rooms, the sudden breezes that rushed past them when all the windows and doors were shut– but she loved to tease her friend about it.

The answer was a short *look*: impatience, exasperation. "I'll help you tidy up and then I gotta go," she said again. As soon as she stopped speaking, there was the sound of a chair being moved in the living room, scraping across the hardwood floor. They both knew from experience that nothing would have moved, and no one would be in the room. "I *really* gotta go," Eloise repeated.

Cassie stopped her with a sudden hand on her arm. "What if it were Daniel?" she asked softly.

Eloise's rigid posture melted and she looked at her friend. "God, I wish for you that it was. I wish he were here for you, if that would help."

A lump formed in Cassie's throat and she nodded. Eloise had never met Daniel, but she knew all about him, all about the three and a half months that had turned Cassie's world upside down and left her in deep mourning through all the long fall and winter, and even into the spring.

"Hey." Eloise took Cassie's hand and squeezed it. "If it is Daniel, then I guess there really is nothing to be afraid of."

"Nothing," Cassie agreed. "And he'd love it if you stayed."

Eloise managed to hang on through half a movie before the small sounds in the kitchen and the upstairs, the drafts of cold air that wafted through the living room and stirred the ends of Cassie's hair, and the heavy feeling that they were not alone as they sat and watched TV, became too much. "If it's Daniel," she said, "he needs to learn to be more subtle while we're trying to watch a show."

Cassie smiled as she walked her friend to the door. "Daniel thought watching a movie was almost the same as a church service."

Eloise thought about the implications and looked at her friend's face closely. "And you're still not afraid? Even if it's not him?"

"No. It's just noise. Just a breeze every now and then. Nothing's ever tried to hurt me. And it doesn't feel threatening. I'm okay."

"Well, call me if you need me. When's your mom getting home?"

"She's usually back by ten."

"I don't know how you can stand it." Eloise dug her car keys out of her purse. "Seriously. Call me if you need to."

"I'm fine. Talk to you tomorrow. "

"See you."

Cassie watched as her friend got into her car and drove away, then shut the front door and locked it. She knew she was never alone in the house, even when her mother wasn't home. It had required some getting used to, but it no longer bothered her. She wasn't sure that he was, but the thought that perhaps Daniel was still with her always made her feel better.

# ~ CHAPTER THREE ~

Michael knew he would have the house to himself that evening, and he relished the thought. He ignored the light switch in the hall. It was dark but sometimes dark just suited him better anyway. He locked the front door behind him and then took the stairs down to the basement two at a time.

The basement was his lair. Half of it was concrete floor and rough wooden storage shelves, a washer, a dryer, and a furnace. Michael's weight bench also lived in that half. But the other part was carpeted and painted, track-lit and wired for music and movies with his sound system, his computer, and his TV stand. Tonight he chose the loudest, rudest music he owned, cranked the volume up to brain-numbing, and headed for his weight bench. His mind felt cluttered and somehow stung. He wanted the thoughtless oblivion of a hard workout. He tossed his backpack into a corner, stripped off his shirt, and settled down to it.

Forty minutes later he still wasn't happy. He had been blind-sided at the bookstore and he hadn't quite gotten over the shock of it. More than that, he couldn't believe he chose to tell that story. He had never spoken about what he had seen that evening up at the cabin to anyone, including Cassie, and now here he was spilling his guts to a bunch of strangers. And to Cassie herself. She hadn't seemed particularly alarmed that she had once described a ghost that *he* was seeing, but then Cassie had always been polite, if not gracious. Starting a commotion in the break room about his story would have been out of character. In the end, though, who knew what she was really thinking?

He frowned at the memory as he toweled the sweat off of his face and arms with his discarded shirt, picturing her behind the counter, picking up those scraps of paper and then turning around and seeing him. She had been as shocked as he was, but the recognition had been simultaneous. He understood the sudden light in her eyes, saw the beginnings of her wide smile as she regarded him. And he had squashed the welcome even before it started. Safer that way. Cassie had known him *before*.

He buried his face in his shirt for a moment longer, waiting for the feeling to pass. The feeling had everything to do with conscience, if he cared to admit it to himself, because of what he had seen in her face. She had been all set to renew the friendship on the spot, as soon as she laid eyes on him.

And why not? They had been good enough summer friends, he supposed, all those annual vacations at that lake in Wisconsin. They probably could have continued that through high school, had Michael chosen. Maybe even gotten to be more than friends. But no, he reminded himself. That choice had been taken out of his hands. He told his conscience to back off; he hadn't done anything wrong. He had been polite.

But then there was the matter of the story. She had teased him, too, right in the middle of it. *Boys are stupid.* He heard it in her young woman's voice and he heard it in her eight-year old voice as well. The teasing had felt the same and he warmed to it even as he pushed the memory of it away. Proximity to Cassie could be dangerous. And now here he was, working with her at the same store.

He rose from the weight bench and went to the basement bathroom, blinking against the sudden harsh lights above the mirror that blazed to life as soon as he flipped the switch. As usual, the scar caught his eye first although there were rare times that he barely noticed it. Most days, he couldn't help staring at it. It had defined the left side of his face for years now, but he still couldn't get used to it. Or everything it represented.

He had noticed Cassie looking at it but somehow that hadn't embarrassed him. She had been staring at him, his whole face, and her eyes had taken in the scar but hadn't lingered. She hadn't stared at it with the same morbid curiosity so many of them did. She hadn't winced away from it like some of the others. She had simply looked at it and then gone right back to looking into his eyes.

Now, *that* memory caused him to cringe a little. Cassie didn't seem to have changed. She still seemed lively and inquisitive, quick-minded and good-natured. He had seen that during their time together that evening.

After a moment, he hung the hand towel over the mirror so that he couldn't see his own reflection any longer, and braced himself with a brisk shower. The water soothed the throbbing in his neck and shoulder.

Later, clad in clean sweatpants, an old tee, and a hooded sweatshirt, he sat out on the front porch in the dark autumn night, closing his eyes and listening. The voices didn't come that night. They never did. But he couldn't bring himself to stop waiting for them. He could not bring himself to stop.

# ~ CHAPTER FOUR ~

Michael ran in and out of Cassie's thoughts in a troubling way, from his bleak expression even when he smiled to the darkness in his eyes. He was so watchful when he spoke, as if he had to measure every word before saying it. He had grown into an attractive young man, and when they had been in the break room together after his story, she noticed that he still had that clean smell she remembered from all those years ago. She didn't know if it was the detergent his mother used, or the soap he lathered up with in the shower, but he always smelled fresh. She sighed at the thought of him. Michael was cluttering up her mind, squeezing in beside memories of Daniel, and all without even trying.

"Hello? Earth to Cassie."

She looked up and found her mother gazing at her from across the table, eating her lasagna and looking amused. "That's the fifth time you've sighed in the past twenty minutes," Lori Valentine said. "What's up?"

Cassie twiddled her fork for a moment, getting organized. "Do you remember Michael Penfield?" she asked at last.

Her mother frowned thoughtfully, an expression that barely wrinkled her brow. Lori Valentine was a young-looking, athletic dark-blonde woman with the requisite porcelain-fine skin and blue eyes. Cassie, all dark wavy hair and dark eyes, sometimes wondered at the fact that they were related. "The name rings a bell, but I can't place him."

"Remember all those summers we went up to the lake? He was the boy I used to play with all the time."

"Oh, I think I remember him. I remember the family. Michael was the one with that mess of brown hair, wasn't he? And a younger brother?"

"That's him."

"So what about him?"

"He lives here, now. And he just started working at the bookstore."

"You're kidding! What are the odds of that happening?"

"I know. He's actually lived here for a while. Nick told me he graduated from St. Thomas's High."

"Well, then it's nice you finally ran into each other."

"We should have run into each other a long time ago." Cassie reminded her mother about her unexpected meeting with Michael at the mall years earlier. "He never called me, though. And if he went to St. Thomas's, he did move here."

"Are you going to ask him about it?"

Cassie shook her head. "I don't think it's that simple. Something happened between then and now. Do you remember how he used to be? He was almost wild back then, silly and funny and loud. Now he's super-quiet and reserved, almost like talking is really hard for him. And he has a scar." She gestured to her own face. "It runs all the way down to his neck. And at least once I caught him wince when he moved, when he thought no one was looking."

"So he was hurt?"

"I think pretty badly. I don't think he wants to talk about it."

"That's his right, isn't it?"

"I wasn't going to bother him about it," Cassie said, a touch defensively. "But–"

"But you still want to know what's going on."

"Well…"

Mrs. Valentine laughed. "I'm sure you'll figure it out at some point. You always do. And he's someone–" she stopped abruptly, the expression on her face betraying a sudden flash of guilt.

Cassie stared at her levelly. "And he's someone who isn't Daniel?"

"Honey, I'm sorry."

"It doesn't matter. I should be past all that by now, right? Everyone seems to think so."

"I've never said that. I doubt anyone else has, either."

"No one has to say anything." Cassie looked down at her plate, half-angry and completely miserable. Mourning was her right.

Her mother was quiet a moment longer before making a stab at changing the subject. "Wasn't Eloise supposed to be here for dinner tonight?"

Cassie battled down the tangle of bitter feelings and tried to meet her mother halfway. "Yeah. She changed her mind when she found out we'd be eating late."

Mrs. Valentine raised her eyebrows in surprise. "I don't remember that ever being an issue."

"No, it's just the house," Cassie said without thinking and stopped. *Wrong thing to say.*

"And what about the house?"

*Great. From her own minefield into her mother's.* "Nothing. It's no big deal, Mom. She just couldn't make it." But it was too late and Cassie knew it as soon as she glanced at her mother's face. It was going to be one of those discussions. Where was Richard when she needed him? "So where's Richard tonight?" she asked, making one last effort to forestall what she could see brewing on the horizon.

"He had to go to Michigan for a seminar. Don't change the subject on me. What does Eloise think is wrong with this house?"

Inwardly, Cassie was rolling her eyes. *Nothing besides your everyday garden-variety haunting*, she wanted to say. Aloud she said, “She’s just not used to it, that’s all.”

“Oh? And what’s so hard to get used to?”

“Mom, let’s not talk about this.”

“Aren’t you the one who always wants to talk about this stuff? All those books and movies about it?”

“It’s just an interest,” Cassie said lamely.

“Honestly!” Her mother finally exploded and Cassie was actually half-relieved. The sooner she started the sooner it would be over. With luck, her mother wouldn’t even mention going back to school this time. “I’ve worked all these years to get us a nice place to live and now that we have it, you and your friends are so convinced there’s something wrong with it. Well, excuse me if we couldn’t get something a little newer or trendier.”

“Mom, it’s okay. The house is fine. I love it here.”

Her mother’s blue eyes were blazing. “But you’d be the first to say this place is– is–” She spluttered over the word.

Cassie couldn’t decide if it would be better to help out or let it go. She chose the former, to get everything out of her mother’s system sooner. “The place is haunted?” she suggested and cringed inwardly as she might if she had just lit the fuse on a stick of dynamite.

“There is nothing wrong with this house,” her mother stated firmly, stacking plates and gathering silverware from dinner. “Absolutely nothing.” She brought the dishes to the sink and deposited them with a crash to be rinsed and placed in the dishwasher.

Behind her, Cassie took a silent deep breath, even as a sudden breeze wafted through the kitchen and stirred the ends of her hair. She almost called out so that her mother could see this for herself, but the breeze ended as quickly as it had begun. Meanwhile, her mother rinsed plates and jammed them into the dishwasher furiously.

"Hey, Mom, I can do the rest. Why don't you go relax and read that new book you got yesterday?"

Mrs. Valentine turned around and fixed her with a blue glare. "You don't have to humor me. I'll finish. You can do the glasses and the baking dish."

"Sure. No problem." She stayed on in the kitchen after her mother stalked away, dutifully scrubbing out the glasses, and her hair stirred with the soft breezes that whispered past her as she worked.

## ~ CHAPTER FIVE ~

"Pay attention, now," Fredo said, expertly wielding a box cutter to open a shipment of paperback thrillers from New York. "This is the history of the store, and I tell this story to everyone Steve hires."

"And there will be a test later," Nick added as he sorted through packing slips.

Michael glanced at him and Nick mimed yawning and falling asleep. Michael grinned in answer.

Fredo ignored both of them. "This bookstore has been around since before World War II. A man named William H. Kendall started it–"

"Fredo's building him a shrine next spring. It's going to have color spot lights and a fountain."

"–and it passed to his son after the old man died." Fredo didn't miss a beat as he pulled stacks of books out of the box and ignored Nick's running commentary. "William's son, Bill Junior, ran the store until his death, but no one else in the family took his place when Junior finally died about fifteen years ago, so it became part of the Kendall estate until Prime Companies bought it a while back. They eventually sold it to Steve, and here we are."

"Happy as clams."

"When you get done with the packing slips, there are a bunch of orders on Steve's desk that need to be checked against the boxes in receiving." Fredo paused long enough to glare at Nick.

"Got it. But not until you finish the story. You're just getting to the good part." Nick looked at Michael. "The part with the sex and the violence."

Michael bit back a laugh.

"The folks here in town, from the Chamber of Commerce to the Historical Society were really worried about Steve taking over the store."

"They thought he might be selling contraband out the back door."

"Shut it, Nick. They were afraid he was either going to change the place into some trendy eatery or boutique–"

"Hollywood Steve's Glamour Wigs and Fashion Accessories."

"–or change the bookstore itself so much that they wouldn't be happy with it. But Steve just updated the building, fixed a couple of structural problems like the roof and a sagging foundation, and kept everything else the way it was. I think now everyone is pretty happy that he took over the place. It'd gotten tired and shabby, and he breathed new life into it. He put in that coffee nook at the back. He makes sure there're always cookies or scones and takes donations for them, but doesn't charge. And he changed the second office into a staff room for us. He even has that Scrabble game up in the corner."

"I noticed that," said Michael. "Who's playing?"

"Oh, it's not a real game. Everyone on staff just goes in and puts a word down when they feel like it, then replaces the tiles on the rack. Although sometimes we need to remove a word from the board that's not quite acceptable." He glared at Nick again.

Nick began whistling, expression completely innocent, stacking the last of the packing slips into a neat pile.

"You'll find Steve to be a pretty easy boss. I came to work for him before he opened the doors for business. Then he hired that one." He gestured at Nick with a sour expression, but

Michael could see a glimmer of amusement in the man's eyes. "Cassie came along last spring. And now there's you. Steve never advertises for staff. When someone asks him if he wants help or can be hired on, Steve decides if the store needs another pair of hands, and then he decides if the person asking would be a good fit. Obviously he liked you." He smiled at Michael. "I still don't understand about Nick, but Steve's the boss."

Michael saw Nick laugh to himself.

"We're pretty friendly around here," Fredo finished. "That's the way Steve likes it. And even though when we're busy we may not talk all that much, there aren't many secrets, either." He broke down the box, story and unpacking finished, and looked up. "Got any questions, Mike?"

"Maybe one," Michael said after thinking a moment. "What's up with the ghost stories?"

Fredo laughed. "I've been asking him the same question for a long time. He's had ghost story night nearly every Thursday since we opened for business." He shrugged. "Steve's always had a thing about ghosts and haunted places and stories of the unexplained. Go figure. He told me once he had a friend who had talent in that area, as he put it, and got him interested in other-worldly things, but he never really explained that. Guess it's one of the man's quirks."

Michael nodded. "I was just curious." He took a deep breath. "Guess I'm ready to go to work."

"Okay, then. Steve's got a couple things he needs you to sign, and then I'll swing by and let you know where we want you."

Michael was released shortly thereafter to his first full day on the job and was assigned to restocking the bestseller table. He couldn't help a bit of nervousness, and with Cassie coming in to boot, he felt a knot of apprehension growing in his midsection. He had really wanted this job, had loved the feel of the store as soon as he had entered it.

How on earth had he wound up in the same place as Cassie? He suppressed a groan, pulling open another box, and glanced up only to see her heading his way. This time, he allowed himself to groan aloud, only quietly and with his head halfway into the box he had just opened. In spite of his best efforts, he could feel himself getting yet tenser at her approach.

"Hey," she said.

He turned to look at her. "Hey," he replied, not very enthusiastically. He didn't know what else to say. She was wearing a pale blue sweater that enhanced the darkness of both her hair and her eyes. The light floral scent she used wafted across the space between them and he tried hard not to enjoy it too obviously.

He wished for just a moment that he could have been anyone else, just some guy who could walk up to a pretty girl who had huge dark eyes and smelled so sweet, and start a conversation. But that train of thought was useless. He busied himself unpacking books but was forced to look up when she continued to stand on the other side of the table.

"I wanted to welcome you to the job," she said. She smiled at him, friendly but a little shy. "Steve's a great guy to work for, and Fredo's a doll. Nick's a lot of fun when you get used to him. I'm only here part-time so you won't have to see me constantly. Lucky break for you," she added wryly. "But anyhow, welcome. And if you need anything, feel free to flag me down."

There was an awkward pause. "Thanks," he managed.

"No problem." She came around to him, placed a cool hand on his wrist, then surprised him by stretching up and kissing him on the cheek. "Just let me know." She headed to the front of the store, already engaging Nick in some inane conversation about whether or not *phat* belonged on the Scrabble board.

He wanted to touch his face where she had kissed him, but

was far too self-conscious to do it. He could still feel the soft pressure of her fingers against his wrist and how her hair had brushed his arm when she reached up to him. The simple gesture and his own mixed feelings left him in silent consternation.

He survived the day largely due to the fact that Steve had assigned him to stocking shelves after he had finished with the bestsellers. Fredo, who was handling receiving, sorted through all the boxes and Steve himself was entering inventory. It was Michael's job to cart boxes and stacks of books and place them according to Steve's direction: new hardbacks, new in paperback, genre, remainders, and magazines.

Michael liked the work; it was solitary and mindless once he understood Steve's system. Unfortunately, that left him plenty of time to think, and Cassie's greeting that morning was programmed into his head and set to perpetual replay.

Girls were no longer the great unknown to him. He had dated in high school, even seeing one girl in particular for a time during his senior year. Cassie, however, because she had known him when they were children, represented a much more complicated situation.

Sooner or later she would ask about his family. She had known them all, what with the summer vacations at the lake. And then he would have to tell her about the accident. His fingers tightened on the stack of books he held just thinking about it: the sound of the impact, the ensuing enormous silence, the pain, the confusion, the broken glass and the fire, and then his mother's voice telling him to move…

He touched the scar on his face briefly, without conscious thought. The scar marked his face and neck and traveled all the way down to his shoulder where it faded out. But there were other scars that mapped the left side of his torso, his hip, the upper part of his thigh. There had been broken bones and torn skin, at least one serous burn and too many surgeries to consider.

But the damage the accident had done to him on the outside was nothing compared to the tangled, ripped, and raw mess on the inside.

After endless weeks in the hospital, Michael had come to live with Grandpa Henry, still in pain, completely lost, shocked into a silence that stilled his voice for many more months. Outwardly he tried to keep up with his physical therapy and what schoolwork he could manage, and inwardly he tried to process the loss of his family and the life he had once known.

Grandpa Henry, his mother's father, had been a rock and an anchor, the first, last, and only person ever to see it when fifteen-year-old Michael finally went from granite and ice to quicksand and mist, weeping, flailing, and crying out in torrents of survivor's guilt and self-hatred on the tortured road to some kind of acceptance.

"You let it out, boy," Grandpa Henry would say when he found him in a jumbled, grieving heap in his room or curled up atop the bench on the front porch, placing a heavy arm around the bowed, shaking shoulders, rough calloused hand wiping the tears away occasionally. "You let all that poison out of you, good and proper."

After a while, hell had receded and a shaky, cautious Michael had emerged from his grandfather's house and from his own chrysalis. But this was no new awakening, no sun-glinted butterfly rebirth. This was a quiet, reserved, fiercely self-protective Michael who spoke rarely and laughed even less. He smiled when it was called for, but not quite from the heart.

He knew his grandfather watched him in silent worry and he tried his best to live up to the older man's hopes. He obediently attended classes, wrote for the school newspaper, brought home an acquaintance or two, even dated from time to time. But nothing claimed his heart or inspired the need for closeness. Loss seemed too probable.

He hadn't thought about Cassie during that time, and seeing her behind the counter the other day had brought all sorts of uncomfortable things to the fore. He had liked her all those years ago, and he would admit it to himself as he would never admit it to anyone else.

Cassie had been the highlight of all those family trips to the lake, a bright, warm, friendly girl who could keep up with him in everything from sports to horror movies. As noted, she wasn't afraid of insects or snakes or even bats, didn't care much about skinned knees or elbows, and actually didn't mind when his parents insisted that Michael bring annoying younger brother Benny along with him, wherever he was going.

And between summers, she had written him letters sometimes, funny, chatty things about school, movies, books, whatever captured her interest. He never bothered to write back, but it didn't mean he failed to appreciate her reaching out to him. When they had run into each other at the mall, he had even hoped–

Michael, emerging from his memories, found he was blushing as he shelved a never-ending supply of cookbooks, and his rational mind immediately kicked in and asked him what he had to be embarrassed about. Even now if he acknowledged that he still liked her, how was that an embarrassment? It was fact, for one thing. In addition, Cassie had grown up to be as pretty as her twelve-year-old appearance had suggested. Better yet, he sensed that she could still keep up with him in most things, still wasn't afraid of insects or bats, or worried about skinned knees or elbows. Or scars. He sensed she would gladly have kept company with both Penfield brothers. So no, he realized there was no need to rationalize any attraction he might feel towards her. But the thought of Benny brought him back to square one.

Sooner or later she would ask about his family and then he would have to tell her about the accident, about the whole horrible mess, including his own injuries. And would he then see pity in those lively brown eyes? Would she see him as he so frequently saw himself –as someone damaged and troubled and not much worth getting to know? And, jumping way ahead of himself, what if he won her –only to lose her somehow? Loss was not an adversary he cared to challenge again.

He glanced up to the front of the store where she was labeling specially-ordered books and alphabetizing them on the cashier shelf by customer name. Her hair swung freely with her movements and the expression of concentration on her face belied the animation he knew was her true nature. He remembered her kiss and for the umpteenth time he wished he could have just been some guy who could walk up to a pretty girl and start a conversation.

# ~ CHAPTER SIX ~

Cassie was well aware of Michael staring at her off and on as she worked at the cash register and he restocked shelves. She didn't know what to make of his behavior. Talk about mixed messages. He couldn't bring himself to smile at her, and yet he went and told everyone a ghost story about the two of them right off the bat. Of course, no one knew it was about both of them. It was almost like he was sending her a secret message, bringing up shared childhood memories. But what that message was, she had no idea. She sighed, vexed, and finished with the customer-ordered books.

"Getting to you?" Nick asked with a grin. He was standing at the other cash register, sketching as he always did during a slow moment, and he looked up at her with the grin still on his face, eyes crinkled up in mischief.

"What?"

Nick nodded out toward Michael, dutifully stacking cookbooks, picking up an impressive number of books at one time in his big hands.

Cassie felt herself coloring. "What about him?"

"Oh, give over already, Cass. This is your Uncle Nicky talking. I'll bet you desire the boy as much as he desires you."

"Nick, you are so full of –"

"Now, no need to be crude. Judging by the way you keep looking at him, I would guess you'd like to check out his muscles. And judging by the way he keeps looking at you, I would guess he'd just like to check you out. Period."

"Stop it."

"And that peck on the cheek this morning was perfect." He pulled his fingers together and kissed the tips, like an Italian chef praising the marinara sauce.

"*Stop it.*"

"On the other hand," he continued, completely ignoring her, "watching you two get together could have all the excitement of watching two porcupines get started."

"Nick!"

"Okay, okay, I'm just saying."

She could never really get angry at him. He was too silly. Still, he was almost always accurate in his observations, and she knew he was accurate about her. She guessed he was probably also on target about Michael.

But it was too soon.

So she told herself. She spent the rest of the day in a bit of a funk. On the one hand, there was Michael, large as life, shelving books and opening boxes, talking to Steve, occasionally hauling the cart out to receiving to give Fredo a hand. She hadn't seen him in years, but there was a familiarity to his stance, his movements. She remembered the tangle of brown hair that was forever falling across his forehead or the way he would stop and study what he was doing with a slight frown on his face. She had always liked him. He had been the best of summer friends all those years ago, and the memory of that tugged at her.

But then there was Daniel, the thought of him shadowing her throughout the day, constant in everything she did. The memories no longer stung every time his face popped into her mind or a particular mental snapshot of him appeared unexpectedly in her thoughts. But there were still times when she would find her eyes tearing up when something he had said came to mind, or if she allowed her very last memory of him to gain a foothold.

Standing behind the cash register, working half-heartedly at reorganizing the shelves below the registers while catching glimpses of Michael as he worked, tinted nearly every memory she had of Daniel with painful irony. She knew before her shift ended that she was going to go home to her room, shut the door, put on the saddest music she could find, and work on her List.

Michael caught her eye when she was leaving and gave her a little half-smile and Cassie waved back in return, her mind filled with Daniel's bright green eyes and the warmth of his arms when he held her.

For Michael, it was too soon. The words were still in her head that evening after dinner. Her mother was working late again, so Cassie was home alone. She made boxed macaroni and cheese, her favorite comfort food and a dish her mother loathed, then cleaned up the kitchen and went to her room and her computer to work on The List.

The List, something not even best friend Eloise knew about, was Cassie's last indulgence to herself regarding Daniel. This month was nearly a year, after all. A year, and she both remembered the date and shied away from it.

She booted up, went into her files, and opened the document, a list of facts she knew about him. Item one said *His name was Daniel Patrick Rhodes*. Item two said *I love him.* She had debated long and hard about the second one, deciding in the end to keep it in present tense. It was true. She suspected it would remain so: she would always love Daniel. Regardless of anything, or anyone, that might happen in her life, his place in her heart was permanent.

The List was meant both to comfort and remind her, and included such details as *His eyes were green* and *His height was six-foot-two* and *His all-time favorite dinner was homemade sloppy joes with potato chips, no vegetable in sight, and chocolate chip cookies for dessert*. Cassie knew these facts would keep him close and she was determined to capture every aspect of him that she could remember.

Sometimes when she wrote, she would remember suddenly how he smelled when she put her arms around him and snuggled into his chest, or how rapt his attention was when they would stream a movie and watch it. He had turned to her once and said, "Think of all the movies I'm going to miss." That memory, like others, came out of nowhere and lanced her with a quick, sharp pain, but she added the quote to her list as it occurred to her. It was item 79.

Item 80 stated *We met at the Donan Mansion at an art display*. It was such an obvious detail that she was surprised she hadn't included it earlier, but now that it came to her, she would put it in. She typed the words and slipped back to that time, a warm, sunny Saturday morning in early June.

*The display at the Mansion was formally titled "Illustrations of Children's Literature by Local Art Students." The suggested donation had been five dollars, and Cassie had slipped her money into the box and wandered into the first of the display rooms, captured immediately by what she saw. Nick had suggested she might like it and he had been right.*

*There were charcoal sketches, pen and ink drawings, paintings, and at least one sculpture, all based on children's literature. She gaped at a drawing of Meg and Charles Wallace from* ***A Wrinkle in Time****, smiled at a rough charcoal illustration of the Mad Hatter, dawdled at the brilliance of a detailed acrylic painting of Neverland.*

*She walked slowly through the four display rooms, impressed with all that she saw, wondering what it would be like to be able to render such work. Cassie had no ability in art. In the fourth room, she stopped in front of a large framed pen and ink drawing of all four March sisters posed with Beth at the piano.*

*She sat down on a convenient bench that was opposite the sketch so that she could further study the light and shadow expression on Jo March's face as she gazed at her younger sister, already looking frail but so happy as her fingers touched the keyboard. And then she became aware of Daniel as he made his way through the room.*

*He was tall, thin, shoulders hunched inward in a way that suggested not weakness, but a guarding against some sort of pain. He peered nearsightedly at the pictures, walking slowly, whether from rapt interest or necessity was unclear. He looked to be her own age, perhaps a year or so older, and Cassie studied him unabashedly as he read captions and studied details, frowning sometimes as if trying to make sense of something, smiling sometimes with an expression of such wonder on his face that she found herself guessing at what he could be thinking.*

*Eventually he turned and their eyes met. They stared at each other curiously and he smiled first, a smile so open and friendly that she grinned back. "Hey," she said in greeting.*

*He moved forward to where she sat, walking as slowly and carefully as he had when studying the pictures. "Hey," he replied. "Are you part of the display?"*

*"Sure. Guess what book I represent."*

*He opened his mouth once, twice, then laughed. "There's no way I can answer that without sounding rude."*

*She liked his laugh. "Cassie," she said, extending her hand. "Cassie Valentine."*

*"Dan Rhodes." They shook hands. "And why are you here? Are you an art student?"*

*"A friend who actually is an art student suggested it. I'm no artist but I like to read. He said a lot of my favorite kids' books were illustrated here. What's your excuse?"*

*"A way to get out." His tone suggested he had escaped recently from someplace dire. "May I?"*

*No one had ever asked Cassie's permission to share a bench and she was surprised and pleased. She patted the space beside her as an invitation.*

*He sat down with a sigh.*

*"Are you okay?" she asked. Up close he looked pale, as if his skin was stretched too thin across the bones of his face.*

*"Just a little tired."*

*"As suggested by your tee shirt?"*

*He looked down and squinted at the black lettering on his green shirt. Not Dead Yet. "I forgot I put this on," he said. "But I suppose you could say that." He leaned back against the wall and closed his eyes, and she stared at his profile.*

*Wispy, toffee-colored hair hung just over his forehead. He had long, dark lashes that curled. A nose that turned up just the slightest bit at the end. About two days' worth of stubble. A finely chiseled chin. He was, as Eloise would have put it, quite yummy. Cassie smiled to herself and turned to lean back against the wall beside him. She could feel the heat from his arm inches away from hers and she liked it.*

*After a few moments, he opened his eyes, bright green, and turned to her, smiling when he found her looking back at him. "Can I ask you out?" he said.*

*They dated cautiously, and the description was Cassie's as she told Eloise about him. "He's half aggressive and blunt, and half timid. I don't mean physically aggressive either, just kind of no-nonsense. He doesn't hesitate when he wants to ask me something. At the same time, I had to be the one to take his hand the first time and that was at the end of our first date. He seemed surprised when I did that." His hand had been warm and strong.*

*"If you're going to keep getting all moony like that, I'm going to puke," Eloise had said. Then, "When do I get to meet him?"*

*But Daniel was not eager to meet Eloise, or Nick, either.*

*"No, please," he said. "I'm not ready to be evaluated." And so Cassie had let it go.*

*On their fourth date, three dates after Cassie had decided she was in love, two weeks after they met at the Donan Mansion, he told her he had leukemia.*

Cassie typed item 87. *His favorite ice cream was cookies and cream.* Item 88. *He wore tee shirts that said Not Dead Yet, One Foot in the Grave, Buying the Farm, Circling the Drain, and Dead Man Walking.* Item 89. *He chose to be cremated in a black tee shirt with Another One Bites the Dust in gold letters.*

She noted that the ends of her hair were stirring in a light breeze that blew suddenly through her bedroom. It was cool and gentle against her cheek and she turned to face it, closing her eyes, until it stopped abruptly. She heard furniture shifting downstairs in the kitchen. Cassie knew her mother wasn't home yet, but the sounds coming from below didn't frighten her. "Daniel?" she whispered.

There was no answer.

## ~ CHAPTER SEVEN ~

Life at Poet's Corner Bookstore became less tangled for Michael by the end of his first week. Learning the systems –receiving, stocking, pulling, check-out, closing– was not difficult. Steve and Fredo were the patron saints of patience, and Michael was grateful for good-humored guidance, spiked occasionally by Nick's less then helpful observations. Still, Nick himself was easy to work with and didn't mind repeated questions or occasional screw-ups.

"You should have seen him when he first started," Fredo had said, tilting his head in Nick's direction. "But no matter how hard I tried, I couldn't get Steve to fire him."

Nick smiled widely. "I love you too, Fredo," he called from across the store.

For Michael, the wild card in the mix was Cassie. Not that she treated him any differently than anyone else. Cassie was always warm, always friendly. Her cheerfulness was tempered a bit from when he remembered her, but what the heck. He had changed a great deal himself so he would be the last to complain about it.

What kept him on edge around her were the odd moments when he would realize she was staring at him, sometimes from across the store, sometimes when he stopped in the break room to get a cup of cocoa or a cookie and she came in afterward. He tried smiling at her, saying "Hey" by way of greeting, even waving. She would reply, or not, and he never could predict what she was going to do. He couldn't figure her out.

Nick didn't help. "Ask her out," he would mutter when they

passed each other on the floor, Michael stocking, Nick carting crepe paper, string, stapler and yardstick, or some other odd article for his next display. After about the fifth time, Michael actually whacked him in the back as they passed each other, and Nick laughed as he walked away.

He probably would have made his move a lot sooner if he didn't feel like Nick, not to mention Fredo and Steve, were watching all of this unfold with undisguised interest. He felt as if he were suddenly back in school, and wondered idly if they were passing notes to each other when he wasn't looking. Or better yet, texting. So Michael did nothing except ignore them, especially Nick, and try to decipher whatever signals Cassie was sending his way. If she was sending any. Hell, maybe he was imagining that she was looking at him, although he didn't think he was.

After a while of keeping eyes and ears open, he realized Cassie had been involved with someone just a year earlier, and the way it looked to him, she wasn't over it yet. He could understand that. Still, she never went on a date, never took calls from any guys as far as he could see, never talked about anyone special. He wondered about it all.

When he had been at the store for a while, he decided he might as well find out where he stood with her. He found himself thinking about her and wondering what it might have been like had he called her when they were still in high school, had things been different. Maybe even if they hadn't.

They were scheduled for lunch at the same time that Friday, and he followed her out of the store to a pharmacy down the block. He could at least ask for her phone number and see how she reacted to that. He saw her heading to the back of the store, past the make-up and the hair care products, and he traced her steps to the magazine rack. And there she was, scanning through an article in some glossy celebrity gossip-type magazine. But she wasn't alone after all.

A young man stood just behind her, a little to the side, apparently reading over her shoulder. He was tall, as tall as Michael himself. He had wispy light brown hair and was dressed in jeans and a dark green tee shirt. The clothes seemed just a bit large on him, but Michael sensed strength despite the lanky build and the thin appearance.

As he stood there, stopped in his tracks, unsure what to do, the young man turned around and looked at him over his shoulder. His eyes were a bright green.

Michael blinked, still not sure what to do, and the thin young man smiled at him, a friendly and welcoming smile. He held his eyes for a few seconds, nodded, then turned back to Cassie and the magazine. *Weird*, Michael thought. Cassie seemed totally engrossed in whatever they were reading. Michael turned away and headed off to get his own lunch without speaking to either of them. He would talk to her later. Much later, since she still had a boyfriend.

Nick, of course, sensed Michael's apparent shift in attitude and called him on it the following Monday. At least he waited until they had gotten off work.

"So why don't you ask her out?" They walked together down the block from the bookstore. Michael was on his way to his car, Nick was heading for the health food store three streets over where Eloise worked.

"It's not that easy."

"Yeah, guess not. You and the porcupine." Nick had already given his friend the reference at an earlier date: Michael had not been amused. "My God, man, how difficult can it be?" he asked, resorting to the Hearty Voice of High Drama, complete with upper-class British accent.

Michael didn't answer right away. "And what about her boyfriend?"

"She doesn't have a boyfriend."

"Oh, I heard it's been about a year. I figure no one's asked her out since, and she's taken this long to get over him. What if he comes back?" Michael thought about the young man he had seen with Cassie. He seemed friendly enough. No point in being a complete jerk by trying to disrupt whatever they had going.

Nick stopped walking and favored Michael with a strange look. "What if he comes back?" he echoed. "That would be pretty tricky."

"Oh, yeah? Why?"

"Because he's dead."

"But...*what*?"

"He's dead. Daniel died last fall. He had leukemia. Cassie was a wreck, dude. She stopped out of school, putting everything on hold, and has never gone back. She didn't see anyone, not even Eloise, for a few weeks at least. And the grieving went on for months. That's why I finally brought her around to meet Steve. He needed the help, and so did she, actually. It worked out okay."

"But..." Michael was stymied. "*Dead*?"

"Yeah." Nick laughed at the expression on his friend's face, then stopped, uncertain. "You look like you've just seen a–"

Michael nodded slowly, emphatically. "I think I have. I think I've seen him with her." He swore Nick to complete silence and was surprised when Nick actually complied.

But Nick was troubled about what Michael told him, asking him for a description repeatedly. "Although it doesn't do any good," he added ruefully. "I don't know what he looked like. He never wanted to meet either Eloise or me."

"Why?" Michael found that puzzling. Why not meet Cassie's best friends?

Nick looked back down at the winged monster he was sketching. "I thought it was kind of weird myself, at first. Cassie never came out and said why, but Eloise and I figured it out. He didn't want any more good-byes." He stopped drawing for a moment, then resumed putting scales on one of the monster's wings. "All Cassie said was how hard it was for him. I think he knew he didn't have a lot of time. I think Cassie took him by surprise, especially since he couldn't get rid of her."

"What?"

"Just something she said once. I think he figured she'd split on him when she found out how sick he was, but she didn't. I don't know if he was secretly hoping she would, but if he was, he didn't know our Ms. Valentine, did he? Stubborn is her middle name. Not to mention the fact that she was in deep over him."

Cassie wasn't in the store or they could never have had this discussion at the cash register during a slow period. Michael accepted Nick's information in silence and thought about it the rest of the day. Cassie, falling in love with a guy who was dying. No wonder she was so much quieter than when they last saw each other years ago. He understood loss, understood it in spades. Now when he caught her staring at him, he would simply smile and then leave her alone. She had enough to deal with as it was. Maybe there would be a chance with her later.

# ~ CHAPTER EIGHT ~

Out of the blue, Steve decided that since the store had been under his ownership for two years, it was now time to clean out the basement and expand the premises. He announced it at a special Sunday staff meeting, pulled together hastily just after the store closed. "We're doing really well, guys, but we can't sit around congratulating ourselves. We need to branch out to stay competitive, especially with the whole e-reader thing."

Fredo nodded. "It's about time. We have enough people come in and ask if we carry stuff besides books."

"What other stuff would that be?" Cassie had already guessed but wanted to make sure she knew what he meant.

"The gift items," Steve said. "The non-book stock. Stationery, calendars. Well, maybe too late for calendars this year, but next year. Clip-on reading lights. Maps. That kind of thing."

"How about music?" That was Nick.

Steve smiled. "Maybe. We'll start really slow with that. Only select artists at first."

"Like only death metal, or maybe all-polka bands?"

Steve ignored him. "And we'll see how it goes."

"So what's up with the basement?" Michael asked.

"We need to clear it out, clean it out, and finish the other half of it. Only part of it was used for storage. I'm going to get it all fixed up, have the wiring redone, put in Wi-Fi, and finish the floors and walls. When that's done, Audrey –that's my wife, since you haven't met her yet– and Nick will take care of furnishing and decorating. Sound like a plan?"

He looked around and grinned when everyone nodded back. "Okay, then. I worked up a schedule for tackling this before the contractors can start coming in." He began patting the pockets of his flannel shirt as well as his jeans, looking for the elusive scrap of paper with the schedule on it.

Cassie couldn't help smiling as Steve went through the familiar routine.

He located the paper in his left hip pocket. "Okay. Tomorrow, Mike and Nick will be downstairs for most of their shift."

"Let's send Mikey down there by himself first, to check things out," Nick suggested. "He sees dead people."

"Sometimes I see soon-to-be-dead people, too." It was the first time Michael had answered Nick in kind at a meeting, and Nick looked pleased at the response.

Steve cleared his throat. "Well, okay then. We need to hustle because I want as much of this done as possible before the Christmas season starts. I figured Cassie could handle the floor on her own if Fredo and I check in from time to time. And you need to call one of us if you get swamped." Steve looked at her.

"Okay, boss."

"We're good to go, then. Meeting adjourned. See you all tomorrow. And thanks, people."

Cassie picked up her purse and glanced around. Steve and Fredo were heading back toward receiving, Fredo talking earnestly about reorganizing one of the systems. Michael and Nick had retreated to the counter to look at one of Michael's muscle car magazines. Good. Maybe she could slip out unnoticed.

Daniel was on her mind, had been since she woke up that morning. He came and went in her thoughts, and she was used to that. But some days were still harder than others. This had been one of those days, the kind of Sunday where if Steve hadn't called a meeting, she would have been hard-pressed to find a reason to get out of bed. Sometimes it was still so easy to pull the covers over her head and just go back to sleep, back to peaceful oblivion. Day-to-day could be too hard.

She was nearly at her car when she heard a soft "Hey." She grimaced to herself, but turned around. Michael stood a few feet behind her.

"Hey," she replied.

He stared at her, unsmiling, unsure, and she looked back at him, waiting a bit impatiently. She wanted to go home and put sad music –*his* music– on her player and bury her head under the pillow. If her mom was out with Richard, as she should be, Cassie would have the house to herself. With no questions.

"Can I talk to you a minute? Are you in a rush?" he asked.

"I have to get back home," she said. Well, she did, didn't she? If she stayed out in the real world much longer she would crumble into a heap. She needed to retreat.

Michael took an uncertain step forward, hands in his front pockets, shoulders hunched. He looked as if he were anticipating a sharp blow to the head. "You know what Nick said back there? About seeing dead people?"

That was unexpected. Cassie nodded. "The farmer up in Wisconsin."

"And someone else." He flinched away from her for a second, then caught her eyes again, his face serious, the scar pulling his mouth into a grim line. "I've been wanting to ask you- well, you know. Maybe ask for your phone number."

"Yeah. I know," she said. She didn't expound on the simple statement but he didn't seem to expect that.

"So I followed you out of the store the other day to ask you about it. You went into the pharmacy down the block and stopped at the magazines."

She cocked her head at him, somewhat surprised. "Michael, are you stalking me?"

"I -*what*? No, of course not. I just wanted to talk to you away from…from…"

"Nick."

"Nick. Steve. Fredo. They all know. Jeez, they're worse than the locker room in junior high."

"I know." She smiled in spite of herself.

He took a deep breath. "Cassie, when you were in the store reading that magazine, I swear I saw him with you."

"Who?"

"*Him*."

The emphasis he placed on the word caught her attention and she suddenly understood, catching her breath. She had never told Michael about Daniel, but of course he would know. By now, he would know everything that Nick *and* Steve *and* Fredo knew, probably with Eloise thrown into the mix, courtesy of Nick. "Tell me," she demanded.

"You were alone when you went into the store so I followed you into the magazine section. I was going to talk to you but then I realized you weren't alone at all. All of a sudden there was this guy standing just behind you, reading over your shoulder. There was no question he was with you."

"What did he look like?"

"He was about my height, but thinner. Light brown hair. He was wearing jeans and a green tee shirt with words on it, but I couldn't quite read it when he turned to look at me."

"Green," Cassie whispered. "Not dead yet."

"What?"

"Nothing." She was impatient for details. "Then what happened?"

"I stopped. I didn't know what to do. I thought you were alone but you weren't. So I stood there for a moment and then he turned around and looked at me. And smiled."

"He smiled at you?"

"Yeah. Real friendly, like it would have been okay if I walked up and spoke to both of you, if I wanted. Then he just turned back and kept reading over your shoulder." He fumbled his car keys out of his pocket, fingering them nervously. "So I left. I thought maybe you were getting back together with your old boyfriend."

"But he's–"

"Yes. Nick told me later. I didn't know at the time."

"You said he was wearing a green tee shirt and jeans. But what did he look like?"

Michael blinked, confused. "You don't know?"

She stamped her foot impatiently. "Of course I know. But did he look sick? Did he look tired, or healthy, or happy, or sad? What?"

"He looked fine. Healthy. And happy." Michael answered slowly, remembering. "Friendly."

There were tears in Cassie's eyes and she blinked against the sting of them. "What are you doing? Right now?" she asked.

"Me? Nothing. The store's closed. Why?"

"Can you come home with me?"

"Now? Yeah, I guess. Sure."

"Just follow me. You have a car, right?"

"Yeah. I'm parked down the block."

"Then drive over here and follow me home. I'll wait for you."

"Sure." He frowned slightly. "Why am I doing this?"

She looked at him, serious and bleak. "I want to know once and for all who's in my house. So go get your car."

No more questions. Michael went.

# ~ CHAPTER NINE ~

"My house is haunted." Cassie made the statement flatly, no inflection in her voice, no teasing, no humor. They were standing on her front porch and she was about to put the key into the lock.

"And you think it's..." Michael didn't finish. The look on her face was one he didn't recognize.

"Daniel? I don't know. My mom and I moved here last spring, right before I started working for Steve. As soon as we moved in, I knew we weren't alone. But it's not the kind of thing I can discuss with my mother. You'll find out, if you ever see her again." She inserted the key and turned it sharply. "Welcome to Chez Valentine," she said grimly.

Michael followed her across the threshold and felt as if someone had punched the wind out of him. There was a heaviness, a thick feeling in the house that made it hard for him to breathe. The furnishings were bright and the sun that poured through the picture windows washed the carpet, the sofa, the walls, with light. But whatever he felt in his gut, in his throat, negated daylight itself.

Cassie wasn't even looking at him. "You feel it too, don't you? Like something else is here?"

"Kind of hard to miss."

She led him farther into the living room and gestured him onto the couch while she took the armchair across from him. "So," she said. "Tell me what you see. Or who."

"Cassie-"

"I'm so serious, Michael. Is Daniel back?"

Michael looked at her and understood how lost, how tightly wound she was. No matter what he said, something in her could very well snap. He'd been in uncomfortable situations before, but this was one for the books. He bought time. "Uh, could I have a glass of water?"

She gave him a hard look and then sighed. "Sure. I'm sorry." She put down the throw pillow she had been holding and went to the kitchen. "Ice?" she called back.

"Great. Thanks."

While she moved about the kitchen, he glanced around the house. No Daniel. He thought he caught a glimpse of someone – something? – standing a few feet before him, in front of the couch, but it was gone as soon as he blinked. Footsteps on the second floor made him jump and he turned to look up the staircase, at least as far up as he could see.

"No one else is home." Cassie handed him a glass of ice water. "It's just you and me. And whatever, whoever is in this house." She looked at him. "Is it…?"

He drained half the water first. "No. I don't think so," he said quietly. He noticed that the noises had stopped, and breathed a silent sigh of relief.

"I guess I didn't really think it was him," she said after a long pause. "I had just been hoping." She was silent for a long beat. "He wouldn't let me be there at the end," she said softly.

Michael didn't understand. "What?"

*"You have to stop following me around, Valentine," Daniel had said. "First the hospital units. Now this place. You're more persistent than a bill collector."*

*They were in hospice by then. No more machines. No more monitors. Just pain medication when needed, music at night, and the sun in the morning.*

*Cassie had looked at him stubbornly. "I will follow you until I can't," she said.*

*He sighed. "Cass, you gotta let go. You've got..." his voice ran out for a moment. "You've got years ahead of you."*

*"Without you." Her lip trembled and she bit it to stop herself from making things worse.*

*"For both of us," he said. He closed his eyes. "Anyhow, I'm too tired to keep up with you. So I have a huge, honking favor to ask you, okay?"*

*She looked at him, a weight in her stomach. "What?"*

*"When I tell you not to come back,* **you can't come back**. *Okay?"*

*"But–"*

*"No argument here. I won't argue about this." His face crumpled in a sudden spasm of pain, and then slowly, ever so slowly, cleared again and he was looking at her with those green eyes. "Let me try and rephrase that more clearly. When I tell you not to come back,* **you can't come back**. *Okay?"*

*"Why?"*

*He looked away. "This is bad enough," he said after a pause. "Flat on my back, too weak to get up most of the time, pathetic..." He moved his fingers restlessly against the sheets. "I know I can't ask you not to visit and I'd be stupid to say I didn't like it when you're here. But when we get to that, you gotta...you gotta do what I ask." He looked at her then and she thought she could get lost in his eyes, wanted desperately to crawl into them, to shelter there, to avert everything that she knew was coming at them with cruel haste.*

*The pain, the despair, the anguish rode her for a moment, turned her inside out. And then she nodded. "If that's really what you want," she whispered.*

*His expression relaxed. "It's exactly what I want," he said. He managed a smile for her. "I need to know this isn't how you'll remember me."*

*She moved closer to him and put her head down on his chest.*

Michael waited for a few seconds after she had finished speaking and lapsed into a heavy silence. He could picture the scene she had just described perfectly, catching everything she didn't explain. She didn't need to explain. Mourning was something he understood quite well. "Cass?" he finally ventured.

She turned to him slowly, her eyes surprisingly dry. "I'm sorry, Michael," she said, her voice faded. "I haven't talked about him in a long time, not even to Eloise. It's too hard."

He nodded. "I get that. I really do."

She looked at him searchingly. "Do you?"

He couldn't hold her gaze, not yet ready to open up about his own loss, and simply nodded. When she didn't answer right away, he looked up at her.

She studied his face, eyes lingering on his scar for just a second longer than usual. Then, "Yes, I think you do," she said. She turned away, resumed staring at some distant point, some far-off memory he couldn't see, and he understood that as well.

"Are you going to be okay?" he asked.

"I'm fine." Voice remote, still faded, so quiet he could barely hear her.

"I'll leave, then. I know you need to be alone." He rose and brought his water glass to the kitchen, placed it in the sink, then went back to the front hall.

She was no longer seated in the armchair, but was waiting for him at the door. "Michael," she said. She raised her hand in a sort of formless, helpless gesture.

"It's okay." He opened the door and stepped out onto the porch, then stopped a minute, considering, and said, "Give me your phone."

"What?"

"Your phone. Let me have it for a minute."

Cassie got her cell phone from her purse and followed him out onto the porch, giving it to him wordlessly.

Michael took the phone and punched buttons. "You call me if you need me," he said, giving it back to her. "Any time." He folded her fingers around it, keeping his hand around hers a little longer than necessary, and then on impulse he reached down and gave her a gentle hug. He knew what she still had to go through and he wished he could do more for her, but realized it was her task alone. And she hadn't asked for his help. "Take care." He squeezed her a little bit, then released her quickly and went down the front steps.

# ~ CHAPTER TEN ~

That Thursday, Steve said, "The boys have been doing serious labor down in the basement for almost two weeks. Everyone's been working really hard lately. You two in the basement, Cassie and Fredo tag-teaming the floor, Fredo and I dealing with receiving, inventory, and contractors. How's about we make tonight's ghost story session a little special? I'll order pizza, Mark offered to bring in soda, and May is bringing dessert. How does that sound?"

"Great." Surprisingly, Michael spoke up first. "I'm starving."

"I noticed all the cookies were gone," said Fredo.

"I'll order the pizzas now," Steve said. "Cassie, go ahead and flip the sign to *Closed* and you guys go clean yourselves up a little."

Shortly after, Steve brought four pizza boxes into the break room, handing one each to Michael and Nick before setting the other two on the table, grinning at their reactions.

"Judging by the way the guys are stuffing their faces, neither Nick nor Mike is going to be able to speak long enough to tell a story," Fredo observed.

Michael, gulping, shook his head. Nick simply continued to eat.

"It's my turn," said May. She had eaten what she called her share of pizza, three small pieces, and wiped her fingers on a napkin. "I've never told anyone this story before. Except for my husband, God bless him. You can think what you like, but it's all true."

She was silent for a moment as if gathering her thoughts. Then she said, "This has all been on my mind lately, and I don't understand why. I've tried for years to forget, but there's no forgetting something this wicked. I never realized what evil there is in the world until this happened."

Cassie felt a sudden chill up the back of her neck. In all the months of ghost stories, May had only ever told one or two others, and both of them had been short and somewhat benevolent: a beloved relative coming to say good-bye some time after death, a pet dog that returned and for two weeks after it died, scratched nightly at the back door to be let out into the yard. The way she spoke now suggested an entirely different kind of tale. Cassie glanced around the table and from the serious expressions all around, realized everyone else had caught the same inkling.

May was quiet a moment longer, then began to speak in her softest voice.

"Some years ago, I worked as a cashier at a food market not far from here. You're maybe all too young to remember, but back then this suburb was more of a small town. We didn't have any of the big chain stores at that time. We had a corner grocery store just downtown, across from the church where that real estate office is now. It was actually one of the bigger stores here, with its own parking lot and all." Her eyes were no longer focused on her listeners or even on anything in the break room.

"I worked at that store for almost sixteen years, until my husband changed jobs and we moved out of state for a time. There was a young mother who worked with me back then. She was sweet, she was pretty. Her name was Jane Norridge. She and her family lived in a cute little house a few miles out of town.

"She was a dear, Jane was. She even had Mr. Parrish and myself over for dinner once or twice. Her husband was a good man, and she had two little boys, sweet but lively. Always running, jumping, hiding." She shook her head as she remembered. "Just a nice family, they were."

She stopped again and her mouth worked silently. Cassie felt the chilled spot on the back of her neck begin to twine itself around her spine. Out of the corner of her eye, she saw Steve half-rise out of his chair, concern for May evident on his face. Mark's face was also crinkling up into an expression of worry. And then May spoke again.

*Jane hadn't come to work. And she didn't call. By ten-thirty that morning, May could see that Mr. Monahan, the store manager, was becoming as worried as the rest of the staff. She wasn't surprised when he beckoned her over to the customer service desk. May took out the cash drawer, closed her register, and went to meet with her boss.*

*"May, would you be okay with giving up your break time to drive over to Jane's house? Maybe there was some kind of emergency and their phone isn't working. Or maybe someone needed to go to the hospital. Can you see if you can track her down?"*

*"We're all worried about Janey, "May said, taking off her smock. "I'll find out what's going on."*

*She hurried to her car and drove out to the Norridge house. Jane lived away from the town proper, but even without four-lane highways, there was not enough traffic on the roads at that time to delay May's errand. She stopped and parked across the street from the house, and saw that the Norridge family car was in the driveway. That worried her. Had Jane or one of the boys been taken ill?*

*"Missus Parrish."*

*May started and looked for whoever had called her name. She was disconcerted to see Jeremy Mott staring at her from across the street. He was standing on the sidewalk just in front of the Norridge house.*

*Now what would Jeremy Mott be doing there? He was young and quiet enough, and it had been kind of Mr. Monahan to take him on at the store as an occasional bag-boy, but he made her nervous. There was something wrong with the lad, always dressed in grimy jeans and faded, fraying shirts. He made himself as presentable as possible when he was working and he was always polite when she spoke to him, but he looked like trouble to her. She didn't quite understand Jane's compassion for the boy, taking him to eat at the local restaurant occasionally, or at one time even buying the boy some clothes and a new pair of shoes.*

*"He has these dreams, May," Jane had said. "He's afraid all the time, and he has no one to talk to. He's too young to be so afraid, so beaten down."*

*The memory twisted something in May's stomach. She looked at him and her own uneasiness sharpened her voice. "What are you doing here?"*

*"Don't go in there, Missus Parrish," he said. "You don't want to be going in there."*

*"Whatever do you mean? Jane didn't come in to work. I want to make sure she's all right."*

*Jeremy's response frightened her. He began to weep, standing alone on that sidewalk. "No, she's not," he said. "Nothing's all right."*

*"What do you mean?" May asked again.*

*But Jeremy didn't answer. He just stood where he was, crying and wiping the tears from his dirt-streaked face onto his stained and filthy jacket sleeve.*

*May crossed the street to the house and brushed past him, climbing up to the porch to ring the bell. The door was ajar. She pushed it open and stepped in, her hand rising to her mouth to stifle a scream when she saw the young woman's body. And then she was backing out of the house and tumbling down the steps, barely noticing that Jeremy was no longer there. She fled to a neighbor's house where she could find a phone and some human companionship.*

"She was dead," May said, her voice flat. "They all were. Someone had come into the house and killed them. Stabbed and slashed them. The young woman I saw who had been their houseguest. Jane herself. Her husband, Martin. I didn't go farther than finding that first body. My legs wouldn't take me any farther. I backed out of that house and ran for the closest neighbor, which at that time was nearly a block away. Jeremy was gone. I had no idea where he went. I called the police, and then I called the market."

She stopped and no one said anything for a time.

Then Steve stirred uneasily. "That's a horrible story, May. But you said there was a ghost…?"

She nodded. "Jeremy was blamed for those murders. The police found him in the lot behind the market, hidden by one of the dumpsters. Had Norridge blood all over him. They said he had overdosed on some sort of drug after killing all those people. They said he probably wanted money for more drugs. They were pretty sure he had to be on something to have killed them all like that."

"So he ran back to the market after you saw him?"

May gave Cassie a wan smile. "No, child. Jeremy was dead when they found him. He had been dead long enough that he was stone cold to the touch."

Cassie saw Michael's eyes widen at the same moment that she understood what May meant. "So what you're saying–" Michael began.

"Yes, that is exactly what I'm saying. When he called to me from across the street and told me not to go into the house,

Jeremy Mott was already dead."

Later, May apologized, passing around brownies and dishing out ice cream, saying that perhaps the story had been completely inappropriate for a Thursday night gathering.

Steve refuted that gently. "We're all adults here. Well, there's Nick, of course. But we ask for stories and you certainly delivered tonight. That's probably the most powerful one we've heard since we started."

"That even rattled me," Mark admitted. "Hardened skeptic though I am."

May shook her head. "I've tried to find an explanation for it, but I never have. I saw and spoke with Jeremy, I'm sure of it. Even though it's impossible."

"Nothing's impossible," Nick announced seriously, and the others looked at him in surprise. "Just ask my cousin." He regarded them all with the same expression and then burst out laughing. "Y'all are looking at me like I just grew horns. Where are those brownies?"

# ~ CHAPTER ELEVEN ~

Cassie walked into her house, switched on the light in the hall, and put her purse down on the nearest chair in the living room. The evening had been draining, tiring, even though she had enjoyed herself after May's ghost story and the mood in the room had lightened, especially when Nick had requested that Fredo be removed from the bathroom-cleaning schedule.

"We don't like it when Fredo cleans the bathroom," Nick had whispered loudly to Michael, hand placed ostentatiously at the side of his mouth. "When Fredo goes to clean, he turns into Scary Frat-Bachelor Guy. Ouch." This in response to Fredo whacking him at the back of the head.

"Liar," Fredo added.

"It's true," Nick protested. "He'll clean the toilet and then use the same rag to wipe out the sink. Then he comes to the break room and–" The sentence was never finished as Fredo chased Nick out into the store.

Cassie smiled at the memory as she went upstairs to her room and The List. She hadn't worked on it in a few days, and she had a few more details to add. She decided on a rock band, and switched on her player. Then she booted up and scrolled down to Item 89, the last one she had entered. Item 90. *He loved skiing.* She entered another thought as it occurred to her and then paused.

From downstairs, she heard the front door suddenly open and then close. Good. Her mother was home. She continued to type, including items about childhood pets, what kind of car he always wanted to own, and his dream vacation. It was several minutes before she realized that she hadn't heard her mother toss her car keys on the kitchen counter, open the refrigerator for a bottle of water, or call out her customary greeting.

The realization came to her gradually, like a slow awakening on a cold winter morning. Cassie's fingers stopped of their own accord and she found herself glancing a bit uneasily at her bedroom door, which was slightly open.

The door to her room was the only thing that ever made Cassie uncomfortable in her own house. Always when she was in a hurry, late, rushing to get out of her bedroom, she would grasp the knob to fling the door open and dash out into the hall. And always, no matter how hurried she was, she would hesitate for a moment, suddenly certain that she would come face to face with *someone* who had been standing outside the room the whole time. And the thought would raise goose bumps on her arms and neck for just a second. She didn't know why she felt this, but it was unnerving. She had an idea that it was just a matter of time before she did open the door to find that person standing there.

Now she heard footsteps coming up the stairs, slower than her mother's, and heavier. The hair at the back of her neck was already rising and she felt a frozen moment of indecisiveness. Should she call out? Should she run to shut her door and lock it? The footsteps were nearly at the top. She knew without a doubt they would be coming down the hall in her direction.

But she was wrong. The footsteps reached the second floor, then headed in the direction of her mother's room, the first at the top of the stairs. Her mother's door opened. There was a short moment of relief – perhaps it was just that her mother was too tired to yell out hello, or even get herself anything from the kitchen. Maybe she was ill. Concerned at the thought, Cassie half-rose from her desk, at the same time hearing her mother's bedroom door creak the way it did when someone pushed it. But before she could call out, ascertain who was actually there–

"Hide!" a voice hissed behind her.

She jumped and turned, moving so abruptly that she nearly knocked over her chair. There was no one else in the room, and she felt panic rising in her. The voice had sounded *urgent*, a stark cold thread of fear laced through it that caught her in an icy paralysis. At the same time she heard as much as sensed the same slow footsteps coming down the hall to her room.

Unwillingly, she looked away from her closet, where the voice had seemed to originate, over to her bedroom door. It was not closed all the way and she waited in a quiet, still panic to see *it* appear in the narrow opening, blocking her view of the hall, partially revealing whomever, whatever was there. The steps shuffled closer. Any second now, any moment…

And then the doorbell pealed furiously, wild, shrill, and Cassie started.

The entire house could have been holding its breath with her, waiting with her for the author of those measured steps to be revealed. But the doorbell broke the spell and all at once the house began to breathe again.

Cassie released her own pent-up breath and checked her clock. It was after ten already. Who would be stopping by so late? Steve had been known to drop by Fredo's or Nick's after hours, delivering a forgotten paycheck or once making baby-sitting arrangements on his way home. Maybe he remembered something that he needed to talk to her about. But she dismissed the thought as soon as she had it. Even he would have been in his own living room by now, watching the news with Audrey. Still, the thought of her boss, so calm and reassuring, enervated her.

She forced herself into movement, striding toward the hall and yanking the door wide open. She still half-expecting to see someone, or something, standing right there waiting for her, a stronger, more visceral version of the feeling she experienced so frequently in this house. But no one was there.

On trembling legs, she managed to navigate the stairs without falling and breaking her neck. She tried to peer through the little windows on either side of the door to get a glimpse of her late night caller, but she couldn't see anything. As soon as she could, she looked through the peephole in the door. A woman stood on the porch.

Curious, Cassie undid the locks and opened the door partway, hiding a little behind it, and addressed the woman through the screen door. "Can I help you?" Her voice shook slightly.

"I am so sorry to bother you." She looked younger than Cassie's mom, stood about average height, was wearing a powder blue jogging suit with a tee shirt beneath the jacket. Her hair, pulled back in a tail, looked almost gold beneath the porch light. She smiled hopefully at Cassie, her blue eyes turning up slightly. "But could you possibly have seen a little boy? He's about this tall." She held her hand out a little lower than her hip. "He would be wearing gray sweat pants and a gray hooded sweatshirt. And Superman shoes. Have you seen him?"

She looked so hopeful that Cassie hated to say no. "I'm really sorry, but I haven't. I've been upstairs in my room. Umm, where would he have been going?"

The woman's expression became rueful. "I must seem like a dreadful mother to you, losing track of my son so late at night. Actually, he had been in bed. But he's always liked to hide, and lately he's been sneaking out. Most of the time he's just in the yard. Would you mind terribly if I looked around back? He's always liked it out there."

"Oh, sure. That's fine. Do you want some help?"

"Oh, no. I'll just check really quickly. I saw your lights and didn't want to alarm you if you noticed someone prowling around the back of the house." She shuddered. "No neighborhood is really safe anymore. Thanks for your time. I'll just go look now." She smiled at Cassie again and turned away.

Cassie watched her go down the steps. "Wait!" she called. "What's your name? Who should I contact if I see him?"

But the woman either didn't hear, or chose to ignore her. She skirted the front of the lawn and went up the walk that ran beside the house.

Cassie slammed the front door shut and locked it, then dashed through the house to the kitchen and the back door, hitting the light switch for the back steps and flooding the yard with sudden brightness. She opened the back door, which squeaked hideously, and stuck her head out to look for either the woman or the boy.

The yard was empty.

Cassie ventured out onto the top of the concrete steps and gave the yard a thorough going over, or at least as far as she could see with the help of the light at the back of the house. No one. Frowning, she went inside and locked the back door, checking it more than once before getting herself a glass of juice and sitting down at the kitchen table. She knew she could go back upstairs and work a bit more on The List, but the thought was not appealing. Daniel would have understood. She decided to wait for her mother downstairs that night.

* * *

*"Michael, come and find me..."* The voice jerked Michael from a deep and formless sleep. *"Come and find me."* The echoes of it played over and over in his head until they faded on their own. God, where had that come from? He pushed the tangle of hair back from his forehead and looked at his clock. Three more hours until his alarm went. But could he get back to sleep? Not likely. He groaned, full of self-pity, and pushed the sheets away, went to the washroom and then to the kitchen for a glass

of water.

Moonlight spilled through the kitchen windows and teased quiet glints of light from the stove and the silver tones of the refrigerator handle. The scent of slightly overripe bananas floated on the air close to the kitchen table, a testament to the fruit in the bowl that had yet to be consumed. Michael gulped the water and stared out the windows above the sink. *Come and find me.* Whose voice? Benny's? Cassie's? It didn't matter. It was a voice from years and years ago, a time of lakeside summers and sun-hot playgrounds, bonfires on the beach, and ice cream that melted before he could finish eating it. All of it was from a different time, a different world, he thought, and best to let it go. But the voice in his head would not leave him alone. Standing in the quiet of the dark, empty kitchen he could hear it again if he chose.

His reverie was interrupted by the sound of his grandfather snoring peacefully in the master bedroom down the hall. He smiled, but there was sadness in it as he wondered how differently his life might have been if only–

But that was the path to madness. He knew that. The path to madness, to imprisonment, to solitary confinement so tight and so close that sunlight couldn't even find him. He had been there once before and he didn't choose to go that route again. But still… *If only* was something that haunted him, tempted him, and he could usually keep it at bay until he had one of his sleepless nights.

He got another glass of water and wandered out to the living room with it, sitting sideways on the sofa and looking out the front window. The porch beyond the curtains and glass was half-illuminated by the moon. He could see the top of the handrail at the front steps, although the steps themselves vanished into the shadow.

He thought about standing with Cassie on her front porch. So he had given her his number and told her to call him, any time. She hadn't. Of course, he had also told her to call if she needed him. The blatancy of her feelings about that smacked him dead center in the face. Still, he knew she was hardly in the market. She held Daniel around her like a shield, and he knew he would never try to breach that. And yet…

He still caught her staring at him at the bookstore. Sometimes she seemed to want to say something, although she never did. What did she want from him?

And then from deep inside, somewhere in the back of his mind, or maybe even his heart, that little *something* was nagging at him, pushing him to talk to her. To open up to her and tell her everything he had consciously chosen never to talk about. When he had buried his story, never speaking to the therapist, or even to Grandpa Henry, he had promised himself he might tell it one day, if he ever found the person who most needed to hear it.

Cassie's face flashed into his mind, her expression distant, remote, totally devoid of her natural vibrancy, and he wondered if confiding in her would help her somehow. In the dark of early morning like this he didn't shy away from the thought, not like he would in the bright lights and reality of The Poet's Corner Bookstore. Would he eventually do it? He drained the glass of water thoughtfully and cupped it in his hand. He had a feeling the time was coming.

# ~ CHAPTER TWELVE ~

Even days later, May's story about the murders of the entire Norridge family and guest, and of the subsequent death of their young killer, clung to Cassie like no other Thursday night ghost story had ever done. Being alone had never bothered her much, but today she felt jumpy, uneasy, by herself. She would have called Eloise, but she knew that Eloise was doing "something artsy" with Nick, as she had put it, so Cassie was on her own.

Of course, there was always Michael. Images of him were beginning to tug at the edge of her awareness. His serious expression when she told him about Daniel. His complete understanding when she needed to be alone. His hand around hers, and the sweet, gentle embrace he had given her before he left her house. She was aware of the strength in that hand, those arms, and equally aware of how delicately he had treated her, as if afraid that hugging her any harder might break her. And for just those few seconds that he had held her, she had felt— *safe*. It was the only word she could think of that seemed accurate. So yes, there was always Michael. But she knew even as she thought of him that she couldn't call him. Not yet.

She walked slowly down the main pathway at Bridgeton Park Cemetery, paying little attention to the rows of headstones on either side of her. The cemetery was quiet, peaceful, even beautiful with the stands of trees turning fiery with the change of seasons. The grass had not yet gone to brown, but was the muted green of early fall, and the chrysanthemums that grew in mounds of deep red, gold, and yellow at the edge of the path were all the more brilliant for the reticence of the grass.

Daniel's resting place was about twenty feet farther and to the left, just below the top of a small rise. He had shown her the site himself when he still had the energy for walking with her. "I'll be just here," he said, and then turned a slow circle at the crest of the hill. "Great view, isn't it?"

Cassie had not known how to respond at the time and even now the memory brought stinging tears to her eyes. She wiped at her face impatiently, her feet slowing when she reached his headstone. It was flat and onyx black and looked shockingly new, bearing his name, dates to mark the short span of his existence, and the single word "Panache." That had been his choice and even as she read it again she couldn't help a small smile. And then a small sigh.

She sat down cross-legged on the grass, knowing he wouldn't mind. "I miss you," she said aloud. A soft wind blew through the grass in reply and she felt less alone. "I've been working on the List, you know. I've got up to 97 things on it. I'll bet you didn't realize I knew 97 things about you. And no, I'm not making up stuff."

She stopped and half –rose to her feet, aware all at once that someone else had arrived. She could feel it. "Hello?" she called out. She twisted around, trying to see in all directions. There was no one there. When she had parked her car, she saw that hers was the only one in the lot.

Uneasy, she stood up and looked around again. No one. But she could feel someone close to her and she knew it wasn't Daniel. From where she stood, she could see a man packing up a rake, a hoe, and other gardening tools in the caretaker's shed, but that was far enough away that she doubted he even realized she had entered the cemetery.

She folded her arms across herself, rubbing her hands up and down for warmth. The air had grown abruptly cold and she recognized the sensation. Sometimes, back at her house… She didn't finish the thought, but a new idea crowded into her mind. *Whoever was in her house could very well be buried in Bridgeton Park Cemetery.*

In her head, she heard Daniel telling her to leave, to go home. NOW, he emphasized. She hurried back to the path and took off at a half-run for the parking lot. The drive home was uneventful, even as she shivered in her seat, and she slammed out of the car in haste when she reached her driveway, flinging herself up the porch with her key clutched in her trembling hand.

At the back of her head, she wondered what refuge she would find at home. Peace and calm at her own haunted house? That was just crazy thinking. Nevertheless, she shoved open the door and rushed inside, panic just barely under control, then closed and leaned back against it. She took quick heavy breaths, her eyes closed as she tried to calm down.

Amazingly she heard a voice call out to her. "Cassie, is that you? Come and have some pizza with us!"

Salvation. Her mother had arrived home early, and with Richard. Cassie opened her eyes feeling better already. Her mother was so much happier when Richard was around, and that had been him calling out to her. He had the sort of deep rich male voice that demanded attention. Not because of what he was saying, but simply because his voice was so— She tried hard to think of a word but couldn't come up with one. His was a deep, calm, warm, and resonating voice, like a hug that could be heard, and it always made her feel good. She couldn't help thinking that he was the best thing that could have happened to her mother.

She put her purse down on the hall table and slipped her keys into it. "In a sec!" she called back, tidying her wind-tangled hair with her fingers before entering the kitchen.

"Cassie! It's so good to see you out of your room!" Her mother greeted her with a one-armed hug as she grabbed plates from the cabinet. "Did you eat? Do you want some pizza?"

"I'll have a piece." Cassie washed her hands and accepted a plate, helping herself to a large triangular slice of sausage pizza, gooey with cheese and fragrant with onions and green peppers as well. "This is really good. Thanks."

"And what are you doing with yourself this fine afternoon?" Richard asked from across the table, his eyes smiling at her from behind his wire-rim glasses. A lock of silvery hair fell across his forehead, as always, and Mrs. Valentine brushed it back for him before taking her own seat at the table.

"Just trying not to freak out." Cassie knew she was venturing into dangerous territory with that statement, but decided to take the chance since Richard was here.

"About what?" He leaned forward as he always did when he found something fascinating, which was pretty much all the time. Richard Carlton had a master's degree in anthropology, a Ph.D. in history, and was semi-retired from his position as a social studies and humanities instructor. But he could no more stop being an interested educator than he could stop breathing.

"The bookstore I work at has a standing ghost-story session on Thursday nights. One of our regular customers told us one last week that was pretty frightening."

Her mother made an impatient noise but before she could say anything, Richard beat her to it. "Really? A frightening ghost story? So it was a good one? Did you believe it?"

"It was a great story," Cassie said, gratified to find that Richard didn't shoot her down as quickly as her mother would have. "And I couldn't help believing it."

"Are you still exploring that nonsense? Honestly, Cassie, if you devoted that kind of time and energy to going back to school–"

"I'll go back when I'm ready. That's why I only work at the bookstore part time. Besides, ghost stories make me think about other issues, like life after death and all the things in this world that can't be explained."

"Can't you contemplate something more worthwhile? Study someone's biography, or something historical."

"In a way, this is historical. In addition to the ghost, the story May told us was about a real crime back in the past."

"Oh, Cassie, honestly. If you just went back to school you wouldn't have time for all of this nonsense."

Richard interrupted before it went any further. "Lori, you look hungry. Have some more pizza. Cassie has told us on different occasions that she will be going back to school as soon as she can. In addition, she is staying out of trouble and learning about the seen and unseen in this world around us. How bad can that be?" He looked at Cassie and winked. "And when she gets her own paranormal talk show we can brag to everyone that we knew her when."

Mrs. Valentine groaned. "Don't encourage her."

"Everyone needs encouragement. Didn't you say that to me just the other day when I was complaining about the quality of service at the restaurant we were at?"

"Well, yes, but–"

"All right, then. End of story. Cassie, have some more pizza. You look hungry."

Back up in her room, content from eating two pieces of pizza and the warmth of Richard's support, Cassie sat down at her desk and opened up the List, scrolling down to the bottom and stopping cold when she saw what was typed after Item 97. She blinked twice, but the words didn't go away.

Dropped down two lines below her last entry, in a slot that should have been for Item 98, were two unpunctuated sentences: *I felt so bad I knew they were all dead*

# ~ CHAPTER THIRTEEN ~

Steve Crawford was the boss his staff would have designed if they could have. He was soft-spoken and kind, the sort of person who remembered others by name, a trait the customers loved. He went out of his way to track down obscure authors, strange titles, or out-of-print books for those of his elderly patrons who didn't like to shop online. His daily uniform was a pair of jeans and a clean flannel shirt, and when he forgot to remove it, a Chicago White Sox baseball cap.

He introduced his wife, Audrey, to the staff, and brought his two little daughters, Emma and Abby, into the shop on a regular basis. He even asked Nick and Eloise or Cassie to baby-sit for them from time to time. He gave out his cell number to all employees in case anyone needed to reach him during non-business hours. As far as Cassie knew, only Fredo called Steve on his cell, and Fredo had known Steve forever.

So Cassie wasn't exactly surprised when he turned up on her doorstep the second day she called in sick. The doorbell rang and when she glanced through the peephole, Steve stood at the edge of the porch, gazing out at the street. He turned when she undid the lock and opened the door.

"Steve?" She wondered what he was going to say this particular visit.

He took off the baseball cap and fidgeted with it, almost as if nervous, a gesture that surprised her. "Hey, Cass, I wanted to see how you're doing. I got a little worried that you called in two days in a row."

She blushed, not sure how to cover it up, and pulled the door open wide. "Would you like to come in?"

"Oh, no, no, I don't have to do that. Is your mother home?"

"No, she'll be at work late again tonight. Always is. Why?"

He shrugged, clearly ill at ease. "It seems like a bad idea for me to come in, if she's not here." He didn't explain further.

Cassie looked at him with some surprise. "I'm over eighteen, you know. It's not like I'm a child."

"No, but you are my employee. Trust me, Cass, it's just about impropriety."

She shook her head. "Whatever you say, boss."

He looked at her. "Are you feeling okay? Did you see a doctor?"

"No." She bowed her head, not sure how to continue. She wasn't ill. "I'm sorry I've been out. I haven't really been sick. It's just…"

"Nick told me." Steve's voice was gentle. "He suspected. It's one of the reasons I'm here. He was worried about you. We all were. So I decided to come see you myself, put everyone's mind at ease."

She gave him a tremulous smile. "That's sweet. But I'm okay. Really."

"You sure?"

"Yes."

"Okay enough to come back to work tomorrow?"

She nodded. "Yes. I was going to call you tomorrow morning to verify. Noon to close, right?"

"That's right. Glad you're coming back. The boys have been pining without you."

"Nick? Pining? I can't even imagine that."

"Okay, so Michael's doing enough pining for both of them."

Cassie noticed the inflection in the simple statement. "We're not going there. Bosses aren't supposed to find dates for their employees. It's just about impropriety."

He smiled at her, his hazel eyes turning up at the corners. "Fair enough."

They both jumped as a loud crash came from the direction of the kitchen. Cassie winced, but Steve frowned. "Are you alone?" he asked.

"Yes. Believe it or not."

"Then what was that?" There was a hard edge to his voice.

She looked at him curiously. The mild demeanor had been replaced by something tougher, something colder. "The house is haunted," she said. She cleared her throat, waiting for him to scoff, but he just looked at her, expecting an explanation. "Really," she said. "Since we first moved in. My mom doesn't notice anything, or she's really good at pretending she doesn't notice anything, but the noises, the drafts of air, even a cold spot or two, all add up to a haunted house to me. Ask Eloise. You can even ask Michael." She smiled. "You look really curious about it. Want to come in now?"

"No, no, I really can't," he said. But he leaned forward and stuck his head through the doorway anyhow. "I like what you've done with the place. Very nice."

As soon as the words were out of his mouth, Cassie felt a cool breeze ripple past her back, tugging at the ends of her hair. If Steve noticed, he didn't say a word. The door was open, so she doubted he thought anything of it.

"Do the noises drive you crazy?"

"Not really. The cold spots are worse. And the footsteps." She grinned at the look on his face. "I don't usually feel too uncomfortable, although that story May told the other week about that whole family getting murdered in their house, and then her seeing the ghost of their killer on top of it, got to me. That was creepy."

"That *was* creepy," Steve agreed. He shook out the baseball cap by holding onto its bill, then placed it back on his head. "So

I'll see you tomorrow?"

"You sure will," Cassie said. She smiled at him, feeling suddenly shy. "Thanks for coming over."

"Of course," he said. "I know the anniversary is coming up and you want a little time alone, but maybe sometimes it would be better to be with your family." He grinned at her and went to his car, waving once before driving away.

*Family*. It was true. The Poet's Corner was very like a family. She sighed and shut the door. And no sooner had she locked it and hurried back up to her room than the doorbell rang again. She frowned slightly, and once again made her reluctant way down the stairs to the front door, taking a glimpse through the peephole. Nick stood on the porch alone, hands thrust deep into the pockets of his hooded sweatshirt.

"Hey, stranger," he said when she opened the door. "And they don't get any stranger than you. Just wanted to see how you're doing."

She peered past him. "Where's Fredo?"

"What?"

"Steve just left. Now you're here. So where's Fredo?"

He grinned. "So we're all a little worried. But the logical question for you would have been 'where's Michael?'"

She frowned at him. "Not funny, Nick."

"It wasn't meant to be. He's worried, too."

She felt claustrophobic, suddenly. "You're all acting like a bunch of neurotics. What's the big deal?" She leaned against the doorway and folded her arms across her chest, glaring up at him. If she wanted to be alone and mourn for Daniel, why should it matter to anyone else? Steve coming to see about her was one thing; Nick's visit was one too many. She was getting angry that he had come to bother her.

He looked at her for a moment. "It *is* a big deal, Cass. You never call in sick. Especially when you're not sick. You wanna tell me what's going on?"

She looked past him at the houses across the street, arms still folded, and began tapping her foot impatiently. "Nothing's going on."

"Bull."

"Screw you."

"See? You also never talk like that. You never talk to anyone like that. What's wrong?"

"How do you know I never talk to anyone like that?"

"Because if you did, I'd be the person you were talking to. Eloise says you've ducked every phone call she's made since the other day. So what's up?"

"How dense are you?" she demanded at last, her defenses in full throttle. *Yes, I'm in mourning*! She wanted to shout at him. *I don't care that it's nearly a year, I am still in mourning! Leave me alone!* But she pressed her lips together tightly and kept silent in that regard. "What do you think is going on?"

*I felt so bad I knew they were all dead*

The thought popped into her head unbidden and she realized she could ask herself the same question she had just fired at Nick. She shoved the strange sentences, and the uneasiness they brought, away from her thoughts and concentrated on frowning at her friend.

He didn't rise to the provocation. "I'm not dense," he said softly. "I know what month it is. I know what date is coming up. Cassie, we all know. And everybody's worried."

"Yeah? Well, tell them not to be. Jeez, can't I get any privacy?"

"There's privacy and then there's isolation."

For answer, she tightened her arms across herself and continued to stare across the street, willing her eyes not to fill, willing herself not to break in front of Nick.

He took a step back and sighed. "Okay, then. I'll leave you

alone. It's just that, well, you don't have to be. All right?"

She looked at him, then. "I need to be," she said.

He shrugged and nodded. "See you tomorrow? At work?"

"Yeah," she said with a sigh. "I've got noon to close."

"I'll be there." He gave her a grin and turned away, hands back in his pockets, whistling something tuneless into the cold air as he shuffled down the steps.

Cassie shut the door behind him and locked it firmly.

# ~ CHAPTER FOURTEEN ~

The day Cassie came back to work, Michael noticed that Nick was keeping a close eye on her although he tried to hide it. At closing time, Nick invited him over for dinner in exchange for a lift home, and much to his own surprise, Michael accepted. It was Grandpa Henry's poker night, anyway, and for the first time in a long time, Michael didn't feel the need to disappear into the solitude of his basement.

"Are you sure your mother won't mind? I mean, would she need advance notice that you're bringing a guest?"

"Are you insane?" Nick said. "Turn left here." Eloise had borrowed his car while her own was in the shop, and Nick was temporarily "relying on the kindness of strangers," as he put it.

"Good thing," Fredo had said when he heard. "If Nick depended on the kindness of those who actually know him, he'd be up the creek." Fredo was still smarting from Nick's earlier reference to him as "El Frodo Grande, a curiously oversized hobbit."

"My mom is used to me bringing people home," Nick continued. "Eloise eats at my house all the time. Besides, this is a Filipino household. We're famous for squeezing people in sideways at the dinner table and sleeping eight to a bedroom." He grinned. "After you get introduced, no one will even notice you."

Michael parked on the street in front of the settled-looking, white frame house –the driveway was already crowded with an assortment of cars– and followed Nick up the walk to the front door with trepidation. He was no longer accustomed to large family crowds.

The walk was littered with toy trucks, a skateboard, several action figures, and a soccer ball. Nick cleared the path by sweeping everything into the grass with one foot or the other. “Kids,” he said, pretending to grump. “My cousin is staying here with her husband and their cubs until their place is ready for them to move. Her husband got transferred here a month ago.”

The front door was unlocked and Nick walked through and bellowed, “I’m home and I brought somebody!”

There was noticeable loud conversation as well as laughter coming from the back of the house and no one responded to Nick’s shout.

“See? Told you no one would notice.” At that moment, a small, blue-striped blur launched itself around the corner and tackled Nick around the knees. “Oof!” He bent down and untangled a small boy of uncertain age from around his legs and picked him up. “This here is Travis. Say hi to Michael, Travis.”

The boy had Nick’s straight black hair, cut in long bangs across his forehead, and the same bright brown eyes. He stared at Michael and then grew suddenly shy, putting three fingers into his mouth and burrowing into Nick’s neck.

“Hey! Don’t you slobber on my shirt, kid!” Nick gave the boy a quick squeeze and put him down. “Go tell your mom I’m here.”

The boy ran off into the back of the house.

“His mom is my cousin,” Nick explained. “I want to make sure you meet her.”

Michael looked at him curiously. “Sure. Why?”

“Because.” He smiled.

After a moment, a short, slender woman came down the hall towards them, bringing with her the delicious scent of cooking. “What’s up, Nicholas? Too lazy to walk yourself into the kitchen?” She smiled as she said it and included Michael in that smile. "Well, hello. My name is Naomi. And you are…?"

"Michael Penfield." He shook hands with her and was startled that her entire hand disappeared into his grip. She was a tiny woman with the same bangs as her son but none of his shyness. She looked Michael over with frank curiosity and then smiled again but almost secretively, as if she had evaluated him and made a decision.

"Do you know Eloise and Cassie?" she asked.

He nodded. "I work at the same bookstore as Nick and Cassie, and if you know them, you know Eloise."

She laughed. "True. I'm delighted to meet you. Before Nick started hanging around with Cassie, all of his friends apparently came from demonically possessed families."

"Well, okay, so some of them had issues." Nick was smirking.

"Issues? Smoking dope or getting caught shoplifting is an issue." She looked at Michael. "But two of them joined a cult, and I think another one of them is on trial for armed robbery."

Michael looked at Nick and Nick shrugged. "So I was a little less discriminating about my friends in my youthful years. You have to learn to ignore some of Naomi's comments. She's like the older sister I never wanted."

She regarded her younger cousin for a moment and Michael had the suspicion that some sort of unspoken message passed between them, but then she smiled up at him. "Come on," she said. "We have a few minutes before dinner. Let's go sit." She gestured them both into the living room, quiet and full of shadows compared to the light and noise that spilled from the direction of the kitchen. She turned on a torchiere lamp situated between a bookcase and a worn green armchair, then switched on the track lights above the entertainment center.

Michael sat down on the couch self-consciously. He had expected to be rushed through a meet and greet of Nick's family, which was how Nick had made it sound, and then parked at the dinner table. He was hungry, and the smells that wafted through the house, exotic and spicy, drove the point home somewhere in the region of his stomach. But he settled down on the couch, covered in tired green fabric that was worn shiny in places, and Naomi sat down opposite him in the fraying armchair.

Nick sat down quietly at the other end of the couch. "Mikey sees–"

Before Michael could stop his friend from repeating the tiresome observation yet one more time, Naomi nodded at them both. "I'll just bet he does."

Michael felt the hairs come up on the back of his neck. "What?" he said.

"Do you mind?" she asked. Before he answered, she touched his wrist softly, running her fingers across the back of his hand, and then turned his hand palm up and studied it under the light of the torchiere.

Michael wanted to pull back, but he sat and let her look at it. She released his hand and placed it back on his own knee, still palm up, and looked at him. He swallowed as he looked back, suddenly tense.

"Unexpected death," she said softly. "I'm so sorry."

He turned his head to look at Nick, wondering how on earth Naomi could come to that conclusion when he never talked about his family to anyone, even Nick. His friend gazed back at him, silent and expressionless for once.

She met his eyes when he turned back. "You're a sensitive, Michael. You're going to see things most people don't. Hear things, too. That can be a problem sometimes, right? I'll bet you ignore your ability, or try to ignore it. Don't. It's there, just like your talent for writing–"

*How did she know that?* Michael wondered.

"–and your sense of isolation." She smiled at him. "Am I

weirding you out? I've been studying hand analysis–"

"Palm reading," Nick interjected.

"–for a long time. My mother taught me, and her mother taught her. It's a family tradition. Some people have a sign in the hand that indicates the kind of ability you have. You seem to have that sign in triplicate."

Michael swallowed again. "How did you know about…death?"

She shook her head at him, her expression sad. "There are marks on your hand. But more than that, there's sadness around you and there has been for a while. It's probably time for you to start coming out of that. You're ready."

He looked away, suddenly conscious of the scar on his face, the intermittent pain in his shoulder and his hip that never left him completely. He didn't know what he was ready for.

She touched his arm. "I'm sorry. I can be a bit blunt at times."

"Yeah. Her family nickname is 'Tire Iron.'"

She ignored her cousin and leaned closer to Michael. "Maybe what I should have said is when you're ready for it, the sunlight is still waiting out there for you." She smiled at him and stood up. "I'd better get my kids to the dinner table before they start grabbing handfuls out of the pot. It was good to meet you, Michael. I'll catch you at dinner."

Michael looked at Nick after she left. "You invited me over to dinner so I could meet Naomi?"

Nick gave him a small smile. "That's part of it. Ol' Nicky Borja has something else up his sleeve, don't you doubt it, son."

Eloise turned up in time for dinner, resplendent in some sort of rainbow-colored tunic and black leggings, bringing whole wheat dinner rolls from the store where she worked. She gave Mrs. Borja a quick kiss in greeting before helping Naomi bring the food to the table.

Nick hadn't been kidding about squeezing people in sideways for a meal. Mr. Borja arrived shortly after Eloise, complaining good-naturedly about being unable to get his car into his own driveway. As soon as he sat down at the head of the table, people seemed to materialize out of the woodwork. Michael was placed at one end of the table beside Eloise, and introduced, rapid fire, to Naomi's husband Sean, Travis's brother Kevin, Mr. and Mrs. Borja, Nick's older brother Drew and his girlfriend Patsy, Nick's younger sister Melissa and her best friend Kirsten, and an older couple whom Nick called "Auntie Helen" and "Uncle Frank" but who were actually friends of the family and not related.

The conversations were loud and lively and Michael was amused when he realized that Nick was no longer the loudest person in the room. He ate rice and stir fried vegetables, strips of beef and shredded cabbage, fruit salad and a noodle casserole, and three of Eloise's rolls, finding that he had to turn down additional helpings when Mrs. Borja and Naomi continued to offer him still more. "I'm so full," he apologized.

"You're so big," Mrs. Borja said bluntly in her accented English, taking his measure with a practiced eye. "You should eat more."

Nick laughed at both of them. "He's tall, Mom. He's not trying for fat."

Mrs. Borja clucked and put down the casserole she had been offering.

They all helped clear the table, even Travis, but Naomi and Sean shooed everyone away from the sink. "There is a scientific way to load a dishwasher," Sean announced.

"A Ph.D. in engineering and all he uses it for is to load dishwashers. So sad." That was Drew, snagging one last roll as he placed the now-empty basket on the kitchen table.

"Dueling post-docs. Pathetic." Nick looked at Michael and

tilted his head at the door. "Let's book."

Michael thanked Mrs. Borja profusely for the meal and was rewarded with a quick kiss on the cheek that she pulled him down sideways to deliver. "Come back," she said. "I like you."

"Now I'm in for it," Nick complained as he herded Eloise and Michael out the door to the front porch. "If you don't turn up for dinner from time to time, I'll never hear the end of it. When Eloise doesn't get here, it's like a congressional crisis. You should have seen the mess when Cassie stopped coming around." He and Eloise sat down on the glider.

Michael sat down on the porch ledge facing them, hands in his pockets, back to the street. "This has been one strange evening, Nick."

"You didn't enjoy dinner?"

"Are you kidding? One more bite and I would have exploded. And I was tempted."

"Oh," said Eloise. She looked at her boyfriend. "You made him meet Naomi before dinner, didn't you?"

"You're not supposed to know that. I'm inscrutable. All Asian people are inscrutable."

For answer, Eloise jabbed him in the stomach with her elbow. "Inscrutable *that*."

"I wanted you to meet Naomi," Nick said, "because I think Cassie needed it."

Michael blinked. "What?"

"Cassie's getting squirrely." Nick sat with one arm around Eloise, a bottle of water in his other hand.

Eloise was uncharacteristically quiet. Michael would have thought she had gone to sleep, but he could see her eyes blinking as she curled up against Nick. He thought momentarily that he would like to try sitting that way with Cassie, and then let the thought go. "How so?" he asked.

"She seems fine at work, right? Laughs with us, jokes

around, chats with the customers. But I know her better than that. Calling in sick two days when she wasn't is a big tip-off. And before that, she stopped hanging around after work. She's been rushing out the door before any of us can stop and ask her what's up or if she wants to do anything. She's also coming in right on time when she starts her shift. She used to get there early and hang out in the break room with Fredo and me before we opened the store. She hasn't done that in a long time." He sipped the water. "Something's going on with her."

Michael looked at him curiously. "How do you know her so well?"

Nick smiled. "Cassie and me – we go way back."

"They even dated once." Eloise's voice was slightly muffled against Nick's shirt.

"Didn't that bother you?" Michael was incredulous.

"I didn't know Nick yet. I met him through Cassie. And they were done before I met him."

"We were done before the first date," Nick said with a laugh.

"Why?" Michael couldn't imagine stopping after one date with Cassie.

"Dude, she's like a sister. Dating her was like going out with my sister. We could barely bring ourselves to kiss good night and when we tried, we both started laughing." He shook his head. "But I know her very well, Ms. Valentine. There's not much she can hide from me. Like when something's not right." He pointed the water bottle at Michael before taking another sip. "And something's not right. Up to you to find out, Galahad."

Michael groaned. "I don't know where to start. She's hot and cold, all friendly one moment and then distant and aloof the next." He thought about giving Cassie his phone number and how well that had gone over. I never know if I'm doing the right thing or not."

"Neither does she. So it doesn't matter what you do. I'll tell you what, though. She needs you around."

"How do you figure?"

"Because you see dead people."

"Nick, if you say that one more time I'm gonna have to–"

"I'm just saying. But I'm also serious. You and Cassie go way back, too. That's her in the ghost story you told your first night at the bookstore, isn't it?" He grinned at the expression on Michael's face. "But it's why I brought you around to meet Naomi, so you could see it isn't just me that knows this about you. I think Cassie may need someone with your particular ability. The fact that you've known each other so long makes you an even better fit for the job. Daniel's been a hard parting for her. If you're seeing him around her, well…"

"Just the once."

"Okay. But she's got something going on in her house and if it's not Daniel, then what? She worries me."

"Why?"

"Because I know all the dark places she can get into. Just like she knows mine." His eyes focused on something remote for a moment and Eloise squeezed up tighter against him.

"We all have our dark places," Michael said softly.

Nick peered at him over the top of Eloise's head. "I know we do," he agreed. "That's why she absolutely needs you."

# ~ CHAPTER FIFTEEN ~

Cassie was lost. She didn't know how else to describe it to herself, let alone talk to anyone about it. She had gone back to The List and deleted that horrible, disturbing phrase she had found.

*I felt so bad I knew they were all dead*

Even after deleting it, the words reappeared in her head. She had no idea where the phrase had come from and the fact that it had turned up in Daniel's list–

She was troubled that Daniel seemed so far away. An absurd observation: he had been gone nearly a year. But always before, she had believed she could feel him close to her. Sometimes the feeling was so strong she couldn't help thinking that if she opened her eyes quickly enough, or turned her head at just the right moment, she would see him standing there, smiling at her. And she knew it was wrong to hope for it, but she couldn't stop hoping, even when reality caught up and walloped her yet one more time.

Before, she had felt him around her, she knew it. But lately, not at all. And she wondered what that meant. Had he been there and was now moving on? Or was she herself moving on, moving away from the memory of him? Part of her fought that idea, terrified it meant that she was allowing herself to forget him and everything he had meant to her. Part of her told her that what she was doing was not only necessary but normal, a natural settling into the direction her life had taken. And she hated it.

She could see concern in Steve's eyes, in Nick's, even Michael's if she chose to do so. She didn't. She put in her hours at work, no more, no less, and then withdrew again when she was done.

She stood at the cash register now and gazed out the picture window to the street outside. The weather was growing colder as autumn settled in, and the people who walked past the shop were togged out in jackets, some of them already sporting thin gloves and scarves. The sight of it made her sad. The year before, the warm weather had lingered longer than it had any right to do, and there had been an almost late-summer feel when Daniel left her, a kind of persisting twilight of warmth and sunlight and longer days. This year, autumn was cold and dark.

She turned away from the window and glanced around the store. Steve was in his office at the computer, and Fredo was coming onto the floor, wiping his hands on a paper towel.

"Hey, Cassie," he said. "Why not take a break? It's pretty slow and I've looked at about as many invoices as I care to for the time being. Besides, Michael's in receiving if I need him and Nick should be here any minute." He smiled at her. "Have you been downstairs lately? It's coming together real nice."

"I haven't seen it, yet. Maybe I'll go take a look." She smiled back at him. "Thanks, Fredo."

"No problem. Take your time."

Cassie went down to the basement to look over the progress that Michael and Nick had made. The finished part that would include the office and the break room was empty except for the air of expectancy that soon-to-be-occupied rooms all seemed to have. The boys had done a good job of cleaning it: the paneling on the walls gleamed under the harsh overhead lights, slated to be replaced by new fixtures that would be easier on the eyes. She stopped a moment and took a deep breath, savoring the smell of wood polish.

And all of a sudden, Daniel was all around her.

She choked, physically shocked, and was submerged into a

corporeal memory of him, feeling his arms around her again, so strong at the beginning and ultimately so weak at the end that his embrace was as soft and caressing as a wrap made of the lightest feathers, but equally heavy with the burden of anguish and parting. She remembered his warmth, his smell, his very taste, and she closed her eyes, overwhelmed with the pain of his absence.

Without conscious thought, she went to her knees, then curled into herself on the floor, and the grief that wracked her drew a storm of weeping like none since the day she had left him in the hospice center for the last time. She put her head to her knees and sobbed, feeling that she couldn't bear anymore, feeling that surely she would be torn apart with this paroxysm of pure anguish.

And then a pair of strong arms lifted her and pulled her close, surrounding her, holding her together. She knew who had come after her. "Nick," she whispered, not opening her eyes, and put her head gratefully against his chest, felt his strength as he held and rocked her a little, while deep inside, her sorrow ran freely from the myriad rents and piercings that all bore the name of Daniel. She dissolved with this fresh wounding, cried until the tears began to stop of their own accord, and still he held her tightly, not letting her go.

Then a voice said quietly, "You can't scare me, Valentine. I've seen you cry before. Of course, we were about nine years old and you had just been stung by a wasp."

"Michael!" She pulled back, suddenly self-conscious of her streaming eyes, her runny nose. She thought how puffy her eyes must look and began groping for a tissue from the pack she always carried in her pocket.

He loosened his hold but didn't quite let her go. "He said to tell you that your Uncle Nicky sent me."

Cassie mopped at her wet face and blew her nose

apologetically. "Oh, Michael, I'm so sorry."

"Don't," he said. "It's really okay. You needed to do that. Needed it for some time, I would think." He saw her glance anxiously up the stairs and added, "Relax. Steve went out for sandwiches for him and Fredo, and Fredo is still at the cash register. No one's going to come looking for you for a bit."

She sighed and moved to put her head against his chest once more, then stopped, suddenly awkward. "I don't know what to say," she began.

He shook his head and pushed damp strands of hair away from her face, his touch slow and soft. "It's okay," he said again. He helped her to her feet and then stepped back, giving her some space. "I'll go up ahead," he offered, "and bar the door from anyone wandering down here. You come up when you're ready. Oh, and there's a small bathroom in the back there. The sink works, but it's only cold water."

She managed a grateful smile and he smiled back, his face lighting up, his left eye nearly disappearing into his scar. And then he was gone, up the stairs and back into the store proper.

She didn't see him again until a few hours later after she had cornered Nick in the break room. "I appreciate your sending Michael down to me," she said to him as he made himself a cup of hot chocolate. "But you didn't have to do that."

Nick looked at her, brown eyes mildly curious. "What are you talking about? I didn't send Michael anywhere." He licked the spoon he had been using and placed it in the sink.

"But he said–" She broke off when Michael entered and their eyes met. He took in the scene at a glance and she saw comprehension cross his face. A slight tinge of pink colored his cheeks and he murmured something and backed out of the room.

Nick raised his eyebrows in surprise. "What did I miss?"

"Nothing. Just something Michael said earlier."

The rest of the afternoon was hide and seek. Michael dodged

Cassie like he might try to dodge a bullet, slipping down convenient aisles or disappearing into receiving for long periods of time.

She finally caught up to him at his car after the store had closed. "Why did you say that?" she asked. "Why did you say that Nick sent you to me?"

He looked away from her and was silent, his face still and bleak. "I just thought it might be easier for you," he said at last.

"Why? Why would that be easier?"

"Cass," he said. "What was I supposed to say to you? That every day I see how much you're hurting? That I've been where you are and I just wanted to let you know I was around? It's not fair of me, I know that. Nick told me how it was for you and Daniel, how much you loved him."

"But you–"

Without warning, he took her face between his hands and silenced her with a sudden kiss, a touch that was sweet and demanding and took her breath momentarily before he stopped. "I'm sorry," he said. He released her and turned away abruptly to unlock the car door. "I'm sorry for all of it," he muttered to no one. He slid into the car without looking at her, pulled the door shut with a vicious yank, and drove away.

Cassie remained on the sidewalk watching the empty street long after his car had disappeared from sight.

* * *

"You've been awfully pulled-in, lately." Grandpa Henry looked at Michael with his sharp blue eyes, the eyes that missed nothing.

"Just a lot on my mind." Michael stared down at his plate and moved green beans around with his fork, movements both anxious and listless, avoiding the older man's gaze.

"No news about the bookstore? It's all you've been talking about since you started."

"Nothing new," Michael said. There was a brief silence. He raised his head and met his grandfather's eyes. "What?"

"Somebody hurt you, there? Someone say something?"

"What?" Michael's momentary confusion was evident. "You mean at the store? No, nothing like that." He put down his fork. "Something else came up," he said quietly.

Grandpa Henry pushed his own plate aside and folded his hands on the table, waiting. It wasn't often that Michael talked frankly with him. Michael was prodded best by silence, if he was going to talk at all.

"There's a girl at work. She knew me, knew all of us, from when we used to vacation at the lake." Michael looked away and the shadow of uncertainty touched his expression. "And I..." he broke off into silence, adding only, "It's complicated."

"Is she involved with someone else?" Grandpa Henry asked after the silence had grown a bit long.

"Not exactly." Michael sighed and took the napkin from his lap, balled it up in his fist and threw it on the table in sudden exasperation. "She had a boyfriend she really loved. He died last year."

"Last year? But then wouldn't–"

Michael shook his head. "She's just like I was, Grandpa. She's hurt and she can't get over him, and I don't have a chance against that." He laughed bitterly. "She's exactly like I was. I know there's no getting through that." It was all he was going to say on the subject and he rose, gathering plates and glasses together to clear the table.

"Michael."

Grandson looked at grandfather, face closed, still, impenetrable.

"Take it slow."

Michael regarded him a little longer, then excused himself and went to the sink to wash and dry the dishes before retiring to his room for the rest of the night.

# ~ CHAPTER SIXTEEN ~

At work, Cassie behaved as if she and Michael didn't know each other. Michael took his cue and avoided her when he could. He also avoided the sharp glances Nick gave both of them, Steve's raised eyebrows, even Fredo's puzzled expression at the overly polite exchanges between him and Cassie. He did the same as she did: went in, put in his hours, went home. Why would he have expected anything different?

After a few days of getting frosted at work, he decided he needed his brain cleared and went for a five-mile run when he finished hitting the weights. In the end his thoughts felt as muddled, but something in him had lightened. *God bless endorphins*, he thought. He ate a sandwich for dinner, showered early, and was deep into the latest David Morrell book to complete his escape when he heard his phone from across the room.

Michael picked up the chiming cell phone and stared at the screen, but the only information was "Private Call". Still, he had a pretty strong feeling who was on the other end. Maybe Cassie was bringing assault charges against him for the kiss. What had he been thinking? *Nice move, Penfield. Push a little harder, next time.* He forced himself to answer the call. "Talk to me."

"Michael? It's Cassie."

His guess had been right. "Hey, Cassie." He tried to make himself sound as casual as possible.

"You said I could call any time." She sounded worried.

"I meant it, too. What's up?"

"Can we talk?"

Hmmm. They had never been together, so she couldn't be breaking up with him. That was the good news. The bad news–He didn't go there. "Sure. Tomorrow?"

"No. Like right now."

He glanced at the clock. It was nearly ten-thirty. Grandpa Henry would be turning off the news and heading for the bathroom any time. "Where do you want to meet?"

"I stole your address from Steve's files. Come outside," she said, and hung up.

Michael raised his eyebrows in surprise. He put on his running shoes and went to the front door.

"Mikey? Are you going out?" Grandpa Henry was already in the bathroom but nonetheless heard the lock click open when Michael turned it.

"Just on the porch. I've got a friend out front."

"Okay. Keep the noise down."

Michael smiled in spite of himself. He suspected that secretly Grandpa Henry wished he could have used that admonition a lot more than he ever had. Michael grabbed a hooded sweatshirt from the peg by the door and went out into the night.

Cassie's car was parked in front of the house and she got out and walked toward him hesitantly when he stepped onto the porch. "I know it's late," she said.

He shrugged. "It's okay. Do you want to come in?"

She shook her head. "No, if that's all right with you. If we get too cold, we can sit in the car."

"That works." He led her to the bench beside the front door and sat down with her. "What's going on?"

She was silent a moment, and he could barely see her in the shadows. Her dark hair and clothing

rendered her nearly invisible. "You said at my house you know how hard it is to talk about..." her voice broke and she turned her head away from him, staring out at the dark street.

Then she snapped back to him, abrupt and fierce. "So you must have a story like mine. Can *you* talk about it?" she demanded at last. "I mean, can you actually sit there and talk about what happened without… without…" She stopped, groping for words, unable to say anything more.

*Uh-oh.* Michael felt the automatic reluctance, a swift kick in the gut that normally signaled him to stop talking and leave immediately. *Run away*, the little voice inside him quoted. *Run very far away.* But he knew that if he gave into that, at a later time he'd just have to face up to what he had done. And he knew that right now, Cassie's willingness to open up and trust him hung in the balance. He knew what would happen if he shut her down or walked away. "I'll tell you right now, if that's what you want," he said, inwardly amazed at how natural he made that sound.

She looked at him and despite the dark he could see her eyes, curious and wary at the same time. "So, what? You tell me yours and I tell you mine?"

"Something like that." He shook his head at her. "This is no good, Cass. You're poisoning yourself. Your house has something weird going on in it, weird enough for you to drag me over there to see if it's…" He didn't finish the sentence. "I get the feeling that if you don't start dealing with all of this, your house, your loss, that you're going to shatter. Don't you think?"

A tear slid down her right cheek and she said nothing.

"Look, you don't have to talk at all, okay? I'll tell you a story, and you listen. It's all you have to do. Can you handle that, at least?"

She nodded.

"Okay, then. Here it goes." He cleared his throat, took a deep breath, and plunged into it. "My parents and my brother were killed in a car accident right after I saw you at that mall and got your phone number."

Cassie gasped in spite of herself. His scar, his personality change, all of it suddenly made so much sense she couldn't believe she hadn't guessed. She remembered his family: tall and kind Mr. Penfield, funny and harried Mrs. Penfield, even little exasperating Benny. The thought of them all being gone hit her with a shock and a stab of pain that made her catch her breath. She had been so self-centered, she hadn't even thought about what could be behind the scar on his face. "Michael, I'm sorry. I am so sorry."

'"Shhh. I'm telling you a story, remember?" He strove to keep his voice light, secretly glad that he couldn't see the look on her face. It would have done him in completely. He looked away and talked to the street in front of them, quietly, relentlessly. He realized he had finally found the person who most needed to hear his whole story.

"After the accident I was in the hospital for months. Then I came here to live with my grandfather, but that was later. When I was in the hospital, my eyes were bandaged shut for about a week. The left side of my face was injured and so was my left eye. My right eye was fine, but they said they had to keep both eyes quiet for recovery, so both of them were bandaged. While I couldn't see anything…" He stopped abruptly and there was a long silence.

"Go on," she said after a bit.

He glanced at her, uneasy. "I've never told anyone the rest of this. My grandfather knows some of it, but I've never even told him everything."

She looked troubled. "Then you don't have to tell me."

"No, I do. I know I do. It's not really a problem, it's just that I've never talked about all of it."

She nodded at him when he looked at her again. "Keep going, then. I'm listening."

He swallowed. "My father was the first one to talk to me. I was just waking up from a nap in my hospital room. When your eyes are shut all the time, it's hard to stay awake. Well, I was probably groggy for other reasons, too. But one time when I woke up he was in the room with me. I told him I was scared and I felt him pat my hand. 'Don't be afraid,' he said. 'Everything's going to be okay, Mikey.' I must have fallen asleep again. The next thing I knew my grandfather was there offering me juice. I told him my dad had stopped by. He didn't say anything about it and I didn't even think about that.

"A while later, and I'm not even sure if it was the same day, my mom and Benny came to my room. At least, that's what I heard. I could hear them talking to each other while I was waking up and I told them I could hear them. 'Hey, the Mike-aholic is awake!' Benny said. Mom shushed him and asked me if I was feeling any better. She put her hand on my face and told me I would be well soon, that the bandages would be coming off in a little while."

He stopped and looked at Cassie. "After that, I would sometimes sense my mom or dad in the room with me. I would hear my father clear his throat and turn the pages of his book, so I knew when he was sitting with me. Sometimes it was my mom. She always touched my face and I could smell her perfume. One time, Benny came in and told me to hurry up and get well." He smiled slightly at the memory but the smile faded quickly. "But you know…"

She looked at him questioningly.

"My mom and dad died on impact, instantly. Benny died on the way to the hospital." He turned his face away for a moment. "I told my grandfather about them after the bandages came off, insisting they had been there. I had heard them. I had touched them. But of course they were being buried while I was still recovering from one surgery and waiting to have another. No one told me. They didn't want to upset me." There was anger in his voice now.

"Michael, they must have been trying to protect you."

He looked down and took another deep breath. ""'So after I told my grandfather about the visits, someone decided I needed some kind of grief therapy. I was still in the hospital. A woman I didn't know and didn't want to know kept coming in to see me. I never talked to her. In fact, I stopped talking to everybody." He shook his head. "I was confused. I was angry."

"You were in mourning," Cassie said.

"I was guilty," he said quietly. "When the accident happened, right after the crash, I lost consciousness for a couple of minutes. My mother woke me up. Yes, I know it's impossible, but it was her. I heard her calling my name until I was all the way awake and then she told me to get out of the car, to move back because the fire was spreading. God, Cass, it hurt so much to move. But she kept at me, telling me to get away from the car. I thought she was with me. I thought she was waiting for me just outside the window. I never thought to check. I never even looked. I just crawled out and collapsed. I should have..." He stopped.

Cassie reached down suddenly to squeeze his hand and didn't let go.

"My grandfather took me home against medical advice. I was healing okay physically, but I still wasn't talking to anyone, not even him. They told him I should stay so I could work through my grief. He told them he figured when I had something to say, I would say it, and that was that. I went home with him and life went on. Except that I was the only one in my family still alive. I still don't understand why — why they all left me."

Cassie sat with him for a moment in silence. "You heard them, but you never saw them?"

"Not once. And I never heard them again after the hospital. I kept waiting. I'm still waiting, but they don't talk to me anymore." He sounded bitter and knew it, tried to bite the familiar anger back. She squeezed his hand again and he allowed himself to marvel at the fact that her small hand was in his. "That's the whole story," he said. "I've never told anyone before. I figured no one would believe me."

"I believe you," she said quietly.

"Thanks." He felt awkward and was grateful they were sitting in the dark.

They sat for a while longer and then Cassie shivered. "I'm getting cold," she said.

"We can go inside," Michael offered.

"No, no, that's okay. I probably should get home before my mom freaks and starts calling my cell non-stop." She stood up and Michael followed her, reluctant to release her hand. "I'll see you at work tomorrow, right?"

"I'll be there."

She smiled at him and turned to go, then stopped at the edge of the first step. "Can I ask you something?"

He shrugged. "Sure."

"Why did you kiss me that other day?"

The question took him so much by surprise it was as if she had slapped him. "What kind of question is that?" He was genuinely bewildered and had no idea how to answer her.

"No, I mean it. Why *did* you kiss me?" She was silent a moment, then added, "Were you just feeling sorry for me?"

"Sorry for you? I don't think so." She looked so uncertain that he kept his distance, as if any sudden move might startle her. He shrugged again, struggling for an answer. "For the same reason I wanted to ask for your phone number."

She smiled at that. "Ask me for it, then. Just not yet."

"When?"

But she was already going down the steps, vanishing in the

shadows between the house and her car. “Not yet,” her voice floated back to him.

Michael watched her tail lights disappear, feeling somewhere between exhausted and elated. “Maybe,” he said to himself. He opened the door to let himself back into the house, vaguely aware of the sound of Grandpa Henry’s bedroom light switching off as he hung his sweatshirt back on its peg.

# ~ CHAPTER SEVENTEEN ~

"So what was it like?" Eloise's voice was sharp, even over the phone.

"What was what like?" Cassie had her phone wedged between her ear and her shoulder as she tried to finish folding her laundry.

"Don't even start with me, Cassie. I had a rotten day, today. Just tell me what it was like dating him last night."

Cassie blinked. "Date? Who said anything about a date? You mean Michael?"

"No, I mean the hot dog guy on the corner of Main and Third. Of course with Michael. Jeez, what's wrong with you?"

"Nothing's wrong with me. But there wasn't a date. Where did you get that idea? Oh, never mind. Obviously from Nick. Well, no date, sorry. Not even close. We talked on his front porch."

"Oh." She sounded disappointed. "So tell me about it anyway."

"About what?" Cassie asked dryly. "His porch? Or our conversation?"

"C'mon, Cassie. Give already."

"I drove to his house and we talked."

"Yeah? And then?"

"Then what?"

*"That's it?"*

"If you want to hear that we fell panting into each other's arms and got crazy wild in front of the neighbors, the answer is 'no.'"

"Oh." Eloise radiated disappointment over the phone.

Cassie had to laugh. "You're insane. You and Nick both are."

"I'm not blind. You've been lusting after Michael in your own repressed Victorian way since he turned up. Admit it."

"I told you I had a crush on him when we were little."

"Yeah? I think you have one on him now that you're not so little."

"And if I do?"

Eloise made a rude noise into the phone. "What'd you talk about, anyway?"

Cassie considered her answer. "Among other things, when he was in the hospital." She figured that sounded safe enough.

There was a pause. "You were talking with your crush about his time in the hospital?"

"Yeah. So what?"

"You were talking about a *hospital*."

"Well, yeah."

"Sounds fascinating."

Cassie put a grin into her voice. "Well, but he's cute."

"I'll talk to you tomorrow." Eloise sounded disgusted. "'Night."

They hung up and Cassie finished folding the last of her laundry and began shoving it into her drawers with relief. She couldn't tell Eloise everything. Michael's story was too personal for that. But she did smile when she thought about the night before. It had almost been like when they were kids together, but at the same time it was different. Different in a nice way. They weren't kids any longer.

She thought of Daniel, and then she thought about Michael, unable to keep herself from some comparison. But it was apples and oranges, as people said. Daniel and Michael were two completely different people and comparing was pointless.

The memory of Michael's kiss lingered with her, as did the warmth of his confiding in her the night before. He had not acted much differently at work today, chatting casually with her if their paths crossed but not going out of his way to seek her out. It had been more comfortable than she had anticipated, and she appreciated his ability to keep the slight shift in their relationship out of the workplace. But there had been a change between them and she knew he felt it, too. She saw it when she caught him looking at her sometimes. She would smile at him and he would smile back before turning away. No wonder Nick thought something momentous had happened.

She put the last of her socks in the drawer and decided to go downstairs and watch some TV. It had been a long time since she had simply sat on the couch with the remote in her hand. She put her laundry basket back in the corner, gathered up the wrappers from some granola bars she had eaten in her room the morning before, and pulled open the bedroom door.

And there was a young man standing there, looking at her.

Cassie froze, wrappers falling from her stunned hands. He wasn't really there, she understood that, but at the same time he most definitely was. He had on a jacket and a pair of jeans and – was that blood on his hands? On his *face*? His eyes held a spark of insanity. "I don't want to do this," he whispered to her in a ragged voice.

Cassie backed away as he came forward into her room. "Don't–" she began, her throat far too closed to allow a scream, her fear far too paralyzing to allow her to try to run past him.

"Please don't make me do this." He took one more step toward her and then disappeared when he was mere inches away. Her bedroom door swung itself shut.

Five long minutes after she had collapsed on the floor, she found the coordination and the will to grope one hand across her bed, scrabbling around the sheets and the blanket until she closed her fist around her cell phone, pushing the speed-dial with shaking hands. She got voice-mail and left a message she forgot two seconds after she disconnected. When the phone rang for her a few minutes later, she nearly cried out in fright.

"Are you safe?" She had been expecting Eloise. The voice was Michael's and he sounded angry.

Cassie wanted to weep with relief. "Michael? I called Eloise," she began.

"Who called Nick, who called me. I'm on my way. All I got was that there was a guy in your house. Are you out of there?"

"No. I'm in my room. Michael, it's not like that."

"Is the door locked? How do I get in?" he demanded.

"There's a key under the cushion on the porch rocker."

"I'm almost there. Just a few more minutes." He muttered something she didn't quite hear, then added forcefully, "Don't you hang up on me."

Cassie closed her eyes and held the cell phone like a lifeline. She thought briefly of Daniel, wished he was with her, wished he could be coming to her.

*Michael, come and find me…* The thought popped into her head, unbidden. How long ago had that been? She was no longer in her room, huddled on the floor in a state of panic, waiting for a friend to arrive.

*She was eight years old, sitting up in a tree, screened by leaves and trying not to giggle. The sun was hot and dappled through the branches as a warm breeze stirred the treetops. She had a glimpse of Benny, crouching beneath the porch. He was giggling, snorting, hand over his mouth.* ***Michael, come and find me!*** *he had shrieked, smacking his brother soundly on the back of the head. He had grabbed Cassie's arm as he ran out the cabin door, pulling her into the game, both of them laughing like conspirators. Michael, shouting with the righteous indignation of* *an injured older brother, had tossed his comic book onto the table where he had sat reading and come hauling out of the cabin after them.*

***Come and find me**, Cassie had whispered, sitting up in her tree. She heard a soft rustling beneath her and looked down at the same time that Michael looked up. She had felt a strange sensation in her stomach when their eyes met. She hadn't understood it at the time; she just knew that she liked it. He had grinned at her, then put a finger to his lips and gestured her down quietly. He meant to turn the tables on Benny…*

The sound of a car pulling up outside the house, of running footsteps on the porch, brought her back to the here and now. In a matter of a few seconds she heard the front door open and his footsteps in the hall. "Come and find me," she said aloud, her eyes squeezed shut, afraid to open them and see that the young man with the blood had reappeared in her doorway.

"Cassie? Where are you?" His voice came from both downstairs and over the speaker of her phone.

"Upstairs," she said, cell phone hard against her ear. "Straight up and on your left." She sat and waited for him in a kind of shocked relief.

His footsteps were swift and surprisingly light for someone with his build. Her door banged open and then he was there like some sort of avenging angel, eyes on fire, hair wild and tossed with hurry. One hand still held his phone, the other was clenched tightly into a large fist. "So where is this guy?"

"You only got half the story," she said. She pushed herself weakly off the floor and managed to get to her knees.

He came to her and pulled her up. "I was scared," he said.

"You?" Cassie laughed and stopped abruptly when she realized how close she was to converting the laugh all the way over to tears.

He looked down at her. "You want to tell me what's going on? Or were you just trying to give me your phone number after all?"

"Let's go downstairs, first," she said. She clung to his hand with both of hers as they went through the door into the hall and back down the steps. The front door stood open, key in the lock.

"Spiderman wouldn't have left the key in the door." She pulled the door shut, removed the key with trembling hands and replaced it on the porch rocker, plumping up the cushions.

"Spiderman wouldn't have needed a key." He regarded her. "Let's get out of here. We can talk in the car."

"I think I'd like that."

He opened the passenger door for her and shut it with more force than was necessary. He came around, got into the driver's seat, and put the key into the ignition without turning it. He was breathing hard, as if from exertion, and Cassie looked at him curiously. "So tell me what happened," he said, and his voice was slightly clipped.

"Are you angry?" She didn't understand but wanted to.

He laughed shortly. "Angry? I have no idea. You tell me. Eloise called Nick, completely out of her mind, barely coherent. She was going on about how she was in the city with her parents, how she just talked to you, and now someone was in your house and he needed to get over here. So Nick calls me instead of the police. I told him to hang up and call 911 but he said no, Eloise specifically said *not* 911. She told him to get his butt over here. But he couldn't. Seems he's in the middle of some school studio project and his presence was definitely required, so he calls me and tells me to get to your house, that Eloise said someone was in your room."

He braced his fists against the steering wheel and looked at her, brown eyes cold and hard. "I just got home from work. I didn't know what to expect. I didn't know what I was walking into, I just knew I had to get over here. If I had been too late, or if something had happened–" He took a deep breath and blew it out noisily.

She put a hand on his arm and found that he was trembling almost as badly as she had been.

He turned his head and looked at her. "If something had happened to you…"

She shook her head. "Michael, I'm okay. I'm terrified and I'm really, really glad you're here, but I'm okay. There was someone in my room, but he wasn't really there. It's the house. The whole time I've been here I always had the feeling that one day I would open that door and someone would be standing there. And it happened tonight. He was young, maybe the same age we are. I think he had blood all over him. I think it was blood." Her voice faltered a little as she remembered, but she went on. "He said something to me about not wanting to do this. Then he started coming towards me. I was backing up, and he kept coming."

She shivered as she remembered. "And then he said 'Please don't make me do this', like I was forcing him into something." She stopped and took a deep breath. "He disappeared while I was looking at him. Just vanished. And then my door shut itself. "

"Are you telling me you saw a ghost?"

"What do you think happened?"

He thought about that, frowning. "Cass, how old is your house?"

"It's older." She tried to remember what the realtor had said to her mother about it. "It's been renovated, I know that much. Most of the houses on this street came later. I don't know how old mine is."

"With all the ghost stories you've been hearing at work, did it ever occur to you to research your own house?"

She laughed suddenly at the thought, but without much

mirth. "No. I'm so stupid! No, it never occurred to me. There was never anything particular there. Just drafts of air, maybe footsteps. This is the first time I've ever seen anything like this."

"So you've never seen him before."

"No. But there was a night a while ago when I heard the front door open and close and then someone came in." She told him about that night, ending with the voice that had told her to hide.

He looked at her. "Something told you to hide?"

"Yes. Just like that. Just one word. But really sharp and really clear."

"Male? Female?"

"Does it matter? I don't know. I couldn't tell. It was whispered, almost. But loud enough to hear it."

"Are you working tomorrow?" he asked.

"Not until afternoon. I've got three until close."

He nodded. "Then maybe you ought to go ask someone about this place." He looked at her. "Are you really okay?"

"I think so," she said honestly. "He didn't harm me. I was just so scared."

They sat in silence a few minutes and then he said her name softly. He was studying her when she looked at him. "Now that I finally have your phone number, you want to go get some ice cream?"

She thought it over. She didn't want to go back into the house just yet, that was certain. "Can I have whipped cream *and* sprinkles?"

He smiled at her as he started up the car. "Some things never change, do they, Cass?"

# ~ CHAPTER EIGHTEEN ~

The evening felt like a date, even though she told herself over and over that it wasn't one. Rational mind, she decided, was the devil's own invention. She wasn't on a date, she thought. But then even if she was, did it matter? Daniel was gone, almost a year. Going on a date nearly a year after the loss of someone who hadn't even been her fiancé should not have been an issue. So why did she feel so sad inside while she sat in a booth across from Michael, eating a turtle sundae topped with extra whipped cream, sprinkles, nuts, and a cherry as well?

She spent a lot of time looking down at her dish, concentrating on what she was doing. She didn't want Michael to see the conflict that was raging in her, even as she sat there quietly spooning up ice cream and chocolate sauce. But she knew he was studying her and she had a pretty fair idea that he knew what was going on. Had he always been so perceptive?

"This was wrong, wasn't it?" he said suddenly.

She looked up, startled, as he put down his spoon after finishing his banana split. "What?" she asked, trying to gain a little time to get her thoughts in order.

"I shouldn't have asked you to do this," he said softly. There was an expression of ineffable sadness on his face and Cassie felt worse as she looked at him. Even his scar looked sad.

"It's fine," she said. "Really. It's okay."

He looked at her, unsure. "Don't say that," he said. "Don't say it if you really don't mean it."

But she did mean it. At least, she thought she did. "Michael, you asked me to come out for ice cream, not to marry you. I'm fine with that."

"But you're really uncomfortable here, aren't you? I can see it all over you."

"You know what? It's okay if I'm uncomfortable. Life has just been uncomfortable for a long time. It's not very happy. It's not always fun. It just *is*, you know?"

"Yeah. I do." He sat in silence for a minute and then said unexpectedly, "Do you want some help with that sundae?"

Cassie looked at him and started to laugh at the incongruity of the question. "Do I look like I can't finish this?"

He shrugged, embarrassed. "I guess I was just hungrier than I thought."

"Oh, God, you didn't have dinner, did you? You said earlier you just got home from work before coming to my place. Michael, I'm sorry. Ice cream isn't meant to feed a starving guy. Let me get you something else. Want a burger?"

"Hey, calm down. I'm not going to keel over, if that's what you're worried about. I can get a burger if I want one."

"No, seriously. Let me get it for you." She studied him thoughtfully. "You were the one who liked only mustard and onions, right? No ketchup."

His eyebrows came up in surprise. "You remembered?"

"Yeah. Because I thought you were weird." She laughed and got up from the booth. "I'll split the fries with you."

She was back a few minutes later with a hamburger, an order of fries, and a root beer on a tray. "Root beer. I remembered that, too."

Michael pushed aside his ice cream dish to make room. "You really didn't have to do this."

"I know. I'll eat some fries and then you don't have to feel guilty. And then I don't have to feel guilty for dragging you away from your dinner."

They ate in silence for a few minutes and Cassie couldn't

help feeling a bit better about the situation. Except for the one thought at the back of her mind that was nagging at her and refused to go away, regardless of ice cream with sprinkles, or a handful of French fries.

The burger vanished in a matter of a few minutes. Cassie, still working on her ice cream, couldn't help but grin at him. "Is one burger going to be enough?"

"Cut it out, Cass. You make me sound like a bear coming out of hibernation, or something."

"Michael, you're not exactly a tiny person. When did you get so large, anyhow? The last time I saw you, we were nearly the same height."

"High school, mostly. I had to do a lot of physical therapy after the accident, just to get moving again. But when the therapy ended, I kept going with the weights and some of the other exercises. I don't feel as well if I don't. I don't move as well, either." He stopped and took a sip of root beer.

"It's been hard for you, hasn't it? I mean beyond the obvious. The operations, the therapy. Are you still in pain all the time?"

"Nah. Every now and then, but it's not so bad. Are you going to finish that melted sundae or what?"

She let him have what was left of it, smiling to herself as he ate it. When they had all been children together, she remembered that she and Benny would be done eating long before Michael. Benny was like a gnat at meal time, landing and taking little bites and then zooming off again. It drove everyone crazy, but pinning him down to sit and eat a meal was next to impossible. At least, during vacation. He was too excited to be doing other things. Cassie herself didn't eat much and didn't take long to finish what she ate.

Michael, on the other hand, in foreshadowing of his adult size, could sit at the table and eat until his mother had cleared away everything but his plate. They all teased him about it, but looking at him now, it was obvious he had been puppy-feeding. They should have known what was going to happen just by checking the size of his paws, she thought. She grinned at the thought and Michael noticed.

"What?" he said.

"Nothing. Never mind. Was that good?"

"Great. I'll have to remember banana splits make good appetizers and melted turtle sundaes aren't bad for dessert."

They left the diner and Michael drove her home in silence. He seemed at ease compared to earlier, but Cassie was on tenterhooks, trying to get up the nerve to do what she knew she must do before they said good night to each other. She stared out at the street slipping by her in the night as they passed the dry cleaners, the post office, the Quick Mart. When the gas station loomed up on the corner, she took a deep breath. They were nearly to her house.

Michael pulled up to the curb. "C'mon," he said. "I'll check out the house with you before I go."

She put a hand on his arm. "Not yet," she said softly.

He looked puzzled. "Okay. What's up?"

"It's my turn," she said. "To tell you a story." After all that he had told her the other night, she knew she couldn't renege on the agreement.

The puzzled look on his face dissolved to one of uncertainty. "Now? Are you sure?"

"I've never tried talking about this before," she said hesitantly. Her voice sounded suddenly hoarse and rusty, as if she hadn't spoken in a long time.

"I know." Michael carefully looked away, looked out through the windshield in front of him. "Would it be easier if we sat on your porch, or in your house?"

She gave him a sad smile. "Thanks, but nothing is going to

make this easier."

"Okay." He nodded.

She sat silently a little longer, then said, "Remember when I told you about him asking me not to come back when it was time?"

"Sure."

"We argued about it a lot. I called it his final ultimatum."

*Daniel had said, "I don't want you there for it. Jeez, Cass, you don't follow me into the bathroom."*

*"What? What does that have to do with anything?"*

*"It's private. So is this. I don't know what's going to happen."*

*"But I want to be there with you."*

*"You will be."*

*"Daniel, I don't want to desert you."*

*"You're not. I'm telling you what I want."*

*"But I don't want that."*

*"Tough. My death, my call."*

Cassie stopped and put her fingers across her mouth for a moment. "I told him that I loved him and he told me that was impossible, that he was just a sack of skin and sickness walking around. Then he said I was supposed to break up with him when he told me he had leukemia. He told me it was the ultimate break-up line and had worked so well in the past. I told him it wouldn't work with me. Then I asked him if he was scared of dying and he said he was, but he figured that by the time he got there, he would be so tired he wouldn't give a rat's ass. Those were his words." She looked at Michael. "That was about two weeks before it actually happened." And then she stopped speaking.

Michael waited her out. Through the windshield, he could

see the porch light go out on a house down the street. At the same time, lights went on in an upstairs window. Bedtime for someone, he guessed. Further down the block, a dog barked into the night. Despite that, it was somehow peaceful sitting there with Cassie. Still, he could feel her shoring herself up, pulling herself together to tell him about Daniel's death. When at last she began to speak, he closed his eyes to the street before him and watched the story that she unfolded for him.

*She had spent the afternoon at his bedside, and they sat in silence as the daylight began to fade from the view out of Daniel's window. The grass grew darker as the light withdrew, and the trees began to cloak themselves in shadow. There were still some evening insects left, stragglers at the end of an unusually long summer, and they began to buzz and cluster around the street lights that came on against the twilight.*

*Daniel stirred on the bed and Cassie turned away from the window to look at him.*

*"You know what's funny?" he said, his voice barely above a whisper. She moved closer to hear him and he smiled at her gently, almost shyly. "When I was a kid, I mean a little kid, really young, I used to love the morning. If I was awake early enough, I'd sit and watch the sun rise. Out on the porch, you know? Shivering in my pajamas, huddled down against the cold, sitting on the top step waiting for that first real burst of light." His smile turned inward for a moment as he remembered, and then he looked at her. "I used to love the feel of a new day, so early, so unused. But now I prefer sunsets." His glance flicked toward the window. "What do you suppose that means?"*

*Cassie heard and could barely reply. "I think it means–" she stopped, unable to continue.*

*"What?" His expression was mild as always, but his eyes were unyielding.*

*"I think it means you want to rest," she said. She looked down.*

*He took a deep breath and let it out in a sigh. "I'm really tired," he admitted, and added, "Finally too tired to give a rat's ass."*

*She knew what he was telling her and swallowed hard. They sat again in silence for a few more moments. She tried not to look at him, unwilling, unable to face the next part. They had finally reached this dreaded, awful place. Inside she was pleading, praying for more time, but time was implacable.*

*"Cassie," he finally said.*

*She took her time raising her eyes to meet his. "Yes?"*

*"Don't come back."*

*She wanted to have heard him wrong. She knew she hadn't. "What?"*

*"Don't. Come. Back." He said it bitingly clear, using the familiar play-sarcasm he had so frequently used over the past few months, and she wanted to cry out against him. "You heard me. It's time."*

*And then her heart broke. She looked at him and let the tears fill her eyes and spill down her face without bothering to wipe them away or pretend otherwise.*

*He raised a weak hand, managed to thumb away one tear, and she caught his hand before it fell back to the bed. He no longer had the strength to reciprocate her grasp, and the clinging was all on her part. "You agreed," he whispered. "You said you would."*

*"I know what I said."*

*"Then go on. You've got somewhere else to be. You ought to go there."*

*"I'll go." She hung onto his hand for a few more minutes. "I'll remember," she began.*

*"Don't remember...not like this." His voice was so tired, so*

*faded, but she understood what he was asking.*

*"Not like this," she promised. "Never like this." She managed what she hoped would look like a smile and touched his face once more. Then she leaned over and kissed his lips, lightly, gently, for the sake of remembrance. "I'll see you again later," she said, placing the palm of his hand against her cheek before she released him. She bent close to him once more. "I love you," she whispered into his ear.*

*He nodded and closed his eyes, turned his face away, but she still saw the tear that trickled down one gaunt cheek.*

*She fled from the building into the shelter of twilight, fled to her car where she could shut the door and be alone, and then she crossed her arms on the steering wheel and put her head down and sobbed.*

She took several short, quick breaths. "I never did go back, just as he asked. I found out from his sister that he slipped into a coma that night and died late the next day. And he managed to do it privately, too, waiting until his dad had gone to the washroom and his mom and sister were talking quietly at the window. They didn't realize he had passed until his dad came back."

Michael held the silence, the air too bruised for him to move just yet. He was aware of Cassie leaning back in the seat, settling into the shadows, and after a long moment, he turned cautiously and looked at her.

She wasn't weeping. She was staring out the window, her gaze focused somewhere up the street.

"Cass?"

"Hmmm?"

"I'm sorry for your loss."

She bowed her head and found his hand with hers. "It hurts, Michael," she said quietly. "It really, really hurts."

He squeezed her hand and they sat in the dark in silence for a long time.

# ~ CHAPTER NINETEEN ~

At ten minutes after three, Michael was ready to start pacing. Research your house, he had told her, and assumed she had started that morning. But Cassie was never late. So where was she? He glanced out the window yet again, but saw no sign of her. Nick was in receiving with Fredo, and Steve had been in his office nearly all day dealing with contractors and deadlines. Business had reached its usual afternoon slump, sure to pick up shortly when school let out and families started coming in for a bit of book shopping before going home to dinner. Where was she?

He flagged Steve down when the man got up to refill his hot chocolate mug. "Did Cassie call in sick?" he asked.

"No, but she did call in late."

Michael nearly slumped with relief. "Okay, just wondering."

"Are you all right out here? Not too busy?"

"No, it's fine. I was just wondering if I was going to be alone the rest of the afternoon."

"She should be here pretty soon. She said she was working on something and it was just taking a little longer than she expected, but she didn't think she'd be more than half an hour late." He gestured to the break room. "Want anything while I'm up?"

"No, thanks, I'm good right now."

Steve nodded. "Okay. Let me know if things go nuts before she gets here."

Working on something. He should have known. When they were nine years old, Cassie had been relentless when she wanted to know about something. Like where he might be going by himself, walking down the dusty road away from the cabins. If she spotted him from her window she never hesitated to come after him, demanding more information. She always wanted to know everything, even back then.

It should have driven him crazy, but somehow it didn't. It had even been mildly flattering in some way he didn't understand, to have this tiny inquisitive girl with huge brown eyes and thick, wavy , dark brown braids that reached nearly to her waist following him around and asking questions about what he was doing and why. On the surface, it could have been pestering. God knows when Benny did it, it was as annoying as a cloud of mosquitoes, a constant buzzing and whining that made Michael want to slap the source.

The thought of Benny popped into his head unexpectedly and he let it slip away without paying enough attention for it to cause pain. Over the years he had finally learned to do that. Benny had been a nosy, annoying kid, as nosy and annoying as only little brothers could be.

But Cassie, asking him questions even more numerous than Benny's, had done so in a way that suggested a fact-finding mission. She never questioned his answers unless she truly didn't understand something. She never ridiculed what he said, or scoffed at what he told her. Sometimes it had been fun to converse with her like that. She always wanted every last bit of information. So he wasn't the least bit surprised that when she finally arrived at The Poet's Corner, twenty minutes late for her shift, she looked to him like someone who had just gone on a trip to hell and taken notes while she was there.

* * *

Cassie's quest to find out about her house led her to Mr.

Dale Cotton. He was a semi-retired carpenter who worked a few days a week at the hardware store several blocks from The Poet's Corner. Hoping he was working the day shift, Cassie entered the hardware store. It seemed almost dark after the bright autumn sunshine outside.

A tired-looking woman in a red smock was behind the counter, restocking a battery display. She turned when Cassie entered. "Help you?" she asked, not stopping as her quick hands gathered up cardboard and plastic packs of size D batteries and hung them on long white hooks.

"I was looking for Mr. Cotton. Is he in today?"

"Should be. Probably find him back in the plumbing section. He said something about a project."

"Thanks."

Cassie wandered down the first aisle, past rows and rows of nails, bolts, and screws in a bewildering array of transparent drawers. A large sign that announced "Plumbing/Pipes" appeared on her right, two aisles down. At the end of the aisle stood a tall, gray man with a length of pipe in each hand, apparently comparing the two although Cassie could see no difference between them.

Dale Cotton really was a gray man: gray hair, gray slacks, a gray plaid flannel shirt neatly tucked and rolled up at the sleeves. He didn't pay any attention to Cassie until she cleared her throat when she stood a few feet away from him.

He looked at her over his glasses. "Need some help?"

"Mr. Cotton?"

"Yup. And you would be?"

"I'm Cassie Valentine. Mr. Cotton, I was wondering if I could ask you a few questions."

"Sure thing. What needs fixing? Plumbing? Electrical? I'm not too bad with electrical, but I'm really better at structural problems."

Cassie was taken aback. "Oh, it's not about fixing anything. It's about my house."

He raised his eyebrows. "Now, that could be interesting. It's about your house, but you don't need to fix anything?"

She smiled. "No. I was told you worked on renovating it."

"Oh. Quite possibly. Where do you live?"

"Over by the Brookhaven Estates subdivision, but not actually in it. I'm on Highlake, right in the middle of the block."

He frowned for a minute, and Cassie could almost see him reviewing job assignments in his head. After a moment his expression cleared. "Oh, that one. Blue siding, tidy little front porch, white front door? Did they ever fix that dang doorbell?"

"Oh, they fixed it. It's pretty loud."

"Hmmm. Well, that's better than the last time I was there. Blasted thing wouldn't ring no matter what we did with it. Well, how's it going? Everything okay? You know if you have complaints, you have to talk to the construction manager. I was just a contract worker."

"I don't have a complaint. Just some questions."

"Right. Questions. You did mention that." He put the pipes down and took off his glasses, wiping the lenses on his shirt. "How can I help you?"

Here it was. Cassie wasn't quite sure where to begin, so she plunged into the middle as always. "No one lived in our house before we moved in, right?"

"Right. It had been empty for years."

"So who paid to have it renovated?"

"Mr. Dunleavy decided to do something about it."

"Dunleavy Construction?"

"That would be him. He got a hold of the place and decided to fix it up. Make it all nice and modern inside."

"Modern," Cassie repeated. "How old is the house?"

Mr. Cotton frowned a bit, thinking. "I don't rightly know

that," he admitted. "Not with certainty. Maybe fifty, sixty years old. Not as old as some of those historic sites we have around here, but not young enough to be new construction." He scratched his graying head. "But the foundation was solid. We just fixed the place up again."

"Mr. Cotton, you did more than fix the place up. Everything in there was new, from the bathrooms to the carpets. The kitchen cabinets, too. All the appliances. I may be young, but my mother and I were reading real estate ads for years. Nothing like our house should have been that cheap. So why was it?"

He looked at her steadily, his blue eyes shrewd in the weathered gray of his face. "What put the bee in your bonnet?" he asked.

"I wanted to know the history of the house," she said, not sure how up-front she was ready to be.

"Oh? And why is that?"

"I'm thinking of majoring in history when I go back to school," she said, nothing else coming to mind.

"The history of your house?" There was a droll expression on his face now.

"Okay," she said. "All right. The truth of it is I think there's something wrong with the place."

"Wrong how?" he asked. "You didn't have any complaints."

"That's not what I meant." She grinned in spite of herself. "You know what I'm talking about, don't you?"

"So you want to know the history of your house." He sighed. "Yeah, I expect I know what you're talking about. Only I don't suppose your mother would appreciate this very much."

"She doesn't have to know," Cassie said. "Unless you think she needs to," she added hastily.

He shook his head. "I will tell you what I know about the place," he said. "And you decide what you want to do with it."

"Fair enough."

"Well, I guess there's no good way to say it, so I'll just say it. There was a murder in that house."

Cassie felt her arms come up in goose bumps. "A murder? When? Who?"

"I guess it'd be, oh, maybe thirty some years ago? Maybe more. Probably more than that, now. Whole family."

"The whole family was killed?" Cassie echoed. She realized she was getting past goose bumps and going to totally alarmed in a fast way.

"I think so. I was living around these parts back then, not here in town, but it was a big story, all right. Nice young family. Mother, kids. The dad was found out a ways, out where they built all those big new houses. That was just an empty field back then. They found him out there."

"But what happened? Do they know who did it? Or why?"

"Yeah, they found the guy. He was dead when they got him. Some kind of druggie or junkie. Something like that." He shook his head. "It was a real shocker, back then. Guess it still would be now."

Cassie shivered, a hard knot of recognition and denial growing in her stomach. "And so the asking price on the house was so low because no one would buy it?"

"Now, I never said that."

"No, but it probably had something to do with it, didn't it? Who'd want to live in a house where an entire family had been killed?"

"In the end, a house is a house," he said.

"Yes, but this one is a little different, isn't it?"

He looked at her keenly. "I'm not saying anything right out. It's not my call to be going and scaring the person living there. But I'll tell you what. There were times that house gave me chills. Not all the time. But every now and then. Like something was waiting. Or like I wasn't alone." He shook his head at her.

"But then it was probably my imagination working overtime. Nothing ever happened to me while I was there."

Cassie wondered what he would say if she told him what had happened just the night before. Instead she asked, "Mr. Cotton, do you know the name of the family that lived there?"

"You're not going to leave it alone, are you?"

"I can't," she said.

He sighed. "There are still some people around here could probably tell you, but most of them would have the sense not to. The name was Norridge. And that's all I'm saying."

She heard the name and it was nearly akin to a physical blow. The knot in her stomach blossomed up and out, reaching and constricting her throat, sinking below her legs, making her shaky. But she remembered her manners. "I owe you, Mr. Cotton."

He snorted. "Come find me when you're old enough to buy beer."

## ~ CHAPTER TWENTY ~

The library was cold, almost to the point of frostbite, and Cassie couldn't help wondering if the air conditioning was still running despite the change of seasons. She hadn't been there in a long time, and the clerk behind the check-out desk smiled at her when she came in. Cassie managed to smile back before hurrying toward the reference section, trying not to feel so cold. It wasn't just the cool air in the library, she knew.

Muriel Henderson was at the reference desk, and Cassie breathed a sigh of relief. She liked Muriel. Some of the other librarians, helpful though they were, gave her the occasional odd look when she requested various materials she needed. Muriel was always charmingly neutral, no matter what kinds of questions or requests Cassie came up with.

"Cassie! It's been a little while. I thought maybe you'd grown tired of us."

"Oh, no, Muriel. Just busy at work and all."

"Well, I'm glad you were able to get away today. What can I do for you?"

"I need to look up something from thirty years ago. In the newspapers."

Muriel nodded. "Let me set you up with one of the machines. That will be on microfilm." She led Cassie into the glassed-off room where the huge reading machines sat like silent metal gargoyles, and snapped one of them on. "What year? Do you know?"

Cassie shook her head regretfully. "It was a murder from more than thirty years ago. The family name was Norridge."

"Norridge," Muriel repeated softly. "I think I remember that family name. They were all killed, weren't they?"

"That's what I heard. The family was killed inside, the father outside in the field beside the property."

"I do remember that one," Muriel said. "I was in college when that happened. What a dreadful thing. Let me see what I can find for you."

"Thanks." Cassie perched on the stool before the machine and waited, wishing she had brought a sweater in addition to her jacket.

Forty minutes later, she wished she had brought a sweater, a scarf, a hat, and a thermos of hot tea. She wished she had brought Eloise, or Michael, or Richard, or maybe even her mother. She was shivering for real and it was not just the cool temperature of the library. The cold she felt would not easily be dispelled.

Scraps of news articles floated through her head, and for the first time she wished she didn't have the kind of memory that hung onto the lists and details that helped her on so many quizzes and exams. "All found dead…" "Community shocked as family is found murdered…" "Police solve crime – but no happy ending…"

Cassie read article after article, never quite becoming inured to the pictures that had run with the stories: her house, her front porch crowded with police officers, just a glimpse of a body bag being brought out.

She saw pictures of the two little Norridge boys, Martin David, Jr. and Robert Steven. She saw the high school ID picture of Jeremy Mott, an average young boy who had been neither handsome nor ugly, his hair a nondescript shade in the black and white photo, looking somewhat lost as he gazed at the camera that snapped his likeness. There was a picture of Mary Velasco, the young woman Ms. Parrish had mentioned as being a houseguest and who had been murdered along with the family. And there was a picture of the Norridge's themselves. A family picture, taken for a church directory, showed a smiling Martin and Jane Norridge, young Martin, Jr. with a missing front tooth, and younger, cherubic Robert, a cowlick popped up at the crown of his fair head.

It was the picture of Jane Norridge that drew Cassie's breath from her, made her feel the cold painfully. "Have you seen my little boy?" a woman in a sweat suit had asked Cassie after ringing the doorbell late at night just a short time ago. The woman in the sweat suit had been Jane Norridge.

Cassie didn't take any notes. She didn't need any. She had a feeling she would remember all too well everything she had read. A Detective Albert Billings had been working the case, but it was Police Chief Walt Donnelly who had made the announcement to the press that the crime had been solved and the case was closed.

She looked at their pictures as well. Det. Billings had been in his thirties, perhaps, when the murders had occurred. He was tall and solid, and the moustache he sported drooped and paralleled a sad, drooping look in his eyes. Chief Donnelly was massive in his suit and tie, with a beefy neck and heavy face that were not yet overweight.

She had seen enough. She turned off the machine but left the little spools of newspapers stacked tidily in their boxes, as Muriel had asked. She had thought to call Steve at work, telling him she would get there soon but was running a little behind in something she was working on, and it was a good thing she had.

It wasn't just the research that would detain her. Somehow she had to digest and process everything she had just read, everything she had just seen, and then go to The Poet's Corner and work a three-hour shift. Michael would be there, but she realized seeing him and not being able to talk freely right away might make her feel worse. She needed to tell someone. At the same time, she didn't know how she was going to tell anyone.

She collected her purse and headed for her car. No point in being any later. Maybe being at work would put everything out of her mind, sort of a little mental vacation while she was busy with her job. The thought withered even as it played itself out to completion. No way.

# ~ CHAPTER TWENTY-ONE ~

"I saw Jeremy Mott last night."

"What?" Michael stopped in the act of putting a French fry into his mouth.

"Who?" Eloise continued to put ketchup on her vegi-burger. She nudged Nick, sitting next to her. "Can I have another napkin?"

Cassie waited impatiently for all the burger prep to die down before trying to start again. Michael had been gazing at her uneasily the whole time.

"Who did you see?" Eloise asked, taking a bite and wiping ketchup from her chin with a paper napkin.

"Jeremy Mott," Cassie said softly. "And I also saw–"

"Why does that name sound familiar?" Nick had noticed the expression on Michael's face and didn't wait for her to finish.

"Remember May Parrish's ghost story? The one she told the other week? Jeremy Mott was the murderer. The dead murderer."

Eloise plopped her burger down in the plastic basket. "What are you talking about?"

"I told you the story," Nick said. "The one about the whole family being killed and May seeing and talking to the dead kid who killed them all. Remember?"

"Now I do." She shivered, turning toward Cassie. "And you saw him in your house?"

"He was the one in my bedroom when I called you and Michael ended up coming over. I found out today that my house is the house where that murder happened."

Michael, waiting for her to finish, leaned forward. "You're sure about it? I mean, you checked it somewhere?"

"I talked to a man named Dale Cotton this morning. He worked on renovating our place. He told me the name of the family that was killed there. He said it was Norridge. So then I went to the library and I found all the articles from back then. I was going to copy them but then I thought maybe not. Maybe I don't want that material in the house with me." She made a grimace of distaste. "But it had pictures of the place. It had the address. It's my house."

Eloise put her hand out and squeezed Cassie's. "I'm so sorry, Cass. No wonder the place…" She stopped. "What are you going to do?"

Cassie shrugged. "There's nothing I can do. I mean, I live there. What am I supposed to do?"

"You're sure that was Jeremy Mott you saw?" Michael was still trying to find a more pleasant alternative.

"It had to be. May said he wore those dirty jeans and a jacket. And that he was found with Norridge blood all over him. Well, that had to be him."

"And he talked to you."

She frowned, remembering. "I think he was talking to me. He was walking toward me. But I wonder." She shook her head.

"So why is he coming to you now?" Nick asked.

"I have no idea. I did notice that the date of the murder was in June. But that was months ago. In June, it was thirty-two years to the date."

Michael frowned. "So he's turning up now? It's already October. Does that make any kind of sense?"

Cassie sighed. "Not really. None of this makes sense."

"Funny you'd see him and none of the family," Nick said. He looked at Cassie's face. "Sorry. I'm not saying you need more dead people in your house. But for the murderer to turn up and not the victims? That seems as weird as anything else."

"No, it's what you said, Nick. I almost forgot to tell you. I *have* seen someone in the family. Mrs. Norridge. Jane Norridge, the woman who was friends with May and with Jeremy. She rang the doorbell that one night, after I heard that…thing come into my house."

Nick shook his head. "Okay, so now you have a dead family member and also a *thing* in your house?"

"There was another incident a few weeks ago," Cassie said. "Actually, I guess it was two incidents." She told Nick the whole story about hearing someone come in through the front door and actually come up the steps; how she thought it was her mother; how a voice told her to hide. "And right after is when the doorbell rang. It was Mrs. Norridge. She told me she was looking for her son."

"Looking for her son?" Eloise echoed. "Aren't they all dead?"

Cassie shrugged. "I can't explain any of it."

"Hey, guys," a new voice interjected. "Group date?" Steve stopped at the table.

"Business meeting," Nick said in a grave voice. "Three of us are sitting here bitching about our boss."

Steve nodded. "Got it. I hear he's a real son-of-a-gun."

"The worst," Nick agreed.

"Do you want to sit with us?" Michael asked.

"Oh, no. No. I don't have too many complaints about the boss, myself. Actually, I'm just here to pick up dinner."

"Good nutrition, Dad," Nick said.

"Right, Nick. And who let the kids eat an entire bag of mini peanut butter cups before bedtime the last time he babysat for us?"

Nick looked at him, puzzled. "Who was that?"

Steve laughed and shook his head. "I'll catch you all

tomorrow." He turned to walk away.

"Hey, Steve," Michael said.

Steve looked back.

"Did I hear you used to be a cop in a former life?"

Steve gave him a crooked grin. "And who told you?"

Cassie looked at her employer in surprise. "I didn't know that. You used to be a cop?" She remembered suddenly the harder edge that had come into his demeanor when he stood on her porch and heard his first evidence of the haunting within.

"Many years ago, like my dad. I didn't last too long." He shrugged. "Not the right personality."

"Hmmm," Nick said, moving his hands up and down as if weighing two items. "Cop. Bookseller. Cop. Bookseller. Definitely different personality types. Good call, Steve."

"Why'd you ask?" Steve ignored Nick.

"Cassie's house," Eloise said. "There was a murder there."

"What?" Steve moved closer to the table.

"More than thirty years ago," Michael said. "The one May Parrish talked about on that ghost story night."

"Are you kidding me?" Steve looked at them all, then turned to Cassie. "And you think that's behind all the, uh, weirdness you have going on there?"

She nodded. "I know it sounds crazy. Maybe it is. But last night I even saw…" She let her voice trail off, afraid he would laugh at her, but his expression was as serious as she had ever seen.

"Tell me," he said.

They all recapped the story, interrupting each other and throwing out details in no discernible order, but Steve got the gist of it. "Are you okay?" he asked when they finished, gaze fixed on Cassie.

"Yes," she said. "I know what's going on, kind of. I know why, I guess. It's just going to take some getting used to."

"Are you going to tell your mom any of this?"

Cassie made a face. "I don't think so. I thought about it, but I don't think it's the kind of thing I really want to share with her."

He nodded. "Well, if you think of anything I can do, let me know."

"Maybe you could let her move into the bookstore." That was Michael and he was only half-joking.

"If you ever need to get away, Cass, we have the room," Steve said, still quite serious. "Audrey and the girls would love it."

She blushed. "It's okay. Really. But thank you."

"No problem. I'll talk to you all tomorrow." He almost turned away again, but stopped, looking like he was thinking something over. "Cassie, you know there's one thing—" he broke off and looked at her with a slight frown.

"What?" Cassie asked.

He smiled at her then. "Nothing. Never mind. Hey, see you at work." He tapped the table with his fist twice and left.

"Wonder what that was about?" Michael said, watching him go.

* * *

The house got crazier.

Cassie told Michael about it in a desperate little conversation in the break room. Jeremy Mott's appearance seemed to have heralded an escalation in disturbances. "I see him in the house all the time, sometimes walking slowly up the stairs, or sometimes in the hall outside my room. Once I saw him in the living room looking down at something I couldn't see." The memory brought a chill up her spine, but when she looked to Michael for empathy he looked away, frowning.

"There are other noises in the house, too," she said hurriedly, thinking that he was growing impatient with her. "There are other footsteps, not just Jeremy's. There are constant cold drafts, absolutely Arctic." She hugged her arms to herself and shivered as she talked to him. Why did he seem so indifferent? She had never seen him so distant and closed-off to her. She told him about the three permanent cold spots she had located as well: one in her mother's room and thus easy to avoid, but one was close to her closet, and there was another in the living room by the couch.

There was a flicker of concern in Michael's expression when she finished, but it was gone in a second, his brown eyes dark as slate. "I'd never make it, living with that in my own place," he said as they finished cups of hot chocolate at the table. "I don't know how you can take it." He sounded angry.

Cassie guessed he wanted to be able to help more and the fact that he didn't know what to do was making him slightly edgy, even grouchy. But she wasn't sure.

"You can come stay with my grandfather and me," he said after a long pause, but the offer was made so abruptly it came off as less than an invitation and more like a quick fix offered in annoyance. She turned him down and hurried back into the store, confused and a little hurt by his demeanor.

An hour later, he found her and apologized. "I don't know how to help you. What can I do, Cass? Tell me and I'll do it. Just tell me."

But there was nothing she could say.

"Are you alone again tonight?" he asked.

She laughed without humor. "Of course I am. Mom's got some kind of super project going on at work. She even goes in on Saturdays, lately. I'd invite Eloise, but she's useless at my house after dark."

Michael nodded. "I'll see you later, then," he said and walked away before she could respond.

He rang her doorbell at seven, bearing a movie for them to

watch. They tried, but at first there was such a flurry of noise in the kitchen, the creak of chairs moving, a drawer opening, the sound of someone moving restlessly through the room, that Cassie kept springing upright on the couch, ready to jump to her feet. Ready to jump out of her skin.

Michael grabbed her hand and pulled her to him, put his arm around her, quieted her against him. "Watch the movie," he said softly.

"But the kitchen-"

"I can't believe you need to explore that. Who do you hope to find in there?" He squeezed her a little. "Stay here with me. It'll be okay."

She trembled against him as he held her but after a while she relaxed, head against his shoulder, and the noises in the kitchen stopped on their own.

"That was an exception," she told him the next day. "The house never quiets down on its own. And even when it's quiet, I can feel something waiting for me. Just – waiting." Something in the house wanted her attention, she realized. Something in the house was demanding – what? What did it want from her? She asked Michael the same question and he had no answer for her. They both knew she could forestall the disturbances by being away from the place or by having him come over for a while, but it did not change anything overall.

She was not sleeping well. "How can I sleep?" she had just about wailed to him that evening as he walked her to her car. "I wake up all the time, which helps to stop the nightmares I've been having. Dark dreams. Just dark." She shook her head to clear it. "But waking up is bad, too. It's so cold in my room. Sometimes I hear the doorknob turning but I never want to see who's coming in to see me. And sometimes I feel someone standing beside the bed."

She shivered, remembering how it felt to sense the presence of another right beside her, looking down at her. She never opened her eyes when that happened, not wanting to see what was there. "I tried sleeping with the door already open so I wouldn't hear someone opening it to come in."

"What about a light?" Michael asked. "Does leaving a light on help?"

"I tried that, too. It helped for a few nights until I saw that it lights up the corner by my closet just enough to see Jeremy Mott standing there, sometimes. I don't know if he's looking at me or not. I never look at him long enough to find out."

"Can you sleep in the third bedroom?"

"And I tried that, too." Her eyes welled up and she wiped at them impatiently. "I snuck in one night when my mom was already in bed so I wouldn't need to tell her what I was doing, or why." She looked at him and one tear escaped and slid down her cheek. "It made things worse," she said. "The cold, the sounds. And the feeling like he was searching for me, like hide and seek with a dead person." She shivered. "As bad as it is, I'm better off in my own room."

Through all of this, her mother sailed blithely through the days, drinking her first cup of coffee and kissing Cassie goodbye on the top of her head on the mornings that they were both up at the same time. She was totally oblivious to the shadows that filled the house and surrounded her daughter. "Well, when Mom's home the house behaves itself," Cassie said.

But her mother was rarely home during the crucial hours after work and dinner, the ones Cassie withstood alone unless Michael could be there. The only restful sleep she got came after her mother arrived home from work and drove the goblins away. Cassie was annoyed with herself, feeling as if she had regressed to the age of five, afraid of the dark and the monsters that came with it. "Except that I'm not five years old and the monsters are real," she said bitterly.

One day she came into the store and handed Michael a piece of paper. On it was typed *Item 97. His favorite horror movie was the old black and white film "Nosferatu."*

And then far below it, at the center of the page, was one unpunctuated sentence: *There was so much blood I had to put my hand in it*

Michael read it and looked up at her. "It's the second time something has turned up in one of my files," she said, her voice brittle. She told him about the first, *I felt so bad I knew they were all dead.* Michael found nothing he could say to her.

Cassie knew that both Michael and Nick were keeping an eye on her at work. She was fine at the store for the most part, but the shadows never really left her any longer, and she knew Steve was starting to look at her questioningly, always on the verge of asking what was wrong. Eloise spent time with her when she could, sometimes bringing Nick along to the house. In the end, though, she knew none of them could help her, and the darkness in Michael's eyes told her that he realized this as well.

## ~ CHAPTER TWENTY-TWO ~

Then there was the incident at the store. Audrey Crawford stopped by with Emma and Abby one Thursday afternoon. The Crawford family was going away for a long weekend, leaving the store in Fredo's capable hands. "And the rest of yours," Steve had added. "I know you'll be fine."

"Sure we will, Dad." Nick has spoken first when Steve told them of his plans that morning. "I promise to leave the flamethrower at home while you're gone. Ditto for the explosives. I won't forget and leave the coffeemaker on 'warm' or anything like that. I won't even leave the water running in the employee bathroom like I did the one time–"

"Okay, so Nick will be escorted off the premises daily," Fredo had interrupted even before Steve could cut into Nick's usual flow of nonsense.

"By all of us," Cassie had added. "Where are you going?"

But Steve just winked and said, "I'll be back Tuesday morning."

"Ooh, secret destination," Nick said.

"No, I just don't want you to be able to find me," Steve had answered, underscoring the "you" as he addressed Nick. "And the girls are coming to pick me up this afternoon, so behave."

Audrey had strolled in at about one-thirty, Emma in tow, Abby in her arms. Emma had dark red curls and green eyes, favoring her mother. Abby, curled up in her mother's arms and sucking her thumb, was fair-haired and had sleepy brown eyes like her dad. As soon as they walked in, Nick was away from his shelving and taking Emma's hand. "C'mon," he said. "Let's go inspect the cookies."

"Okay," Emma said, gladly putting her little hand into Nick's much larger one. "What's 'inspect'?"

"That means trying all of them to make sure they're good," Nick's voice faded away as he led the little girl back to the coffee nook.

"Great. A long car ride with Emma wired on sugar," Audrey said ruefully. She smiled at Cassie. "How's it going?"

Cassie gave her a hug which Audrey returned with one arm. "Good. You know how Steve is. World's easiest boss."

"Easy? Hmmm." Audrey looked around the store with her quick green eyes. "Nick's display for Halloween reading is great, but don't tell him I said that. His head won't fit into the stockroom." Then she saw Michael standing at the cash register. "You must be Michael Penfield," she said.

Michael came around the counter and shook the hand she offered him. He stood nearly a foot over Audrey, as he did with Cassie, and still managed to look shy and intimidated. "Mrs. Crawford," he said.

"Oh, no, that's my mother-in-law," she said with a laugh. "It's Audrey. And this is Abby. Can you say hi to Michael, Abby?"

Abby regarded him from around her thumb and said nothing.

Michael nodded. "I get that," he said with a smile.

Abby stared at him a little longer, then reached chubby arms out toward him. "Up," she said.

"Wow," Audrey remarked, handing the little girl over to an awkward Michael. "She rarely does that."

"Nick," Abby said next, clear as a bell.

"Oh, I see. You think I can get you to Nick, huh?" Michael smiled and his eye crinkled into his scar. "Let's go see if we can find him before all the cookies are gone."

"Are you two an item?" Audrey waited until Michael was

half the store away, and then turned to Cassie with a grin.

"Not exactly. He and several others here would like that, though."

"Well, he's a cutie. Those arms and that chest. Whoa."

"Arms and chest?" Steve came up and kissed his wife on the cheek. "You must be talking about me."

"Dream on, honey. Ready to go?"

"Sure. Just let me give a couple things to Fredo and we're good." Steve started back to the receiving area, a handful of papers in his grip. "Hey," he called back. "Come with me, Aud. You haven't seen Fredo in a while, either."

Cassie waved them off and went to the cash register in case someone wandered in to make a purchase. She moved Michael's car magazine under the counter, stacked Nick's drawings to one side, then picked up the latest Preston and Child novel that she had just started reading.

After a while she heard Abby's voice and then Michael's in answer. She looked up in time to see Abby put one tiny hand on Michael's face, tracing the scar. Cassie winced, not sure how Michael was going to react.

"Hurt?" Abby asked, still touching his face.

"Not anymore," Michael said. He smiled at her. "I'm better, now."

Abby put her thumb back into her mouth and curled herself under Michael's chin, her other little hand still caressing his face.

"Looks like you've got a friend," Cassie said with a grin.

He looked bewildered. "She took a cookie from Nick, but didn't want to stay back there. She wanted to come up here with you."

"That's sweet." She came around and kissed Abby's plump cheek. "You're too sweet, Abby. Did you know that?"

Abby looked at her and smiled around her thumb, then looked past her. "Who?" she asked, pointing.

Cassie turned and Michael looked in the same direction. There was no one there.

"Who, honey?" Cassie asked.

"Him. With you." The little girl leaned forward a second or two, as if trying to see something better, then settled back into Michael's arms again. "With you, Cassie," she said. "He's with you."

Cassie looked back again at the empty front end of the store and then looked at Michael. Neither of them were smiling anymore. "Abby," Cassie whispered. "What does he look like?"

Abby was still staring at no one. "Dirty," she said with finality. "He's too dirty."

The Crawfords left the store ten minutes later with the usual flurry of child-herding, last minute reminders, and goodbyes. Cassie joined in the cheerful leave-taking, but as soon as everyone was back to their usual stations, she turned to Michael at the cash register. "Why couldn't you see what Abby saw?" she demanded of him.

Michael was taken aback. "What?"

"If you see dead people, why couldn't you see Jeremy, too?"

He shook his head. "Cassie, I don't know–"

"We should both have seen him because he was here for *me*." She sounded furious. "It doesn't matter. He got his point across. Dammit, it's not just the house that's haunted," she said. "It's me."

There was nothing Michael could say to her to make it otherwise and he nodded. "I think you're right."

"I thought it was okay here," she said, the fury seeping out of her voice and leaving sadness behind. She gestured vaguely, taking in Nick and Fredo at the back, Steve's office, Michael himself.

They looked at each other in silent, helpless agreement.

Cassie didn't want to mention to anyone that Abby had

spotted Jeremy Mott at the bookstore, and she asked Michael to keep the confidence as well.

"As if not talking about it will make a difference?" Michael asked.

"I know it won't," she snapped back. She regretted the tone of her voice as soon as she said it, but she was always so tired, always so on edge. "I just don't want to deal with it *here*. Okay? I can't do a thing about my house, but when I come to Poet's Corner, I don't want to know if he's coming here with me." She held up her hand to preclude what she knew he would say, that being at the store instead of at home obviously did not matter. "Please, Michael," she whispered. "I want to feel like there's some place…" She didn't finish and after a bit he touched her shoulder.

"Okay," he said. "I won't say anything."

They were both on edge at work for a few days, but Steve came back and nothing more happened. They began to relax. *Maybe Jeremy's presence had been a one-time occurrence*, Cassie thought. Maybe she really could leave the craziness at home. The store began to feel more of a haven again. It was the only one she had.

## ~ CHAPTER TWENTY-THREE ~

Shortly after Jeremy Mott had first appeared at Cassie's door, she called Michael in a panic. "Come over here," she had started. She tried twice to get something else out, stumbling into complete silence both times before she managed a blurted-out explanation. "My mom had to go out of town. She's gone. Michael, don't be grumpy with me again. Just please come over. And stay over."

Stay over. Now that was a request he could only have hoped for, but he knew what she meant. She sounded terrified. He threw some things into his backpack and then went to wake up his grandfather. It was all a formality, actually. Michael knew that his grandfather would converse with him, give him his blessing, send him on his way, and never remember the next morning that they had talked at all. Grandpa Henry had the rare ability to have entire discussions without ever waking up. Michael left a note on the refrigerator as back-up before driving over to Cassie's place.

The Valentine house was cold when he arrived. Michael didn't ever remember it being so cold, not even the night the kitchen had come alive for them while they watched a movie. Cassie, clad in jeans, a sweatshirt, and a jacket, didn't mention it, as if she frequently dressed in layers for an evening at home. Michael had a sleeping bag with him, and he looked at her expectantly when she led him into the living room.

"Thanks for coming," she said, and the relief in her voice was a tangible thing. "I can't sleep anymore. I can't even think straight." She pulled her hair back into a tail and fastened it with an elastic band, her movements quick and impatient. "And with my mom gone—"

"Hey, relax," he said. "Should I sleep down here?"

"Down here?" she repeated and her voice squeaked a little. "What good would that do if I'm upstairs? C'mon."

He followed her up the carpeted steps and noticed that the air was decidedly chillier as they approached the second floor, but he didn't say anything.

Cassie folded her arms and hugged herself, shivering. "Isn't this ridiculous? I turned the heat up hours ago. It should be at least comfortable in here by now." She led him to her room, ablaze with light. The overhead fixture, the desk lamp, the bedside lamp, even the closet light were all switched on.

Michael blinked at the brilliance of it. "Okay," he said. He put his backpack down in her room and began to unroll his sleeping bag in the hall.

"What are you doing?" She sounded on the verge of panic.

"I'll sleep out here," he said, fumbling with the bag, too awkward to meet her gaze. "Me being in your room right now – it wouldn't be right. Not with all this going on." He didn't even bring up the subject of Daniel. "I think it might be unethical or something. And I'm not trying to take advantage…" He changed the subject hurriedly. "Got an extra pillow?"

She had been staring at him during his halting explanation and now looked both terrified and exasperated, but she clambered over him and went to the linen closet, grabbing a pillow and a case that was done in green and blue rectangles. "Here," she said. She sounded like she was wired tightly enough to explode.

"Cassie." Still on his knees from spreading out the bag, he grabbed her hand and pulled at her until she looked down at him. "Hey, I'll be right here. And that's when we're both ready to sleep, okay? In the meantime, I'll hang in your room with you.

We can play cards. We can stream movies. We can go down and watch the tube. Whatever you want. Just relax, okay?"

She took a deep breath and blew it out through her teeth. "You must think I'm pathetic."

"I think you're tired. Tired and cold. It's like Antarctica in here."

"It's going to get worse," she said softly. "It's going to get colder and colder until after ten-thirty. My mother never notices it. If she does, she never says anything." She wiped her eyes impatiently. "I'm sorry," she said. "I'm so tired."

He was still holding her hand. "C'mon," he said. He got to his feet and led her over to her bed. "Take a nap. I'll sit here and read and you can get some sleep. I think it's going to be a long night."

She got onto the bed, still in her jeans and jacket, and let him pull the blankets up for her.

He put his hand out to the lamp switch and then stopped. "Lights on?" he asked.

"Lights on," she said.

He nodded. "Get some rest. I brought a book." He turned away and her hand shot out from under the covers, grabbing frantically at his wrist.

"You're not leaving, are you? I won't be alone when I wake up, will I?"

He had never seen her like this, not Cassie. Not iron-willed, stubborn, courageous Cassie, and the undercurrent of worry he carried for her deepened in a way he didn't like. "Cass," he said patiently. "I'm not going anywhere. I'm going to sit down in that corner over there and read. Any time you want you can open your eyes and see me, okay? You can wave and I'll wave back."

She was still clinging to his arm. "Sit closer," she whispered.

"Okay, you got it." He got the book out of his backpack and sat down on the floor beside her bed and next to her nightstand with his back against the wall, knees up, facing her. “This good for you?”

She nodded and smiled weakly. “Thanks.”

He nodded back. When he looked up five minutes later she was sound asleep. He sighed, wondering what it would take to frighten her so badly. Even Jeremy Mott turning up hadn’t driven her crazy like this. Cassie had always been the one who never flinched. He went back to his book, his eyes following the words until he realized he was rereading the same sentences. He was feeling suddenly drowsy himself. The house was so quiet.

…He woke with a start and realized he had been awakened by the cold. The clock said he had napped for about an hour. Great. Well, he wouldn’t tell Cassie he had gone to sleep while on watch. She was still deeply asleep as he looked at her, studied the dark lashes against the paleness of her face, the dark hair that had gotten loose from the elastic band and was spread across her pillow. Even in her sleep she looked troubled.

He yawned and after a moment put down the book and went over to his pack to retrieve a sweatshirt, glad he had brought one. It was ridiculously cold. He wondered if he would be able to see his breath, and tried it. Not quite. He had his head through the neck of his sweatshirt and was just pulling on one of the sleeves when he heard it.

A small sound. Just the slightest *snick* of a sound, like a closed door being pushed against until it caught. He finished putting on the sweatshirt hurriedly and went to the doorway, glancing nervously down the hall. For all Nick’s teasing about seeing dead people, for all Naomi’s statement that he, Michael, was a sensitive, he had never seen anything that Cassie said was in her house, not in all the times he had been there. He still couldn’t see anything. Or could he?

*Something* was coming from her mother’s end of the hall, he thought. Could he really perceive a shadow that was darker than the dark itself? Or were his eyes playing tricks? His eyes and his mind. Cassie had said the cold would get worse and not ease up until after ten-thirty. Her clock, when he had glanced at it after awakening, had said about ten minutes past ten. Whatever the case, he could *feel* something coming towards him. There was a vast coldness approaching Cassie's bedroom, a wall of ice bearing down on him inexorably, eating up the distance between them until he felt the first of its wintry presence against his face. He gulped and drew back, but it was already upon him. And just as suddenly it was past, entering Cassie's room, heading directly for her.

Michael spun, suddenly aware that he could indeed see his breath as he opened his mouth to call her name. He didn't want to be awake and alone with this. Jeez, was this what she had been dealing with all this time? Alone with it, and her mother not there for her? Brave Cassie. The thoughts pin-wheeled through his head, quite independent of the dead terror he was feeling, and he willed his legs to move toward the bed. *Get her out!* something inside of him was screaming.

Cassie sat up at his first weighted step, but she did not look at him. Her eyes were open but her focus was that of a sleepwalker. "Yes," she whispered. "I can hear you." She pushed the covers aside and got up.

"Cass!" he whispered at her fiercely. Somehow he could not take another step. And why was he whispering? As if whatever was in the room was unaware of him? But he found that his normal voice was impossible to use; it simply was not working.

She didn't look at him. She walked slowly, dreamily, in the direction of her vanity and stopped in front of the mirror. Her right hand drifted down and selected something he couldn't see. She raised her hand, then, and began to write on the glass, forming letters with easy strokes. From where he stood, he could only see a *T*. After a few endless minutes, she stopped writing and gave a small sigh.

As suddenly, Michael found that he could move again and he ran to her just in time to catch her as she collapsed. Her eyes were closed and her breathing was deep. *Still asleep*, he thought. He carried her back to her bed. It was only after he had placed her gently down, covered her with blankets, that he turned to see what she had written.

*Tell him*, the top letters said. Underneath was written *Find him Tell*

Michael stared at the message a little longer, then turned back to Cassie. She looked as if she had never moved.

The room was becoming warmer again. The clock at her bedside read ten twenty-eight. Still shivering, Michael retrieved his sleeping bag and the pillow from the hall. The heck with what was right and ethical. He sat down again with his back against the wall, facing her, the pillow up behind his head and the bag around him like a cloak.

And of course that was when he heard, just in his head, May Parrish's little bit of advice while they were at the bookstore his first night there, how talking about these things would make them all come to you. It occurred to him as he tried to get comfortable that Ms. Parrish had omitted a key piece of information: talking about these things not only made them come to you, it made them stick around as well.

He huddled down into his bag, drawing it tighter around himself. Sooner or later, he supposed, he would be able to doze off and get a little rest. In the meantime, he would watch over Cassie. As if his being there made a difference. As if he were able to do anything to help her.

* * *

Cassie awoke from the best sleep she had had in ages, and

marveled at how good she felt. She stretched leisurely, luxuriating in the warm cocoon of her blankets, and turned her head.

Michael was sound asleep sitting up against the wall, the sleeping bag pulled around him, his head tilted toward one shoulder. The pillow had slipped sideways with his head. She had forgotten that he would be there when she woke up and she felt a rush of gratitude. No wonder she had slept so soundly. Michael had managed to make her feel safer than anyone else could have. She thought fleetingly of Daniel and that stung a little, but Michael was the one sitting in front of her.

She smiled at how he looked asleep, relaxed, the side of his face that was unmarked by the scar appearing smooth and slightly rosy against the dark of his hair. There was the shadow of a moustache and a beard coming in, and she was almost startled to see it. Sometimes she still thought of them both as kids.

"Hey," she called out softly to him. He didn't stir. Should she wake him? She supposed she should. They both had to work that morning. She reached out and prodded one of his knees. "Michael. Wake up."

He started then, awake all at once, even alarmed. "What?" he said. "What is it?"

"Nothing, silly. Just time to wake up." She laughed at him. "I feel a lot better this morning. Thanks for letting me get some sleep."

But he didn't smile back at her. He looked at her gravely and said, "Did you dream last night?"

"Why? Did I say something gross?"

Still he didn't smile. "Cass," he said. "Look at your mirror."

The weight in his voice tipped her off. She sat up slowly and looked toward her vanity. "Tell him," she read. "Find him. Tell." Then, "Why did you write that?"

He shook his head at her. "I didn't. You did."

"No, I didn't. I was asleep."

"You were asleep," he agreed. "Or something. But you wrote it. I watched you."

She gaped at him, her face blanched and suddenly pinched-looking. "I wrote it? When? What happened?" Her voice rose in consternation. "Michael, why didn't you stop me?"

"I couldn't. I couldn't move until you finished." He pulled the sleeping bag more tightly around himself although her room was warm and there was sunlight against the blinds, brighter than the lights that had remained on overnight. "Your house is possessed, Cass. I'd swear to it in a court of law. The cold, the door clicking shut at the end of the hall. That – that thing coming toward your room—"

Cassie, wide-eyed, didn't reply. She just stared until he started talking again.

Michael looked uncomfortable. "Something came down the hall from there. I couldn't see it but I sure as hell could feel it. Like ice. I was standing in your doorway and I could feel how much colder it got as it came this way. I could see my own breath when it got here." He glanced away, unwilling to look at her any longer. "It went past me to you, Cass. I felt it. And then you—" He stopped.

"Then what? What about me?"

"You sat up and said 'I can hear you.' Something like that. Then you got out of bed and went to the mirror and wrote that."

She felt sudden panic. "I said something? And got up and wrote that? And you didn't stop me? You didn't wake me up?"

He looked helpless in the face of her new terror, all too well aware of the situation and unable to do anything about it. His expression soured at her horrified questions. "I couldn't stop you," he said, his voice defensive. "I tried calling your name but I couldn't do more than whisper. And as for physically stopping you, I couldn't do anything. Something wouldn't let me even move. I didn't get to you until you finished."

"Thanks for that." There was an edge in her voice.

"Before you hit the floor," he added, somewhat unkindly.

She looked at him, not understanding.

"You collapsed after. I carried you back to your bed."

"Oh." After a moment she said, "Thanks for that."

"Whatever."

This was going all wrong. Michael had been there to face the nightmare with her. Instead of running back to the safety of his own house, he had stayed as he had said he would, and stayed close as she had asked. Now he sat, morose and slumped against her wall, still cloaked in his sleeping bag as if warding away something dreadful.

She held out her hand. "Hey. Truce," she said.

He looked at her, uncertainty in his face, and that hurt her.

"I mean it, Michael. You stayed with me."

After a moment, he took her hand and squeezed it, lacing his fingers through hers. "Do I get breakfast?"

"Any cold cereal you want."

"I don't think so. I was thinking more like pancakes and bacon and hash browns. You got paid last Friday, didn't you?"

"So did you. And you work full time, not me." She smiled but it was gone in a second. "What do you suppose that means? 'Tell him'?"

"No clue."

"And I really wrote it?"

"You really wrote it. Or–"

"Or what?"

He regarded her. "Or something wrote it through you."

She shivered, but threw back her blankets. "I want to show you something."

"Great!" He laughed suddenly and his eye crinkled into his

scar. “Should we take off our clothes?”

“*Michael.* You’ve been hanging around with Nick way too long.” She rummaged around in her desk, found a piece of paper and shoved it at him.

He took it, realized it was upside down, and turned it around. “Find,” he read aloud. He turned the paper over but the other side was blank. “Again with the finding. What is this?”

She was looking at her mirror. “I think it’s the same message. I woke up one morning maybe a month ago with a pen in my hand and that word written on the paper. I didn’t want to think I wrote it, but if you saw me—” She turned to him with troubled eyes. “It has to be the same thing with the computer, doesn’t it? I must have typed those words myself.” She looked ill. “What do I do?”

The look on his face reflected her own feelings, her own worries, but somehow that was reassuring. It meant that she wasn’t alone. “First,” he said, standing up and stretching, long arms nearly reaching to her ceiling, “you take me out for breakfast.” He yawned hugely, stretched one more time, then bent to start rolling up his sleeping bag. “Then we call in an expert. I think we might have a place to start.”

## ~ CHAPTER TWENTY-FOUR ~

Meeting with Naomi meant that they had to tell Nick what had happened. "You spent the night together?" he asked repeatedly. "*Really*?" Michael eventually threatened him with organ removal to get him to stop. But once they were able to tell him the whole story, he nodded agreement. "I'll talk to her," he said. "You could probably come over tonight, if that works." He looked at them both for a moment. "You know, if you two had gotten together in high school, you'd have been voted 'Couple Most Likely to Scare Everyone Else the Hell Out of the Room.'"

"Thanks, Nick. That was extremely helpful," Michael said.

Steve looked unhappy when Michael told him about the previous night's occurrences while Cassie was out for lunch. "Is she really okay?" Steve asked. "Are you both okay?"

"I'm fine," Michael said. "But she's scared out of her mind and she should be. Whatever is going on in that house…" He let his voice trail off. "And her mother either can't or won't see it, for some reason. I don't know how she can miss it. The place was like a deep freeze, last night."

"Oh, I could see that happening." The expression on Steve's face was grim. "Got any ideas?"

"Do you know Nick's cousin? Naomi?"

"The one who reads palms and gives Nick half the ghost stories he tells here? I think I met her once."

"Nick's setting it up for us to talk to her tonight. I don't know if she can help, but she seemed a good person to start with. Maybe she'll have some ideas."

"I hope so." Steve looked at him. "Let me know how it goes. I know Cassie doesn't want me in on this, but I want to know what's going on, okay?"

Michael nodded. "I wish she'd take you up on that offer of a room at your place for a while."

"That makes two of us."

Naomi met with them that night after her sons were in bed, sliding into their booth at the Ice Cream Shack.

"I'm sorry to get you out so late," Cassie began.

"Are you kidding?" Naomi laughed. "It's very nice to get together with people who don't spill everything they're drinking and who can go to the bathroom by themselves." She smiled. "Sean knows I need some away time, and this works just fine."

Michael had gone ahead and ordered the Shack Attack, which consisted of sixteen scoops of ice cream, four different sauces, whipped cream, nuts, and four cherries.

"Dig in," Nick said when the mountain of ice cream arrived, and picked up his spoon. "If we let Mikey start on it first, no one else will get any of it."

They ate for a while in silence until Naomi put down her spoon with a sigh. "That's great, but I can't eat anymore." She looked at them all curiously. "So what's this about?"

Nick continued to eat, signaling Cassie to go ahead and tell her story.

"This is going to sound really weird," Cassie said. "I'm not sure if Nick has told you about my house."

"He's mentioned it a few times. But he told me something else has happened?" She put a question into her voice.

"I'm getting messages," Cassie said, and then stopped with a laugh. "Wow, that makes me sound like I ought to be wearing foil on my head and blacking out my windows with black paint."

"Just a little," Nick offered. "You didn't say anything about voices."

Naomi ignored him. "Messages? Like what?"

Cassie handed her a printed paper that contained the list of everything she had either written or typed, unaware each time that she had done any of it. "I feel like I'm losing my mind. In fact, I think I would have believed I was, if Michael hadn't seen me write that last one last night while I was sleepwalking. Or something."

Naomi studied the list. "Do you know about automatic writing?" she asked.

Cassie nodded. "A bit. I started looking into it this afternoon at work." She felt embarrassed. "Steve has a section on the paranormal."

"Cassie, I think that's what you're doing," Naomi said. She read the list one last time and handed it back. "And Nick said you pretty much know what's going on at your house? You know the background?"

"A whole family was murdered there." She was silent for a moment. "But I think the person I'm seeing is the one who murdered them, not one of the victims."

"Hauntings are usually the energies of a troubled person. Someone who killed an entire family–"

"–is one hell of a troubled person," Cassie completed. "Agreed. But why now? Why me?" She looked at Naomi and sighed. "Never mind. I know you told me what you saw in my hand. I just wish I knew what seeing him around the place has to do with messages I write in my sleep." She sat for a moment in silence. "Do you think you could come to my house and get a better idea?"

Naomi made a face. "I wish I could, but I can tell you right now I'll basically be useless. I don't have any ability in that area at all. You and Michael are pretty scary that way–"

"Tell me about it," Nick interrupted.

"–but I don't have any of that kind of talent myself. I'm

really sorry."

"Me too." Cassie smiled nonetheless. "But I'm glad you came out tonight."

"It's good to see you again, Cass. Don't make it so long before you come back to the house, okay? You can just come by with Eloise some time. And now I'd better get going. Knowing Sean, he's got the kids up watching some crazy monster movie instead of sleeping." She gathered up her jacket and her purse. "Thanks for inviting me, guys. The ice cream was terrific."

"Don't go hitting any bars on the way home," Nick called after her. She simply waggled her fingers at him as she walked away, not bothering to turn around. "I guess that was useless," he added after his cousin had gone.

"Well, at least I don't feel as crazy. She didn't laugh at me or tell me I was imagining things."

Michael looked at her. "I didn't imagine any of that last night, either. You need all those guys you see on TV who look into this stuff."

Cassie groaned. "I can see me explaining that to my mother." She picked up her spoon and went back to what was left of the ice cream. "Hey. You guys didn't have to eat *all* the whipped cream."

## ~ CHAPTER TWENTY-FIVE ~

The incident with Abby notwithstanding, Cassie still felt the safest at work. It was bright. It was usually crowded. Best of all, she was surrounded by people who made her feel safe: Steve, who in addition to being her boss came across as both father-figure and big brother; Nick, insane and guaranteed to make her laugh at some point; Fredo, who she suspected would happily tear the arms off of anyone who tried to hurt her; and Michael, of course, who was openly protective and willing to face anything with her, as he had proved.

Yet it was with some trepidation that she approached Steve's office late the next morning, summoned by Michael with no other explanation than "he wants to talk to you about your house."

She knocked and stuck her head into the office. "Is this a good time?"

Steve was surrounded by spreadsheets, stacks of paper, envelopes, and an adding machine that had spewed at least three feet of printed tape. Still, there was a peacefulness in the office that Cassie loved. The room suited its owner very well with its crammed bookcases, the framed pictures of Audrey, Emma, and Abby. The windows had some dust on them but not enough to stop the sunlight from filtering through. There were two or three somewhat wilted plants on the sill and a model airplane hanging in front of one of the panes. There was a sense of industry and yet harmony, and Cassie always thought whenever she entered that the room reflected Steve inside-out.

He looked up and smiled at her. "This is a great time!" he

assured her. "I'd like nothing better than to stop for an hour or three. Come in and have a seat."

She shut the door behind her and sat down across the desk from him, the same place she had sat during her job interview just months earlier. "Michael told me you wanted to see me."

He nodded, the smile fading abruptly. "Cassie, I have a confession to make, and I'm not quite sure how to start."

"That sounds terrible," she blurted out, and then blushed. "Sorry, boss."

"No, you're right," he admitted. "It does sound terrible. All I can ask is that you hear what I have to say with an open mind before you decide anything."

She swallowed. "Am I losing my job?"

He looked confused at the question. "What? No! Of course not. Oh God, I didn't even think about that. No, this isn't job-related. It's a bit more serious than that."

"Oh." That did not make her feel much better.

"Remember the day I hired you? And I told you that you had the job the moment you were able to identify that poem for Nick when he interrupted our interview?"

"Sure."

"Well, if you had been anybody else, knowing the title "Two Tramps in Mud Time" would have nailed the interview for you. But I think that you might have had the job even if you didn't know Robert Frost from Dr. Seuss." He looked at her. "There really is no good way to say this, so I guess I'd better just say it. I've known you since you were born. I know your mother. I knew your dad. I was his best friend. So when you walked in last spring and asked if you could work here, of course I hired you."

Cassie opened her mouth to say something and closed it again without a sound. The silence hung in the office for a long moment before she managed a weak "What?"

Steve looked away for just a second. "I was the best man at

your parents' wedding. I'm even your godfather. Haven't you seen the pictures? I've been kind of waiting all this time for you to say something to me, but you never did."

"I didn't know." Cassie shook her head, stunned. "My mom put most of the pictures away. There are a couple of my dad, but he's alone or with her or with me. I've seen some wedding picture but not since I was a lot younger. She would get so upset when we looked at them that I just stopped asking."

Steve nodded. "I suppose I had a bit more hair then," he said with a grin. "But if you haven't seen them, then I guess I shouldn't be surprised you wouldn't know me. I wasn't sure how to bring all this up, especially when you didn't say anything. And then I thought when you told your mom about the job and gave her my name, that might bring it all out in the open."

Again Cassie shook her head. "I don't know if I've ever given her your whole name. I think I've always just referred to you as 'Steve, my boss.' Nick and I have always called you that, and she never asked."

"I had been wondering about that. I figured this needed to be cleared up and now was as good a time as any."

"But why didn't I know you? If you were my dad's best friend, why did you never come to see me or check on me? When my dad died–"

"When your dad died, it was pretty much implied that I would keep an eye on you, yes. And believe it or not, I did. I know where you went to school, how you did at your studies, where you and your mom used to live. I knew when you moved to the house, even before you came to work here and told me all this stuff. Yeah, I've been keeping an eye on you, but from a distance."

She wasn't sure how to feel, and she realized he was watching her as she worked it through. "But," she would begin and stop. Finally she said, "My mom never told me about you, ever. My godfather? My dad's best friend?"

He nodded, watching her carefully.

"She never said a word. She doesn't talk about any of that, not even about my dad." She pinned Steve with a look. "How did he die?"

He blinked. "How did your dad die? Lori never told you?"

"She told me it was an accident. But now that I know she's never even told me about you, I want to know for sure."

He nodded. "It's true that it was an accident. It was a rainy night and your dad, being who he was, had stopped to help someone change a flat tire. While he was doing that he was hit by another driver."

"Was the driver drunk?"

"No. It was a genuine accident. The driver didn't see your dad until it was too late. If it helps any, it was fast. Instantaneous. No time to think or feel. No lingering in a hospital bed. Your dad would have preferred it that way, I think."

"But wasn't it a hit and run?"

"Yes. The driver took off, but he turned himself in later. He was just an older guy who got panicky about the situation."

Cassie nodded.

"And what about my mom?"

"What about her?"

"How was she, after? Did she change?"

He frowned at her thoughtfully. "We all kind of changed. Losing someone will do that to you, you know. But your mom? I guess there were some changes, yeah. She got distant from all of us on the police force pretty quickly. I used to go over and visit, but I eventually stopped. She told me she wanted to move on with her life, and I understood. She stopped working at the hospital and that's when she got the job at the insurance company. She was probably right. I think it paid more, and she had you to think about."

Cassie looked at him sternly. “I need the whole story, Steve, so don’t give me any of this ‘eventually stopped’ stuff. She told you to stop coming over. Didn’t she?”

Steve smiled faintly. “Not just a daughter. Gus Valentine, Junior, as your dad would have said. Okay, yes. The truth of it is, your mom just about kicked me out of your apartment the last time I saw both of you.”

She nodded. “Now tell me why because I know she won’t.”

“Your mother,” he began and then stopped short. “Well, it was my fault, too, I guess.” He looked embarrassed. “I was hounding you, she said. Because I was trying to make you do something ridiculous and possibly dangerous.”

“Dangerous? What does that mean?” Cassie began.

“Let me explain that better. Your dad died when you were just four. After that happened, I used to come over and visit, bring pizza or Chinese food or something, just to make sure you and your mom were both doing okay. At first, your mom and I got along great. We were both in mourning and we could talk about your dad all we wanted without anyone feeling uncomfortable. We understood each other.

“Well, one night when we were watching the evening news there was a story on about a little boy who had been kidnapped the day before. You looked up at the TV and said, clear as crystal in that little voice of yours, ‘He’s dead.’

“Your mom and I both leaned forward and looked at you.’Do you mean Daddy, honey?’ your mom asked. You just pointed at the TV and said again, ‘He’s dead.’“

Cassie shivered. “I did that?”

“Like you were announcing that you liked chocolate ice cream. Just a simple statement and then you went back to the puzzle you were playing with. Your mom put you to bed and we didn’t talk about it. Until you did it again. This time there was a story about people who went missing after a plane crash. You told us that three of them were dead, but not the fourth. You said the lady was alive. You were right about all of them: the little boy, the plane crash victims." He looked at her. "And that was very much like your dad," he said.

"How do you mean? Like my dad?"

He picked his words carefully. "Your dad could do certain things. See things. Like *you*," he said, his voice weighted.

She began to understand. "That's why Mom doesn't like me to talk about hauntings or ghosts or anything that might be going on in the house, isn't it? She doesn't like this stuff?"

Steve nodded. "Lori was never comfortable with any of it. She married a man with some kind of strange ability that she didn't understand and didn't like, and then it started turning up in her daughter."

"So tell me about when she kicked you out."

The embarrassed expression returned. "There were some missing person cases over that summer, all children. A couple of times I came to ask you if they were still alive. The last time I brought a picture of a missing girl, Kelly Hargreaves. I still remember her name. You told me she was dead. And then your mother told me I was no longer allowed to come and see you."

He sighed. "I apologize, Cassie. I really was exploiting your ability when you were too young to know it. And it got me kicked out of your life so that I couldn't keep as close an eye on you as your dad would have expected."

"Oh, I get the feeling Gus understands," she said, and then stopped in shock. She had never referred to her father by his name before, and she certainly would not have done it had he been alive. Or would she? For the first time her father, never much more than an abstract concept or a face in a few snapshots and a wedding picture, began to come clearer in her mind.

Steve looked at her sharply. "You called him Gus when you were a toddler," he said.

"I did?"

"Your mother couldn't stand it, but he thought it was funny. He figured he had years to change that back to 'Dad.'"

Cassie took a deep breath. She was almost on information overkill. But she still had questions. "Steve, those pictures of children that you brought to me, asking if they were dead or alive. Was I right?"

"About every one of them, when they were found."

"Were they –dead?" She found herself hesitating.

"Two of them. It wasn't a serial killer. They were separate incidents, but there was a rash of cases that summer."

"And I was able to tell you about them."

"Yup."

She looked at him. "And Gus?"

He held her gaze. "Gus was the best cop I ever saw, and not just because he had an ability like yours. When he died, well, I guess I kind of lost some of my own taste for police work. He was older than I was and like a big brother. His death pretty much took the wind out of my sails. A little after I lost contact with you, I left the force."

Cassie looked away from him, stared out the window for a few moments. To the left she could see the little outdoor courtyard where patrons could go and read in the warmer months. To the right, she could see the back of a building that housed a shoe store and an insurance office. There was the sound of a truck beeping as it backed up, faint in the distance. And the sound of children laughing somewhere.

"What you're telling me, really, is that Gus would have had the same problem with my house. Right?" She turned her head and stared at him, hard.

Steve sighed. "I think he would. He would have known something was going on. One time when we were working together, he told me he had seen the ghost of a monk at Queen of

Sorrows Church."

Cassie's eyebrows went up. "The story you told that one Thursday. That was because of Gus?"

"I thought he was pulling my leg but he was actually serious. I didn't find out until later that the place is supposed to be haunted by a monk. I've never seen it. And that was just one thing he told me about." He looked at her. "Cassie, do you know much about your dad's background?"

"No. I know he was adopted, that he originally immigrated to this country with his mother, who died pretty soon after they got here. I know that both of his adoptive parents have passed on. He didn't have any biological family here."

"That's true. That was one of the things that made us close, I think, both of us being adopted. Gus was close to his adoptive mother, but when she was gone, he pretty much went out on his own. His adoptive father died while he was still in the police academy. You look a lot like your dad, Cass. You could both have been gypsies." He grinned at her. "Maybe that's the problem. Maybe you're both Romany and that's where all this spooky stuff around you comes from."

"You're not helping." She smiled in answer but then frowned a moment later. "So what do I do about the house? Gus isn't here to help me."

"I have a feeling you might be able to figure this out on your own. Something in that house wants your attention. Isn't that what you've said?"

She nodded slowly.

"Well, then I would guess something or someone there has a message for you."

"I don't like the messages I'm getting," she said. "When I write them it's all about finding and telling. When I type them it's about blood. And considering a whole family was murdered in that house and it's the murderer and the mom that are hanging around…" She looked at him. "Nothing makes any sense."

"Not yet. I think it will."

"Easy for you to say."

He nodded. "You're right, of course. I'm not living there. I'll tell you what, though. I still have friends on the force. In fact, we both do. Mark Hemmler's a cop, did you know that?"

"Mark 'I'm a skeptic' Hemmler? From Thursday nights?"

"The very same. Why not let us both look into that murder, see if anyone knows anything that could shed some light on what's going on at your house."

"You think it'll do any good?"

He raised his shoulders in a gentle shrug. "It's what I can do. If I think of anything else, I'll let you know."

"Okay." She sighed. "I guess I'd better go back to work."

"I suppose that means I have to do the same." He looked down at the mess on his desk and grimaced, then rose and walked over to open the door for her. "Cassie, if you need *anything*, you come to me. Got it? Gus would have expected that."

In spite of everything, she felt a little quiver of delight that Steve was almost as good as an uncle. Or at least as close to one as she would ever get. Then she had a thought. "Should I tell my mom I'm working for someone who's forbidden?"

Steve gave her a crooked smile. "You're an adult, now. You do whatever you think is right and I'll back you up."

On impulse, Cassie reached up and hugged him tightly, gave him a quick kiss on the cheek. "Thanks."

* * *

Out on the floor, Michael glanced across the store from the cashier's station and saw Cassie hugging and kissing the boss. What was that about? And what was that proprietary grin on

Steve's face as he watched Cassie walk away? And why did Cassie suddenly look so happy? Something sharp twisted inside of him and he realized with a start that he was jealous. Of Steve? How crazy was that? He tried to shrug it off, but couldn't help noticing *how* happy Cassie really looked, the first time in days. He frowned briefly and went back to sorting through discarded receipts.

Five hours later when they walked out together, he was still a bit unsettled about it. Cassie didn't explain anything, not even when they overlapped on break together for a few minutes. When he asked about whether Steve had been able to refer her to some kind of expert, she had said "Not really," but had given him a happy smile before going back out on the floor.

"Okay, so what can Steve do to help?" he asked at last, walking her to her car.

"He said he was going to look into the murder. He and Mark Hemmler. Did you know Mark was a cop? I didn't."

Michael looked confused. "That's it?"

She had been putting her key into her car lock and she looked up at him, squinting against late sunlight and a gusting wind. "It's about all he can do."

He hesitated. It wasn't like he and Cassie were dating, not really. He had never seriously asked her out for fine dining or an evening in the city. They didn't talk on the phone nightly. Well, maybe they had recently, but that had more to do with circumstances than with the blossoming of a relationship beyond friendship.

Still, he realized there were already certain expectations on his part. What had happened the night he stayed at her house, all the trouble he had been trying to help her face, lent an intimacy to their relationship that he now saw was possibly just in his own head. But no, he didn't want to accept that it was all in his head. She called him first, when something was bothering her. Didn't that count for anything? *Besides, Steve's married*, he kept thinking. *She can't be serious. He can't be serious.*

"But then what–" he started and stopped. She would think he was a huge idiot. Worse, he *knew* he was a huge idiot. But it still bothered him. She had never hugged him like she had just hugged Steve, had she? She had kissed him, Michael, on the cheek and held his hand, but maybe more out of sympathy or relief. He hadn't had one of those impulsive, warm, wrap-around things like she had just showered on Steve, not even when they were kids, and five hours of feeling left out in the cold suddenly came to the fore. "What was all that with Steve?" he finally asked.

"All what?" She was genuinely puzzled.

"C'mon, Cass. You know." She was looking at him like he had suddenly started speaking in Mesopotamian. "That huge hug? That kiss?"

"Oh. Oh, yeah, that." She stopped as if thinking. "That was just us setting up a tryst," she said. "He knows a great motel about ten miles out of town." She stared at him seriously a moment longer and then burst out laughing, which did not make him feel any better. "Michael, are you crazy? Steve is my boss. You know he's married. You know I sometimes baby-sit Emma and Abby. And I adore Audrey. C'mon. You've met her. You've met all of them and Abby even gave you her seal of approval, which is saying something."

"I know. It's just–"

She made a face at him. "Look, I have to get home early today. My mom is actually coming home for dinner, and I want to be there. Can we talk later?" She got into the car and was gone while he was still standing there, feeling two steps behind her as always.

# ~ CHAPTER TWENTY-SIX ~

Dinner at the Valentine house was a sweet affair, and if she had not been so overwhelmed by everything Steve had shared with her that afternoon, Cassie probably would have enjoyed herself quite a bit more. Her mother had chosen to make barbecued chicken, one of their favorites, and cheerfully worked over the grill with tongs and marinade brush in the last of the autumn afternoon sunlight. Inside the kitchen, Cassie made rice pilaf and doctored a bagged salad with fresh cherry tomatoes, diced celery, bacon bits, and a hearty sprinkling of shredded cheddar cheese.

While she worked, Richard came in and watched her, silently drinking a beer.

Cassie looked up at him after a bit. "We're both way too quiet," she said with a grin. "What's going on?"

As if he had been waiting for her to ask, Richard stood up and came to the counter where she trimmed and sliced celery. "What do you think?" he asked. "Is this okay with you? And do you think the odds are favorable?"

Cassie looked up at him, not understanding, and saw the black, velvet box in his hand. Her eyes widened in delight when he opened it and showed her the platinum diamond ring. "Richard–"

"Think she'll say yes?" he asked humbly. "Now, don't do that. If she sees, she'll guess," he added, fending off Cassie's excited hug and shushing her squeals of delight.

"Of course she'll say yes. She has to. If she doesn't, then I'll change her mind."

"Well, that's very kind of you, Cass, but if you have to be the one to change her mind I think that means I have a problem. But on the up and up, now. Will you be okay with this? You and your mom have been a team of two for a long time. If you have any doubts –"

"Don't be an idiot," Cassie said, laughing. Then she smiled at him, delighted, excited. "That's a beautiful ring. I've never seen one like that."

"I got it out of state, when I went to Michigan a few weeks ago." He took one last look at the ring, then closed the box and put it in his pocket.

"Oh, the seminar in Michigan. I remember that. I got in trouble that night and kept wondering why you weren't there to help me out of it."

Richard raised his eyebrows. "What, were you out drinking and carousing, you little delinquent, you?"

"That probably would have been easier for her to deal with. No, it was the usual. Me and my paranormal."

"Ah." He nodded. "I don't know why she has such a hard time with that."

"Oh, I have an idea," Cassie said. She didn't get any further.

"There they are, the two weather cowards," Mrs. Valentine said with a laugh, coming in with a platter of fragrant chicken dripping with barbecue sauce. "Hiding in a heated kitchen while I slave away in the autumn chill."

"Hey, I was working," Cassie defended herself. "The salad's ready. And so is the rice."

"And I was supervising."

"Huh." Mrs. Valentine went to the refrigerator and helped herself to a beer. "Let's eat."

Richard proposed in the living room after dinner while Cassie was in the kitchen loading the dishwasher. She heard her mother's cry of joy and smiled to herself, slotting forks and knives in the basket. She was struck by the irony of learning as much as she had about her father on the same day that her mother became engaged to another man. She wondered what Michael would say about the situation.

The thought brought her up short. *Michael*? Where did that come from? Didn't she really mean what would Daniel have said? Daniel. That was who she meant to think about, wasn't it? And then her mother was shouting for her to come into the living room, sparing her the need to analyze her mental slip any further.

Richard looked almost amazed at his fiancée's reaction, but he also looked smug. Cassie hugged her mother, then reached over and gave Richard a high five.

"You *knew*?" Mrs. Valentine demanded, looking from one to the other.

"Well, I couldn't very well ask you to marry me without Cassie's permission," Richard said with a wink.

Mrs. Valentine looked at the ring on her finger. "I want to announce this," she said.

Richard gestured at the door. "The street's right there. I'm sure the neighbors will happily call the police if you get a little too boisterous."

"No, really. I know! Let's have a party. What do you think, Cassie? Let's have one for your friends. You never have parties, not even when you graduated high school. Well, you have all these people at the bookstore you talk about constantly. Let's invite them over and have a little celebration."

"My friends?" Cassie echoed, trying not to sound doubtful and put a damper on her mother's excitement but at the same time thinking about inviting Steve and what was likely to happen when he showed up. "Are you sure?"

"Of course. We can make it casual. And we can have it on a Sunday, so the store is closed that evening and everyone can get here. I want to see Michael and Nick again. And I want to meet

Fredo and Steve, you talk about them so much."

"Sounds good, Mom," she managed. She smiled at them. "I'll just leave you kids alone, now. I'm sure you need some private time."

* * *

When Cassie did call him later that night, Michael thought she sounded somewhat subdued. "I need to talk to you," she said.

"Sure. Talk." He was in the middle of making a grilled cheese sandwich and was trying to balance his phone against his shoulder while manipulating the browning slices of bread in the skillet. It was his fourth sandwich and his appetite was just beginning to wane. His grandfather was out at one of his card games. Michael had worked out, cooled off, showered, and found he was ravenous.

"No. I mean, can I come over?"

He flipped the sandwich in surprised silence. "You want to come here?" She hadn't done that since the night of his story.

"I want to get out."

That made sense. "Okay. You need me to pick you up?"

"Michael, I drive."

"I know that. But if I drove you home later, I could stay with you a while at your house in case Jeremy drops in again."

"Oh." Mentally, he could picture her weighing that out. "No, it's okay," she said at last. "My mom's home and the house will be quiet. I'll leave now, okay?"

"Sure. Do you want–" he started to offer her some dinner, Michael Penfield-style, but she had already hung up. He finished cooking and sat down to eat.

She arrived fifteen minutes later when he was drying dishes. He opened the door for her, took in the dark spill of hair that framed her too-solemn face, the bulky sweater that hid her slender shape, the small hands that slipped her car keys into her purse. He led her back to the kitchen, his heart glad to see her even though he knew she had come to talk about something serious. "Want something to drink?"

"Not yet." She sat down at the table and folded her hands on top of it. She looked like a repentant grade-schooler.

"What's up?" He hung the damp checkered towel on the rack beside the sink and joined her at the table.

"My mom told me tonight that she wants to have a little get-together. She and Richard are going to announce their engagement."

He looked at her, trying to find a clue. He hadn't seen her mother since he was twelve, and he had never met Richard. "Is this bad news?"

"No, not that. I like Richard a lot. He's a good guy. But this get-together. Somehow, it's for me. She told me to invite my friends."

"And that's a bad thing because…?"

She looked at him and he thought she looked exhausted. "I'm not explaining this very well. I'm sorry. I want to invite my friends, of course. You and Eloise and Nick. Fredo and his wife. And Steve and Audrey. They can even bring the kids if they want." She sounded hesitant.

"So what's the problem?"

She sighed. "Steve told me something incredible today. You know that hug and kiss you asked me about?" She looked at him directly, brown eyes troubled. "He's my godfather."

Michael nearly choked. "What?"

"I'm serious. He and my dad were best friends. Steve used to come over and check on my mom and me after my dad died, but my mom eventually kicked him out of our apartment and told him not to come back. He told me he still kept an eye on me after that, like my dad would have wanted him to, but from a distance. When I came in and asked for a job, he said he was happy to hire me. He just didn't know how to tell me everything he told me today. He even expected me to bring it up at some point, but I didn't because I never even knew about him, so he just let it ride."

Michael obtained a drinking straw from a drawer behind him and chewed on it. "So what made your mom kick him out of the apartment?" He sounded suspicious, even to himself.

"That's part of what I need to talk to you about."

He eyed her, curious. "So tell me already."

She was silent a little longer. "I guess this really started with my father. His name was Gus, by the way." And then she told him. She told him about Gus and his abilities. She told him about the summer of the kidnappings when she was a little child. She told him about her mother's aversion to the whole spectrum of hauntings, ghosts, ESP, anything having to do with the paranormal. She told him about Steve finally giving her the story that afternoon, after he had heard what was happening at the Valentine house.

Michael listened, silent, as Cassie laid everything out for him, and was silent for a time after she finished. "So you and your dad both have this psychic thing going on?" he finally asked.

"I gather."

"And I guess another thing you're saying," he added, "is that Steve thinks you might be your own expert in this situation?"

She nodded reluctantly. "I guess. I think that about covers it."

"And now to top it all off, you have to tell your mom that you work for the Forbidden Man?"

"That's all of it."

He took the straw out of his mouth and looked at her. "Well, it pretty much sucks to be you, doesn't it?"

She looked at him then, and tired as she seemed, she laughed.

# ~ CHAPTER TWENTY-SEVEN ~

Lori Valentine was home for several evenings in a row and the house behaved itself. Although the cold spots remained, there were no rustlings in the kitchen, no footsteps, no surprise appearances from Jeremy Mott. Cassie basked in the stillness and was able to sleep, but she was still aware of a sense of waiting. It was as if the house was on temporary good behavior. Cassie figured she would take it while she could get it.

And while she was home, Mrs. Valentine was full of plans for her little party. She changed the menu at least five times, checking each change with Cassie for approval. Richard stopped by almost nightly, for dinner or to bring a dessert later in the evening. He helped with the menu planning, offering suggestions and volunteering to cook, which in Richard's case meant either tacos or a caterer.

Sometimes they just sat at the table and after discussing the party, started talking about everything that came to mind: long-distance communication from telegraph to text messaging (Richard), lengthening of life expectancy and what it could do to the health insurance industry (Mrs. Valentine), paranormal beliefs in different cultures (Richard and Cassie, with her mother rolling her eyes the whole time).

Once, Michael had been there and Richard included him in the conversation, teasing out the younger man's opinions and ideas, which Michael explained thoughtfully and with a great deal of respect. "I like your young gentleman," Richard said to Cassie that night after Michael left. Cassie had been ridiculously pleased that Richard had said so, even as she was mentally correcting him on the idea of Michael being her young gentleman.

Sooner or later, the talk would drift back to the get-together and Cassie knew that the time was coming when she would have to explain about Steve so that neither he nor her mother would be completely blind-sided by the situation when they saw each other face to face again.

"Think about it," Michael had said to her in one of their break room discussions. "What's the worst that could happen? What's the bottom line? Your mother could buy a gun and shoot you, I guess. Or maybe shoot Steve. She could poison your dinner one night. She could go on TV and do a show called 'My Daughter's Ghost Stories are Ruining My Life.' They could find a bunch of psychic hotline callers to fill the audience."

"Shut up." But she had laughed in spite of herself. "All right. I guess it's no big deal. I just have to tell her."

After a little further deliberation and a discussion or two with Eloise, Cassie decided it would be safer to tell her mother when Richard was there. Just for balance, she told herself, although she realized she was also hoping for an ally.

Over a week had passed by the time Cassie got the nerve up raise the subject with her mother. She was bracing herself when Richard turned up at the front door bearing a still-warm pumpkin pie and a spray container of whipped cream.

"Sweets for the sweet," he said when Cassie opened the front door. "That is this week's password, right?"

"She's in the kitchen," Cassie replied with a grin.

"You can be sweet as well," he said. "She doesn't have a monopoly on the trait."

Cassie just ushered him to the back of the house.

Mrs. Valentine groaned in mock exasperation when she saw what he had in his hands. "Richard, I must have gained five pounds just this week."

"Good," he said. "Then I'm not the only one. Cassie, how about some dishes? And do we want coffee or tea with this?"

Cassie waited until they were all seated around the kitchen table and nearly finished with dessert. She savored the last bite of the spicy pie, the smooth whipped cream, and said, "Mom, there's something I have to tell you."

"Sure. What?" Her mother forked another mouthful of pie and looked at her daughter.

"About the party."

"Yes?"

"And about my boss, Steve."

There must have been some sort of undercurrent in Cassie's voice because her mother put down her fork and looked at her. "Oh, don't tell me there's some reason he can't get here on a Sunday night."

"No, it's not that." She took a deep breath. "Mom, Steve's last name is Crawford. He was Gus's – dad's best friend when he was alive. You know. Back then." She faltered into silence.

The expression on her mother's face went from mild inquiry to concern to extreme disapproval, mouth tightening at the corners, brows down, blue eyes going flinty.

Richard, completely and blissfully in the dark, took another hearty bite but began chewing more and more slowly as the tension around the table rose. He swallowed and asked, "But this is good news, isn't it, Lori? Cassie working for an old friend?"

Mrs. Valentine's immediate answer was a shake of her head. "All this time and you never said a word? Cassie, how could you keep that from me?"

"I didn't know," Cassie replied, a bit more defensively than she had planned. "I didn't know about it myself, until a week or so ago. Besides, I told you his name when I took the job and you didn't say a word so I had no idea. Mom, you never even mentioned anyone named Steve. How was I supposed to know anything about him?"

"Steve. Steve Crawford. When I heard his name I never dreamed he would be the same one. And so now you tell me."

"I invited him to the party. I needed to tell you so it wouldn't be a surprise when you saw him."

"Surprise? Try shock. For years I've kept that dreadful man away from you. He was so willing to subject you to all this ridiculous–"

"Dreadful? Mom, he's my boss and he's my friend. And it isn't ridiculous."

"Cassie, you were only four years old when–"

"And I am my father's daughter." Cassie let her voice go flat and stubborn. She felt compelled to defend Steve as well as her father. "That's really the problem, isn't it?"

"Oh, so he told you all about it, did he? Do you know how long it took me to get that nonsense out of your system?"

"Nonsense?" Richard echoed, distressed by what he saw happening and not understanding any of it. "Ladies, let's talk calmly about this."

"It isn't nonsense, Mom. What Gus had, what I have... You may not like it, but I can't help what I am any more than he could. And this house–"

"Oh, will you stop about this house? There is nothing wrong here. *Nothing*."

"There's plenty wrong here. It's not just me, either. Eloise knows. So does Michael."

"You're just kids. What else would I expect?"

"We didn't imagine the murders that happened here. A family was killed right in this house over thirty years ago. I know their names. I know who killed them. And you know what? I've seen at least two of them here."

"Two what? Ghosts?" Her mother's voice fairly crackled with anger and derision.

"Yes, Mom, two ghosts. They're here whether you believe me or not. It doesn't make any difference. They're here."

Mrs. Valentine pushed her plate away in exasperation, her motions short and abrupt.

Cassie stood up, gathering her dish and her fork. "I'm sorry you're angry," she said. "I wasn't trying to make you mad. But Steve is my friend. And I still want him here at the party." She put her plate into the sink and left the room.

"Cassie!" her mother called out behind her.

"Let her go," Richard said in his most soothing voice. "You both need a break. Now, a little more pie. And then you can tell me about Steve."

Cassie, heading upstairs on legs that were weak and shaking, didn't hear anything more.

* * *

She referred to that evening as "Nuclear Friday."

"Yeah, I thought I saw a small mushroom cloud to the south that night," Nick said.

Monday morning was slow as usual, and Cassie and Nick were moving archived files down to the basement while Steve waited on customers and Fredo sorted through the documents that could be brought downstairs for storage.

"Nick, you have no idea. It was hideous. If it hadn't been for Richard, it would have been even uglier. She's just so stubborn about this."

"Gee, I wondered where you got that trait from."

"I'm not stubborn."

"Oh, no, not you. What was I thinking?"

"Shut up." But she was already laughing.

They worked in companionable silence, looking up briefly when Michael came down to join them. "Hey, Nick. Steve wants us to unpack some shelves in his office and bring those down, too. Now."

"Us? Wouldn't it make more sense if you and Fredo did it? You *are* the two largest people in the store, you know."

They were still arguing about it as they went up the stairs. Cassie, left alone, was organizing vendor files when she heard light, slow steps on the staircase. She looked up and was surprised to see May Parrish coming down to her.

"Hi, May. A little early for a ghost story, isn't it?" Cassie greeted the older woman.

"Cassie. I've been meaning to talk to you but I was away the last two weeks, visiting my cousin. The one with the rheumatoid arthritis and the three dogs. You know, I can't imagine what she was thinking, taking in those giant mongrels. She barely has the wherewithal to let them out into the yard."

Cassie smiled politely and waited for May to finish venting. The woman didn't do it often, but when she did say something, everyone in the store knew she had been holding back for some time. Nick once remarked he wanted to hear May blow a gasket and use every four-letter word in the language. "In that proper little voice of hers? How awesome would that be?" he had asked.

"Oh, never mind me," May finished at last. "There are just some things in this life." She located the only chair in the store room and sat down on it tiredly. "Cassie, sweetheart, Steve told me about your house."

"Oh." Cassie hadn't been expecting this. "Yes. It was a bit of a surprise."

"Surprise? I would think it was a shock. A horrible shock." She leaned forward with concern. "Dear, how is the house?"

It was a simple question, but Cassie knew what was being asked. She looked away momentarily. "The house is disturbed," she said, carefully staying away from the word *haunted*. "There are things that happen there that are a little...unsettling."

May nodded. "I was afraid of that. I was worried that the story I told might have started something."

"Oh, no," Cassie protested. "No, not at all. This was going on long before you told us that story. It started as soon as my mother and I moved in. You can't blame yourself for any of this just because you told us a story. In fact, your story helped clear up some things."

May pursed her lips. "Such a horrible thing, and there you are in the same house."

Cassie looked at her curiously. "There is something you could tell me, though."

"Anything, if you think it will help."

"How much do you know about Jeremy?"

"Jeremy? Why?"

Cassie thought about her reply before she spoke. "Because he comes to me. Because I think that his story is as sad as it is dreadful. I keep wondering how that could have happened to a young boy like that. I saw his picture in the paper when they ran the story of the murder. He looked so lost, even when he was younger. Where was his family, that he needed a woman he worked with to buy him clothes or feed him lunch? Why wasn't anyone looking after him? When you told us the story, you mentioned Mrs. Norridge saying that Jeremy had dreams and was afraid all the time. Do you know what she meant?"

May leaned back in the chair and thought a bit. "It's been a very long time, Cassie. Let me see what I can remember." She frowned and was silent for quite a while, but Cassie was afraid to move, afraid to break the older woman's concentration. At last May looked up again. "I'm afraid I don't remember much. It has been so many years. But when Jane mentioned dreams and no one to talk to, I believe she was saying that Jeremy saw things. Sometimes he knew things. Do you understand what I mean?"

"Yes," Cassie said simply.

"Perhaps you do." The woman's smile was sad. "I think you and Jane would have gotten along quite well. What little I can remember is that Jeremy came from a strongly religious background. His family was from a town downstate, a small community of hard-working, God-fearing people who lived and died by their Bible. Now, I'm not saying anything is wrong with that. Maybe we need more of it in this world, who knows?

"But someone like Jeremy was going to have a problem. He couldn't talk to anyone about what he saw without being accused of deviltry, or some other such evil. He did confide this to Jane. I think it took him a long time to realize that she wasn't going to condemn him if he told her about himself." She shook her head. "I'm afraid I don't remember much more."

Cassie looked at her, something else occurring while May spoke. "Were you afraid of Jeremy?"

"Afraid? Oh, no, dear. He was really too sad to be frightening. Even when it came out that he was the murderer, there was a part of me that didn't accept it, although I don't know how it could be otherwise. There was nothing more to be said. The case was closed and my friends were buried." She studied Cassie in her own right, curious herself. "Why are you asking all of this?"

"A few reasons, I guess. There's something about Jeremy that's bothering me. Something that's not right about any of this."

May smiled gently at her. "I have a feeling you might have gotten along with him the way Jane did."

Cassie nodded. "I sometimes think so, too."

The boys took over the basement shortly after with shelves and packing boxes, and Cassie left them to the lengthy and quite loud business of sorting it all out. May left the store to meet a friend for lunch, and Cassie went back to her usual spot at the cash register.

Steve, relinquishing the post, looked at her a little more closely. "You don't look too good."

"Why, thanks, Steve. That's exactly what Nick said when he saw me. Now all I need are Michael and Fredo and it will be unanimous." Michael had run up the stairs to ask a quick question and she saw them look at each other over her head. "And don't act like I'm not here."

"What's up?" Steve asked her mildly after answering Michael's question with a simple "That's fine."

Michael, curious, took two steps into the background and began pulling on his work gloves again.

"I told my mom about you on Friday night." She got furious all over again just thinking about it. "And she said– she said…" she could not quite bring herself to finish the statement.

Steve gave her a quirky little grin. "I can imagine what she said."

Cassie looked up, embarrassed. "Steve, I really wanted you to come to this thing, but if you decide not to, I'll understand. I can't blame you for not wanting to deal with this."

He took her shoulders and shook her a little. "I wouldn't miss it," he said, a wicked little gleam coming into his eyes. "And if Audrey and the girls are at her mother's I won't have anyone reminding me to behave myself."

Michael smiled. "I gotta see that."

Steve's grin broadened. "Don't worry, Cass. It won't be too exciting. I'm sure we'll be civilized as all get-out."

"If you say so," Cassie said doubtfully. "I just feel bad about it."

"Well, don't. We're all adults. We'll handle it like adults."

"You were a cop. Will you be coming armed?" Michael asked.

"Damn straight."

Cassie sighed. "You two." She looked at Steve. "Speaking of

cops, did you say earlier that you found the detective who worked the Norridge murders?"

"Yeah, sure did. Mark got me in touch with him. Can you stay a bit after work? I'll tell you about it. You, too," he added to Michael.

The rest of the day dragged for all of them. Even for Nick, who usually played his way through the workday, juggling paperbacks –"I can do four of them at a time, now!"– or adjusting the display window, reconfiguring the book tables he had just set up the day before or even finding young children in the picture book section and reading them excerpts with great animation, seemed eager for the hands on the clock to speed up. "Eloise and I have plans," he said mysteriously, explaining nothing more.

They toiled their way through each crawling hour, checking the time, cleaning up in between customers to minimize after-closing chores, and finally saw the last of the shoppers through the door. Nick signed out and disappeared immediately. Fredo followed him in a matter of minutes. Cassie and Michael finished their closing rounds before going to the break room.

They could hear Steve puttering around in his office the next room over, opening and closing drawers, shutting down the computer. At last he entered, tea mug in one hand and a notebook in the other. "Nick?" he inquired when he saw the two of them sitting at the table, Michael restlessly tapping a pencil and Cassie with her arms folded in front of her, leaning forward expectantly.

"Gone," Cassie said.

"Oh, right. Eloise." He sighed and took a seat opposite the two of them. "So let's get to it."

# ~ CHAPTER TWENTY-EIGHT ~

Steve opened the notebook and read for a few seconds. "Okay. The detective on that particular murder was one Albert Billings. He retired a few years ago, but he remembers the case. It was his most memorable, so to speak. He says he never saw anything like it, before or after. You want some details?"

Cassie nodded, shivering just a little. Michael put his hand over hers and squeezed it. His touch was warm and reassuring.

"Okay. Martin Norridge, that was the father, was found out in the field beyond the back yard. He was stabbed to death. They all were, actually. Multiple wounds on all the victims. Mr. Norridge was found last because he was outside the house, but Billings says he had probably been killed first. Make it easier for Jeremy Mott that way. No one knows what Mr. Norridge was doing outside the house, if he was lured out or was just outside. It was summer, after all. If he had been in the back yard it would have been easy to get him a little further out just to talk. Especially since the Norridges knew Mott.

"After Mr. Norridge was killed, apparently Mott entered by the front door. There was blood on the door knob and a few smears on the doorjamb. Mary Velasco was killed in the living room."

Cassie thought about seeing Jeremy Mott standing in her living room, looking down at something she had not been able to see, and felt suddenly sick.

Steve glanced up. "Sure you want me to keep going?"

"I need you to," she said. Without thinking, she tightened her grip on Michael's hand.

"Okay. After Ms. Velasco died, they figure Mott went upstairs and killed Mrs. Norridge in the master bedroom, then came down the hall to the kids' room."

"That explains a lot," Cassie said softly. "The cold spot in my mom's room, the footsteps on the stairs that go to my mom's room before coming down the hall to mine. And the kids?"

"Were killed in their bedroom."

"Right outside the closet." She shivered again. "There's a cold spot in my room, too."

He read a little further into his notes. "As far as the police could tell, Mott took money from Mrs. Norridge's purse and Mr. Norridge's wallet, since both the purse and the wallet were found in tossed into a field about a block away from the house with no money in either of them. You already know that Mott was found dead of an OD in the parking lot of the grocery store."

There was a silence around the table when Steve stopped speaking. Then Michael cleared his throat. "So when they found him that was the end of it?"

"Pretty much. They typed the blood that was on him since they didn't do DNA back then, and it was all the same as the Norridges'. Some of the blood on his hand matched Mary Velasco's type. They even found a bloody kitchen knife in the dumpster he hid behind to shoot up. It matched a set in the Norridge kitchen."

Cassie thought about the sounds of someone opening and closing the kitchen drawer at her house. "But wait," she said, something occurring unexpectedly. "If he used the kitchen knife for the murders, how did he kill Mr. Norridge? That happened before he went into the house."

"Why, Ms. Cassie, I do believe you are Gus Valentine's daughter." Steve put on a fake southern drawl and grinned at her. "I asked the same question. The answer is that there is no answer. No other murder weapon was found. And the knife wounds in Mr. Norridge's body did not match those of the kitchen knife, although the wounds on the other victims did."

Michael frowned. "And no one had a problem with that?"

"Not when they had a dead murderer with enough evidence to prove he had killed the rest of them, no." He smiled. "You watch too many cop shows on TV."

"And read too many books."

Steve slapped the notebook shut. "So there it is in a nutshell. Only…" he paused a moment, as if trying to remember something. "I kept getting the feeling there was something Billings didn't tell me."

"Really? Why?" Cassie looked at him curiously.

"I don't know," he admitted. "It was just a feeling. I think I'll wait a few days and take another run at him, see if I'm right or just letting my imagination get the best of me."

Cassie took a deep breath. "Thanks for the information, Steve. It does clear up a few things about the house."

"No problem. Hey, do you want me to bring anything to your mom's soiree?" He grinned at her, pure mischief in his eyes.

"Wine?" Cassie suggested.

"And a Kevlar vest," Michael added.

* * *

The air at the Valentine house was strained. Cassie and her mother were polite and circumspect around each other, talking carefully in neutral tones about the party and the menu. They finally agreed on a Sunday a few weeks away, an arrival time for their guests, and when to serve dinner. Richard, clearly unhappy about the tension in the house, nevertheless held his peace and behaved as if everything was perfectly normal. Cassie found reasons to escape frequently, including extra night hours at work.

She got an unexpected surprise one evening when an elderly gentleman came into the store.

Fredo was off that evening, and Michael, having done a full shift, had already left. Nick was in receiving, and Eloise, who had come in after getting off from her own job, was manning the cashier's station with Cassie. Eloise was always so helpful that Steve stopped just short of offering her a job: she had never asked. She was happy enough at her health food store and brought in things like flaxseed and sunflower cookies, or soy cheese. It drove Nick to counteroffer items like potato chips and mass-produced cream-filled snack cakes.

Both Cassie and Eloise looked up when the older man came into the store. "Hi," Cassie said.

He removed his hat and looked at her, then smiled. "Good evening. I'm just going to look around a bit."

"Enjoy," Cassie said. "If you have any questions, we'll be right here."

He disappeared down the history/reference aisle and Eloise moved closer to Cassie so they could continue their conversation in quieter tones. Eventually, Steve put his head out of the office and asked Eloise to come back. "Sorry," he said. "But I could use a hand with something."

"No problem." She went to the back of the store right away, skirt and scarf trailing behind her.

Alone, Cassie took out her book.

"You must be Cassie Valentine."

She looked up and found the elderly man standing at the cash register.

"That's me." She looked at him curiously.

"My name is Henry. Henry McCormick." He put his hand out and Cassie shook it. "I'm Michael's grandfather."

"Oh, hi!" Cassie was pleased to meet him and smiled broadly. "Are you looking for a book? I'm surprised Michael didn't offer to get it for you. He gets the discount, you know."

Grandpa Henry smiled at her. "Oh, I wasn't really looking for a book. At least, nothing caught my eye."

She nodded, waiting for him to say something more, but his keen silence and the way he was looking at her made her face warm. "Mr. McCormick," she began.

"Please. You might as well call me Grandpa Henry, too. All the boy's friends did when he was younger." He winked at her. "Now, Mikey has been a bit remiss in inviting you over for dinner so we could meet properly."

Cassie shook her head. "It's not his fault, really. Michael's been... um... helping out at my house a lot lately." She blushed again and looked at him. "Has he told you what's going on?"

"Some of it. He's not always the most forthcoming person."

"So I noticed." Cassie laughed. "It helps that we knew each other before."

"I hear you were up at the lake with him when you were both younger."

"Every year for quite a few years," she said.

"So you knew his whole family."

She nodded. "I was really sorry to hear what had happened."

"It was a sad time, a hard time." He looked at her with sharp blue eyes. "I wanted to meet the young lady that seems to be helping him to turn it around."

She didn't know how to react to that. Helping Michael? He had been helping her, had been more than helpful, and still she had mixed feelings about the situation. Her attraction to Michael was growing, but part of her still resisted letting go of Daniel. She cast around for an appropriate answer.

But Grandpa Henry wasn't finished. "He was quiet and moody for years, not speaking to anyone, not going out unless it was for school, or to run during the warmer weather. Since he started working here, though, and after spending time with all of you, he's coming out of himself a bit more. It's good to see. I just wanted to tell you." He leaned forward and whispered, "And you don't have to let him know I was here. At least, not for that."

She smiled. "I won't. Thank you for stopping by. It's good to meet you."

"Thank you, Cassie." He paused a moment. "I will tell Michael it is time for him to invite you to dinner and we'll see how he reacts to that." His eyes glittered with amusement briefly. Then he leaned forward. "About your house…"

"Oh, the house." She made a little face. "If Michael's told you about it, you must think I sound like a crazy person."

But he surprised her. "No, not at all. I've been around long enough to know that not everything can be easily explained. And I remember that murder. If Mikey is helpful to you, then I'm glad."

Cassie looked at him. "Did you know the Norridge family?"

"No, but I do know Dale Cotton." He smiled at her and his eyes crinkled, very much like his grandson's. "We play cards together. He told me about a very interesting young woman who came to ask him about her house."

"You heard about that?"

"Dale and Mike have both told me there's something not right about your place. You be careful, Cassie."

# ~ CHAPTER TWENTY-NINE ~

The invitation to dinner at Grandpa Henry's house, when it came, was delivered with true Michael Penfield flair. Cassie was in the break room getting ready to eat lunch when Michael popped his head around the door. He had been working in the basement, setting up "yet two thousand more of those infernal bookshelves" as he put it, and his hair was wilder than usual. His face was streaked where he had carelessly rubbed his work glove alongside his jaw, and his shirt, coming un-tucked from his jeans, was littered with bits of cardboard and Styrofoam packing.

And yet when she looked at him, Cassie was alarmed at how attracted to him she suddenly felt. At the back of her mind something still whispered "Daniel," but Michael, all clear brown eyes and puckered scar, with "that chest and those arms" as Audrey had put it, looked different to her at that moment. She blinked, but the slight alteration to his appearance, the subtle change that made him unexpectedly appealing, whatever it was, didn't go away. She suddenly thought of sitting up in that tree near the lake, looking down and meeting his eyes unexpectedly, and she was not prepared for that same long-ago plunging sensation in her stomach.

"Hey, Cass," he said, totally oblivious to what was going through her head. "So do you like pork chops with twice-baked potatoes and asparagus, or what?"

"What?" She heard the question and even understood the words, but somehow the message was getting lost.

"My grandfather told me to invite you to dinner. So is Friday night okay?"

"Hey, Mike, you jerk! Where'd you go? Get back down here and give me a hand with this other box, will ya?" That was Nick calling from the basement.

"Gotta go." Michael gave her a brief smile. "Let me know before I leave today, okay? Thanks!" And he was gone.

The invitation threw Cassie into a quandary even as she accepted it before he left at the end of his shift. She went home to brood about it. Michael. Daniel. It always came down to that and she sighed, impatient with herself. She knew she was supposed to get on with her life. She *knew* this. So why did it feel like she was betraying someone when she said yes to Michael's invitation? His entire face had lit up and the smile he gave her was as open as it had once been, years ago at the lake in Wisconsin. Grandpa Henry was right. Michael's relationships at the bookstore, including with her, were finally turning him around. *But what about me*? she thought. There was no answer.

She wound up talking to Richard about it. Her mother had run to the store to pick up something she needed for that evening's meal, and Cassie, coming home from work, had found Richard sitting on the couch reading a book about vitrified forts in Scotland. He put his glasses back on to look at her when she entered, smiling when she came over and kissed him on the cheek.

"My Cassandra Valentine," he said. "Named for both a seer and a messenger. And how are you? You look a bit cloudy today."

"Yeah? I feel a bit cloudy today." She threw her purse onto a chair, took off her shoes and sat down on the couch with him, tucking her feet beneath her. "Can I talk to you about something?"

"Certainly." He put the book down. "What can I offer you?"

"How about some direction?"

"Academic, I hope?"

"No. Relationships."

"*Ach, Gott in himmel,*" he said. "Why me? Shouldn't you be talking to your mother about this?"

"Maybe. We're not discussing too much of anything, these days. At least, not beyond dinner menus."

He sighed. "Are you still doing that? Both of you?"

Cassie grew stubborn. "If I bring up Steve again, we'll just get into another fight. It's not like I planned to go behind her back. How could I go behind her back when I didn't even know there was an issue at hand?"

"That's an anatomical way to put it," he said. "I understand, Cassie, I really do. Your mother does, as well. We saw a certain defensive reflex that night, I think."

"For what? It's not like Steve ever did anything to harm either of us."

Richard shoved his glasses up and massaged the bridge of his nose. "You really do need to talk to your mother about this whole Steve situation."

"Later. Right now I want to talk to you about something else. Is that okay?"

"Of course. You said something about relationships. If you are running away to Las Vegas to get married, remember that you are an adult and have to deal with the consequences of that decision all on your own."

"Richard, don't try to get out of this."

"You can't blame me for trying."

"How do I move past grieving?"

That stopped him cold. "Can you give me particulars?" he asked after a moment.

Cassie looked down and started picking at threads in the ribbing of her sweater. "You remember Daniel."

"Of course I do. And I am sorry for your loss as I know you

are still in pain from it. But you mentioned wanting to move past grief?"

"It's Michael," she said. She didn't elaborate, realizing from the expression on his face that he understood where she was going.

"Michael is here, and you are feeling disloyal to Daniel? Or to his memory? Is that it?"

"That's exactly it. Michael invited me to dinner and I accepted. I know it was the right thing to do. It made him really happy when I did. But it still feels so wrong to me. Daniel's been gone over a year now. I tried not to notice the date when it came and went, but of course I did. I still remember everything about him so well. And yet–"

"And yet he's gone away and left you here and now Michael has turned up. Tell me something, Cassie. How long do you think you would have expected Daniel to mourn you if the situation had been reversed?"

She squinted up at him. "I don't even know how to answer that."

"Do you think you would have wanted him never to date again?"

"Of course not."

"Do you think he expected you never to date again?"

"No," she answered in a small voice. "I think *I* expected me never to date again."

"Because you never thought you could have feelings for anyone again after Daniel?"

"Is that what it is?"

He smiled at her. "Again, you ought to talk to your mother about this. She's been there, Cassie."

She thought about it, realizing he was right. "How has it been for you?" she asked. "If it's okay to talk about it. Does Gus ever get in the way? Or did he?"

"I guess our situation is a little different from yours. Gus has been gone a lot longer than Daniel. Still, your mother was very much in love with your father, and she held herself back for a long time. We first started dating, what, five years ago? And how long did it take before we even became exclusive? Your mother has scars that run pretty deep. But I understand that. I don't expect to replace Gus in her heart. I'm not trying to, and she realizes that."

Cassie shook her head. "Doesn't it bother you?"

"That another man found your mother as loving and beautiful as I do? I'm not that insecure." He looked at her. "Are you ready to give Michael a chance?"

"I don't know. I'm afraid." She didn't know how to express the jumble of feelings she had for Daniel and for Michael as well.

Richard put an arm around her and gave her a quick squeeze. "Don't worry so much," he said. "Just do what feels right and comfortable, and the rest will take care of itself. Daniel loved you, didn't he?"

She nodded, unable to speak as she blinked back the tears that suddenly stung her eyes.

"Then trust that he would understand. Okay?"

She sat with Richard a few more minutes, then kissed him on the forehead when she got up to leave. "Thank you," she whispered.

Upstairs, she booted up her computer and went into The List. Item 98. *He was the most beautiful guy I ever knew.* Item 99. *I will never forget him.* Item 100. She left that blank and saved the document. Item 100 would need to be something really special and she meant to take her time with that.

* * *

Mrs. Valentine suggested out of nowhere that the party take place that Sunday. "I know it's short notice, but everyone knew about it, right? I can see another long project coming down the pipes at me very soon and my free hours are now numbered, so how about it? Say six o'clock?"

Cassie, whose feelings toward her mother had softened considerably since talking with Richard, agreed. "Sure. I'll tell everyone at work tomorrow and I ought to be able to give you a firm head count by tomorrow night or the day after at the latest. Is that okay?"

"That's fine." Mother and daughter smiled at each other and Cassie was surprised at how much that simple conversation cleared the air.

She went to the bookstore with the news and got acceptances from nearly everyone there. Fredo thanked her for inviting his children, but told her that he and his wife had been looking forward to a child-free evening and would be coming without them. Steve also gave regrets for Audrey and the girls. "They will be at Grandma's that evening. Hope you don't mind me turning up by myself?"

"I'm just glad you're turning up at all," she said when he told her.

Steve gave her his crooked smile and said, "Wild horses couldn't keep me away."

"He always says that," remarked Nick, "yet I've never seen him tangle with any wild horses. Not even tame ones. Not even a couple of ponies."

Cassie just shook her head and walked away from them both.

"Hey," she said when she ran into Michael as he came out of receiving. "Can I bring something to dinner on Friday?"

But the dinner was postponed. Michael seemed heartbroken when he told Cassie about it. "It's someone he was in the army with," he said. "I guess the guy's got no other family and when he went into the hospital, Gramps got the call. He'll only be gone for a few days, he thinks, but it kind of screws up Friday." He looked at her hesitantly. "Would you consider a rain check?"

"Don't be silly, Michael. Of course. Your grandfather had to go when he got that phone call."

He nodded, apparently relieved at her answer. But something more was on his mind. "Um, about Friday?"

She smiled at him. "You still want to get together?"

"Yeah! I mean, well, yeah. We can go to dinner. I'll bring you somewhere that serves pork chops and baked potatoes."

"We don't have to go that extreme," she said. "You want to hook up with Eloise and Nick?"

He looked across the store at Nick, chatting with Steve in the break room. "Not really," he said.

Cassie bit back the smile at his rather strained reply. "Okay," she said. "Let's go eat somewhere, and if we feel like it, maybe catch a movie."

"Great. Really. I'll pick you up at six-thirty." Another hesitation. "Unless you wanted to drive and meet me."

She felt sorry for him, he was trying so hard not to tread too heavily. "No, you can pick me up. Seems silly to have two cars. Unless you'd rather I drove?"

"I'll pick you up at six-thirty." The answer was firm.

She didn't watch him walk away, but had the strongest feeling that he punched his fist into the air a couple of times when she wasn't looking at him. The thought made her smile and she didn't bother to hide it. And then she remembered about her mother's dinner party. "Oh, hey, Michael?"

He turned around and his face seemed so unusually soft and happy that she was startled. It took her a second or two to remember what she needed to tell him. "I've got an invite for you, too, for this Sunday at my place. Six o'clock. My mom's decided the party would work best for her sooner instead of later.

So far we have Nick, Eloise, Fredo and Gloria, and Steve by himself. Can you make it?"

"I'll be there," he said.

# ~ CHAPTER THIRTY ~

Almost by unspoken agreement, neither Michael nor Cassie ever mentioned to Nick or to Eloise that they were going out on an actual date that Friday night. Nick invited Michael out to Friday dinner with him and Eloise, going into the city to try a new Mexican restaurant. Cassie heard Michael decline, the casual reply absolutely perfect. If it hadn't been, Nick would have pounced on Michael for a reason why. She knew that was true because she had already given the same sort of answer to Eloise. When Nick and Michael left the store together at closing time late that afternoon, Cassie stayed behind to clean up the break room and give the cashier's station one last tidying.

Steve stopped in his doorway and looked at her. "Don't you need to go home and primp or whatever it is all you females do before a big date?"

Cassie turned to him, open-mouthed. "What? How did you know? Who said something to you?"

Steve grinned. "No one said anything. I'm just not as blind as Nick." She stared at him and he shrugged. "So Michael spent the last half of this week looking like he had a string of light bulbs up his sinus cavities. No kidding. Now I know what they mean when they say someone glows."

"Steve, if you said anything to anyone–"

"Relax, I didn't. Audrey knows, though. Can't keep secrets from the wife." He raised his chin toward the front door. "Go on. The store is tidy enough. Have fun but be careful out there, okay?"

"You sound like Officer Friendly. Thanks, though. I'll see you here tomorrow."

He nodded and waved her off.

Later at home, waiting for Michael to ring the doorbell, Cassie found that she was nervous. How stupid was that? She had known him for years, after all. Nick would helpfully point out that they had even spent the night together. Michael had seen her at her worst, whether it was those summers she had the braces, or that afternoon when he had found her crying in the store basement. What on earth did she have to be nervous about?

Yet, here she was, pacing while she watched the minutes tick by on the clock face. She couldn't have been more nervous if she were expecting Jeremy Mott to knock on her bedroom door. Check that. Jeremy Mott would have won hands down over Michael in terms of making her nervous. But her mother was down in the kitchen cooking dinner with Richard, and so Jeremy Mott was effectively banished from the house. Or so she hoped. This was ridiculous. She didn't need to be worrying about hauntings at the same time that she was anxious about Michael, and for no good reason.

She went downstairs to wait. Richard heard her rambling around in the living room and came out to see her, smelling slightly of her mother's garlic and basil spaghetti sauce. "Hey," she said when she saw him.

He smiled. "You look very nice."

She blushed. "I feel ill," she said. "I can't believe how nervous I am, and I've known him my whole life, practically."

"Ah, but not like this," he said. "He's been a buddy and a pal and a friend and a co-worker. I have serious doubts, however, that he has ever been a suitor."

"When you put it like that, it sounds twenty times worse."

He raised his hands. "Sorry. Not my goal. Just cut him some slack, okay? I'll bet you he's about *forty* times more nervous than you are."

"You think?"

"Look at it from his point of view and see what he might be thinking of as a personal Waterloo."

Daniel's smiling face appeared in her mind's eye. "I get it," she said.

"That's my girl." He gave her a fatherly hug and went back toward the kitchen. "Before your mother notices that I'm not at my post, grating cheese," he added in a whisper. The doorbell rang and he grinned at her. "Have fun."

Cassie closed her eyes and took a deep breath, then went to the door.

Michael was gorgeous. Peeking over and around her double filter of loss and guilt, she looked at him and saw the tall, well-built young man with hopeful brown eyes, the optimistically combed mop of hair, the scar that made the rest of his face appear so smooth and young. He stood in his familiar stance, hands in his pockets, shoulders hunched slightly forward in a way that implied both uncertainty and anticipation. He was wearing a dark blue button-down shirt with a striped tie knotted loosely below the open top button and collar, a leather jacket she had never seen before, and new jeans.

His eyes widened when he looked at her and Cassie blushed slightly. She had chosen, after about thirty-seven different clothing auditions, a fitted lavender sweater and her best black jeans. She had pulled some of her hair back in a clasp, and had even put on a trace of make-up, something she hadn't done for anyone in over a year.

"Ready?" he asked and his voice failed slightly. Nerves.

She nodded, grabbing up her wool jacket. "Yes. Let's go."

The entire night took her by constant surprise. After the first few minutes of feeling awkward and strange in the car, they looked at each other and Michael laughed out loud. "Boys *are* stupid," he said. "I can't remember how to talk to you." And after that, they were fine.

He took her to a Chinese restaurant she had never been to before, where he showed her how to eat with chopsticks. "That's the kind of thing you pick up when your grandfather's served overseas," he explained. They ordered family style and ate off the same platter, drank tea, and shared the fortunes in their cookies.

Then they drove a few towns over for dessert, stopping in at a family style restaurant for pie and ice cream and then going for a walk along the river. "I should jog about five miles before bed tonight," she said. "I've eaten way more than I have any business eating."

"We could probably find a way to burn it off," he said, swinging her hand as they walked. She turned to look up at him and he smiled, then tugged her around by the hand and bent down to kiss her, tilting her face up to his, fingertips gentle under her chin. She kissed him back and after a moment he pulled away. "Whoa," he said. "Slow down, Penfield," he added, and she laughed at him. "Slow way down, boy."

They walked a little longer, stopping in front of shop windows, talking about the old days in Wisconsin as well as what they saw ahead of them in the coming years. "I wasn't ready for college," Michael said as they gazed into the windows of a bookstore. Then abruptly, "Nick does better windows, doesn't he?"

"He sure does." Cassie met his eyes in their reflection. "So are you going back to school?"

"I'd like to, I guess. If I can figure out what to study. I've been talking to Steve about it lately. He majored in political science, wound up at the police academy, took some night courses in business, worked a bunch of places, and then opened a bookstore. I don't know that I want that kind of path exactly, but it made me feel better to think I don't have to do one thing for the rest of my life."

"No one does that anymore, do they?" They turned away from the store window, still holding hands. "I don't know what I want, either," Cassie said. "I was thinking history. I like research, too, but I also want something that lets me help people. But what kind of job does all that add up to? I was taking general classes, but I only finished one year before…" She broke off, not sure whether to finish the thought aloud.

"Nick told me. He said you didn't go back afterwards."

"I couldn't." She sighed. "Michael, we need to talk."

"Uh-oh." He squeezed her hand and looked down at her. "Should I take you home, now?" His voice was carefully neutral and again she was struck at how hard he was working to put no undue pressure on her.

"No, you don't have to do that. But we do need to talk."

"It's a little cool out," he said. "Let's go back to the car."

They sat in his car, parked beneath a light on a small one-way street, and watched the night wind scoop and toss the branches of the trees that lined the sidewalk. "What's up?" he asked.

"I was talking to Richard about this the other day, and now I need to talk to you. It's about Daniel."

"Yeah. I thought it might be."

She looked at him. "I really like you, Michael."

He looked puzzled. "That's not about Daniel."

"Yes, it is. I really like you and I don't want to hurt you."

"Oh, God, that actually means 'I don't want to hurt you, *but*,' doesn't it?"

"We're friends, right?"

He winced and then groaned quietly. "That's even worse. *I don't want to hurt you and we're friends*." He looked at her. "It's okay, Cass. I get it. I'll take you home, now."

She took his hand away from the key in the ignition and tugged on it. “We’re friends, right?” she asked again, insistent.

“Yeah, of course we are. I guess I was just hoping that–”

“Then shut up and listen to me. I’m trying to tell you something.”

“I thought you just did.”

“No, you leaped to a spectacularly obtuse conclusion because you’re not listening to me.”

He blinked once or twice. “Okay. I’m listening.”

“You said we’re friends and I’m counting on that. Michael, I do like you. I really do. I think I liked you all the way back when we were eight or nine and I didn’t even understand what I was feeling then. I just knew I liked it when we looked at each other. But in between there was Daniel, and I was totally in love with him. No, don’t do that. Don’t turn away from me. Let me finish. I do like you, but I’m still trying to get past Daniel’s death. There are going to be times I’ll miss him or still mourn for him, and if your friendship can’t get you past that with me, then maybe you should reconsider asking me out any more.” She stopped and the silence in the car was absolute.

She hadn’t been looking at him when she rushed through the last of what she had to say, words spilling all over each other, but he was silent so long she finally looked up at him.

He felt the heaviness of her gaze and he turned back to face her. His expression was somewhere between sad and unreadable, the scar pulling his eye and the corner of his mouth down. “I just need to know,” he began. He sounded close to hopeless. “I just need to know that I maybe have a chance with you,” he said, the last half of it nearly whispered.

“Michael,” she said, surprise in her voice. “With everything I’ve got going on, I was asking if I had a chance with *you*.”

* * *

By the time he had walked her to her door and kissed her good night several hours later, Cassie understood what Steve meant about the string of light bulbs. Michael *did* glow.

# ~ CHAPTER THIRTY-ONE ~

Michael was at the Valentine house by three-thirty in the afternoon that Sunday. Cassie had asked him to come early to help set up and he was kind enough to agree. They cleaned up the last specks of invisible dust that her mother kept finding. They wrapped plastic-ware in thick paper napkins and stacked them in a basket on the table. They put out glasses and plates, ice buckets and platters, small snack dishes with nuts and mints and M & M's.

Cassie set out candles on the table in the dining room, the coffee table, and the side board against the wall by the kitchen. Michael arranged folding chairs in the living room, cleaned up the TV trays in the garage and brought them in, and put bags of ice in the coolers. When at last Mrs. Valentine dismissed them so that she could go and get dressed, Cassie and Michael escaped to the front porch and sat on the top step.

"Nervous?" he asked, turning his head to look at her as he sat with his arms folded across the tops of his knees.

"Just about Steve. How'd my mom seem to you?"

"Unusually calm. Almost preternaturally calm."

"I was thinking the same thing. That's bad."

"Really? Why? Doesn't it mean everything is under control?"

"Everything's under *hyper*-control. She could blow like a volcano if something goes wrong."

He grinned at her. "Then we go to plan B. Nick and I talked about it. He'll make the popcorn and I'll pull up the chairs."

She burst out laughing at the image but stopped just as

abruptly. "It still shocks me a bit," she admitted. "The idea that I knew Steve a long time ago and didn't even know it. I used to call him 'Uncle Tee.' He told me but I don't remember. I don't remember the last afternoon he was here or that he ever visited us. Michael, I've been trying and I can't even remember my own father. Do you know how weird that is, to know there was a person in my life and I can't even get a glimpse of him?"

"Jeez, Cass, you were a little kid. Take it easy."

"But I can't. It's like there's something missing and I didn't even know it until these past few weeks. And now that I do know it, I can't ignore it. I mean, what was Gus like? And why didn't my mother ever tell me any of this stuff?"

"Why do families do *anything* they do?" Michael sounded quietly bitter and Cassie realized they were venturing into dangerous territory.

She took his hand. "Okay. Sorry. I just hope Steve will be okay."

"Steve will be fine. He's a cop."

"Was a cop. Now he's a bookseller."

"Okay. So maybe he brings both a gun *and* a Bible to scary situations."

"Sounds like a vampire slayer."

"Or some religions." Nick and Eloise were coming up the walk. "Ready or not?" Nick asked.

"Not," said Cassie.

Eloise climbed up the steps and bent over to give her a lemon-scented hug. "It'll be okay," she said. "We're your back-up."

Fredo and his wife, Gloria, arrived ten minutes after Nick and Eloise, and were soon in the kitchen with Mrs. Valentine, helping her put appetizers on trays and clean up some of the piles of utensils and dishes in the sink.

Steve would have been the last of Cassie's guests to arrive

had he not walked in with Richard. Cassie wondered if Richard had timed that to happen, and she made a mental note to thank him for it later. She answered the front door with her mother close behind her, and she was very aware that the others had stopped conversing in the living room and were watching the front hall with unabashed curiosity.

"Lori, look who I found," Richard announced in his huge, warm voice, leaning forward to kiss her on the cheek and then taking her hand and placing it firmly in Steve's. "An old friend."

Steve looked genuinely happy to see her. "You haven't changed a bit, Lor," he said, shaking her hand and staring into her face. "Not one bit."

At first she stared back at him with nothing more than a polite smile, but suddenly the façade cracked and her smile widened with genuine warmth and pleasure. "Neither have you."

Richard put an arm around them both and began walking them in the direction of the dining room. "Let's find something to drink," he said.

Cassie watched them go, relieved and almost baffled.

"Well, dang," a voice said behind her. "That's it? Cassie, the whole evening is now shot for entertainment."

She turned and looked at Nick. "You could always juggle."

Dinner was a friendly, casual event with Mrs. Valentine's homemade stuffed manicotti, home-made dinner rolls, and spring greens salad a success. Cassie was pleased to see how easily everyone got along with her mother and with Richard. Eloise helped play hostess and Fredo did so much in the kitchen that her mother chased him away. Richard raised his glass in a toast to his fiancée midway through the dinner and announced their engagement with a wedding date as yet to be decided. "We have to clear that with Cassie first," he added with a smile. There were congratulations and more toasts, and Eloise and Gloria had the opportunity to gush over the ring.

After the tiramisu, Fredo and Gloria excused themselves early as they had left their two youngest children in the charge of the oldest. "We want to make sure the house is still standing," Gloria said.

"Our oldest is nearly as mad as Nick," Fredo added.

"Ouch. That hurt me badly, but I forgive you," Nick replied gravely. Then he laughed and said, "So when do I get to meet this kid?"

* * *

After the Donardos had gone, everyone else settled into a sort of relaxed stupor, full of good food and happy to sit and talk. Michael scooped a handful of peanuts out of a dish and munched them, standing at the sideboard and watching as Richard and Eloise discussed the significance of tattoos to a certain tribe in South America. Nick was talking to Steve and Cassie's mother – and where was Cassie?

He turned and saw her coming around the corner, a glass of iced tea in her hand. She caught his eye from across the room and smiled at him before heading in Steve's direction. Steve welcomed her to the conversation with a light arm around her shoulders, and Michael, turning away for a handful of M & M's, missed the start of it. As soon as he turned around, though, the change in the room was impossible to miss.

He saw Cassie drop the full glass of tea. It hit the hardwood floor with a splash that made everyone look around.

"Cassie, run and get a rag," Mrs. Valentine said, bending over to retrieve the glass and the ice cubes. Then more sharply, "Cassie?"

Michael grew cold even as he was just starting to cross the room. For some reason he felt compelled to look at his watch as he moved and saw that it was ten minutes after ten. *Witching hour at the Valentines',* he thought.

"What–" he heard Eloise begin.

"You," Cassie said in a hoarse and whispery voice. She was talking to Steve. "To tell. Tell…" she faltered and seemed to be struggling to speak, her mouth opening and closing, her hand drifting up senselessly to touch Steve's shoulder.

Michael got to her side even as Steve was already taking her by the hand.

"Cassie!" her mother said again sharply.

"I don't think that's Cassie," Michael managed. Steve looked at him and Michael nodded. "Talk back," he suggested.

"Cassie, stop this," Mrs. Valentine tried again.

Richard took her arm to quiet her. "Let it go a minute," he whispered.

Steve looked into Cassie's face. "Who are you?" he asked. "What do you want?"

"Found," she croaked with difficulty, voice labored. "You. Found. Tell you. Tell you I didn't…I didn't…"

Steve cupped Cassie's face gently in his hands, turned her head up to look at him. "Who are you?" His voice was calm but persistent. "And what do you need to tell? What do you want us to know?"

She stared at him, blank eyes growing wider, and then for a split second, Cassie was present in that glance. Just as suddenly her eyes rolled up, sightless, and she collapsed without another sound.

Michael caught her, picked her up. There was a moment of silence, and then everyone was talking at once.

"Call nine-one-one!" That was Mrs. Valentine.

"She doesn't need nine-one-one." Michael was shocked that he found himself defying Cassie's mother, but he knew that he was right. "She needs some rest and some quiet. I'll bring her upstairs."

"I'll go with you." Eloise followed him down the hall to the stairs even as Mrs. Valentine was still shouting that they needed medical help and calling for Michael to bring her daughter back downstairs.

"Medical help for what?" Michael heard Steve ask. "She was in a trance. She'll come out of it. Didn't you ever see Gus do that?"

Cassie's mother sounded furious. "Do not even start with that nonsense in this house."

"This house is the problem," Steve retorted, starting to lose a little bit of his equanimity.

"She must be on something. She must have taken something."

Then Richard's warm voice chimed in. "In all the years you've had with this child, have you ever known her to use *anything* like that?" he asked reasonably.

"Of course not." The answer cracked like a whip. "But there has to be some kind of explanation."

"There is," Steve said. "And drugs ain't it."

"Lori, put your phone away and let's give Cassie a little time." Richard's suggestion was soothing, placating. "I think she's fine with Michael and Eloise"

The rest of the discussion was lost to Michael as he reached the top of the stairs and turned for Cassie's room. Eloise ran ahead to smooth out the bedspread. Michael deposited Cassie gently down, taking the time to position the pillow under her head. She was so still and fragile-looking, lying there with her dark hair fanned out on the pillow. He was almost afraid. And then he looked at Eloise–

–who was just about in tears. "What do we do?" she whispered. "Is she going to be all right?"

"She should be fine. She did this once when I was here. It was almost like sleepwalking, and she wrote instead of talked, but this looks like the same thing. I just want to make sure she's not alone when she comes out of it."

"I can stay," Eloise said. She was already looking around the room uneasily.

Michael smiled in spite of the situation. "It's okay, Eloise. Go on back down with the others. I'll stay. This room doesn't bother me." *Not much*, he thought to himself, but she didn't need to know that. "Maybe you ought to get down there and give Steve some support. Right now all he's got is Nick." That won him a tremulous grin.

She nodded and left the room, but the next minute she returned, hauling a large wooden rocking chair. "It's her mom's," she said. "It's got to be more comfortable than Cassie's computer chair."

"Thanks. Let them know I'll just stay up here with Cassie until she comes around."

Cassie was on her bed when she came back to herself. She sensed someone next to her and turned her head with some reluctance. Michael sat beside her in her mother's rocker. His long legs were straight out in front of him and he rocked the chair in a short arc by alternately digging his heels into the floor and pushing back, and then relaxing again. His elbows rested easily on the chair arms and his hands were clasped loosely at his waist.

He looked at her when she moved. "How're you feeling?"

She groaned. "What have I done?"

"You didn't do much of anything, Cass. You went into a trance, or something. As we speak, Steve and Eloise are doing battle with your mother, who is convinced you need to go to the hospital. Or maybe detox. But I think Richard is on their side, so they ought to be able to convince her eventually."

Cassie closed her eyes again. She could hear their voices

from somewhere downstairs, rising and falling in uneven cadence. She felt tired and wrung-out. Everything hurt, inside and outside. Before she could stop, tears began to leak out from under her eyelids.

"It's okay, Valentine, no one got hurt."

He was being kind and rational and that made it so much worse. The tears came faster.

"Hey! Calm down, Cass." She heard him get up and in a moment he was sitting next to her on the bed.

She said his name and it was all she could manage. She sat up, moving close to put her head against him, and cried. To his credit, he put his arms around her and simply patted her back, or her hair, and let her weep. After what seemed like an embarrassingly long time, she found her sobs were slowing down.

"You want to talk about it?" he asked, and she heard his voice both out loud and through his chest, where her head now rested.

"Just don't let go," she whispered.

"No sweat."

She nestled up to him, clinging to him like he was her personal life preserver. "What did I do?" she asked.

"You talked to Steve," he said. He told her about the strange conversation, what Steve had said and how she had responded. "Do you know who–" he began and stopped.

"Who it was?" she finished. "It'd have to be Jeremy, don't you think? Jeremy is the one who's always here. He's the one I always see."

Michael was silent a moment, thinking it over. "And what does he want told?"

Cassie pulled back and looked at him. "I think he's trying to tell us that he didn't do it. He didn't kill the Norridge family."

The next second the lights flared up to a shocking brilliance and then the power cut and the entire house went dark. From downstairs they heard Eloise shriek.

The first word out of Michael's mouth was obscene. "Sorry," he muttered. "I can't see a thing. Can you?"

Cassie was already scrabbling around under the bed. "Flashlight," she explained. She found it and clicked it on. "That's better."

"A bit. Should we stay here?"

"No. Let's go back downstairs," she said decisively. "I have a feeling we need to get down there." She got off the bed, grabbing Michael's hand without even thinking about it, and they went down the stairs together.

The first floor rooms glowed softly from the candles Cassie had set out earlier. Steve looked up at their descent, coming forward to meet them and give Cassie's shoulder a little squeeze. "Okay? Both of you?"

Michael shrugged and nodded.

"A little woozy," Cassie said. "But I'll live."

There was an uncomfortable silence. Then, "Is it me or does anyone else want a Scooby snack?" That was Nick.

Michael glanced at him and they both laughed, but Eloise whacked her boyfriend in the stomach. "Stop it."

Cassie looked across the room and saw her mother staring at her, a strange expression on her face. "Mom," she started.

Her mother held her gaze a second longer, then turned away. "Well, can I get something for any of you? There's still plenty of ice in the bucket so we can at least have cold drinks." She walked briskly in the direction of the dining room, Richard following in her wake, a confused expression on his face.

Steve intercepted Cassie as she took a step forward. "Hang on, Cass," he whispered. "You guys need to talk, but I think she'll have to get there gradually."

Cassie, hurt and puzzled, looked up at him. "You think so?"

"She tends to react like that. It'll be okay. Just give her some space." He studied her, concern on his face. "Are you sure you're all right, though? Can I do anything for you, or get you anything?"

She shook her head. "No, it's okay. I'm just embarrassed, basically."

"Don't be. Gus was never embarrassed. He always just said, 'And some people snore.'" He smiled when Cassie managed a small laugh. "That's better. Something in here is trying really hard to connect with you."

"Tell him your theory, Cass," Michael said.

Steve looked at her questioningly.

"I have a feeling Jeremy Mott didn't kill the family," she said after a moment. "I think that's what he's trying to tell us. I think he wants us to know that he's innocent." As soon as she stopped speaking, the power kicked on and the house was full of light.

## ~ CHAPTER THIRTY-TWO ~

A few days after the party, Steve left Fredo in charge of the store and took Cassie on an outing, as he called it. "Det. Billings is retired and probably busier than he was when he was working, but today is a good day to see him. Are you feeling up to this?" he asked when he told her what he had in mind.

"I don't know," Cassie was honest. "I've been kind of out of it since Sunday, like I'm just getting over the flu. But it's more than that. I've been seeing things," she said quietly. "Not just in my house, but in my head, as well. I get images and quick flashes of things, so fast I can't even understand them. But I know it all relates to the murder."

"You don't have to go," Steve began.

But Cassie was adamant. "No, I think I do. I think I have to. For Jeremy."

"Well, then, you let me know if this gets to be too much, or if you need to get out of there. This is all going to be about the murder, and if it's too hard to listen to..."

"It'll be okay." Cassie smiled wanly. "I need to be there."

Retired Det. Billings was gray-haired and trim, a man who kept himself in shape and had the build to prove it. He greeted Steve at the screen door and then looked at Cassie, bemused. "More questions?" he asked as he let them into the house.

"A few things." Steve let Cassie pass ahead of him, then followed the two into the living room.

"I'm just having my second cup of coffee," Det. Billings said. "Can I get you some? Or some water or juice?"

"No, thanks," Steve said, and Cassie shook her head.

Det. Billings sat down in his easy chair and indicated the sofa for his guests. "What more can I do for you?"

Steve cleared his throat. "About the Norridge-Velasco murders," he began. "What was it that you didn't tell me?"

The older man regarded both of them for a long moment. "Before I say anything, may I inquire about the young lady?"

Cassie felt embarrassed. "I'm sorry," she said. "I should have introduced myself. I'm Cassandra Valentine. I work with Steve."

"At the bookstore?" Det. Billings raised graying eyebrows.

"She's also my goddaughter. And she's currently living in the Norridge house. She and her mother moved in last spring."

The gray eyebrows went up a degree higher. "And this concerns you?" he asked Cassie.

"It concerns her," Steve said before she could answer.

There was another long moment of silence before Det. Billings responded. "Your call," he said. "Ask away."

"What didn't you tell me about the Norridge case?" Steve asked again.

"Why do you ask that?"

Steve answered with a skeptical, "Come on."

The retired detective sighed. "Everyone liked Jeremy Mott for that murder," he said flatly. "Everyone except me, in the end."

"Why?"

"Too much wasn't answered if we pinned it on him." He sipped his coffee. "For one thing, what happened to the knife that killed Mr. Norridge? It wasn't in the dumpster like the kitchen knife was. Also, nothing in Mott's background leads up to something like this. Yeah, he was a troubled kid. Dropped out of school and ran away from some small town in downstate Illinois before winding up here.

"I went down to that little town on my own time and poked

around, after the case was closed. There were the usual stories about a troubled kid, a loner, maybe even some rumors about mental illness, but nothing about violence, and absolutely no drug abuse. From what I learned, he was the kind of kid who was more likely to get picked on and kicked around than to kill someone else, let alone an entire family." He took another sip of his coffee. "Sure I can't get you anything?"

Steve shook his head and Cassie murmured a quiet "No, thank you."

Det. Billings nodded and took a deep breath. "Then there were the drugs. We could never find anyone who sold him enough to OD on, that night. The premise was that he stole the money from the Norridges', bought drugs, and died.

"So does it mean this kid, fresh from a mass murder with blood all over him, went somewhere to buy the stuff and bring it back, still wearing his bloody clothing? And then he decided to shoot up and conveniently die in the parking lot of the grocery store where he and Mrs. Norridge both worked? What kind of sense does that make? If he were a junkie and overdosed, he would probably have done that a lot closer to where he bought the stuff.

"And if he really killed those people for the money to buy the drugs, sooner or later we would have found someone who remembered a kid covered in blood making a purchase. But we never did. I kept looking for his supplier for years after the case was closed, any time any kind of dealer got picked up, or even anyone who used. No one saw Jeremy Mott or sold him any drugs." He took a long drink from his coffee cup.

"There's more, isn't there?" Steve asked.

Det. Billings nodded. "After the case was closed and before I was officially told to leave it alone, I checked into the background of Mary Velasco, their houseguest." He looked at them with an almost predatory gleam in his eyes. "Turns out she and Jane Norridge were childhood friends. Also turns out that Mary Velasco was recently separated from one Dominick Walsh-Latham, the son of a very wealthy family from Massachusetts. I learned he was handsome, charming, rich, abusive, and possibly crazy. Mary had gone back to using her maiden name even though she was still married. Her husband was not happy about any of this, least of all her up and leaving him like that."

"So you're suggesting," Steve began after a brief pause.

"I'm not suggesting anything," the older man said. "Those are just facts I dug up. You can draw your own conclusions. But here's another fact for you. All of the victims had multiple stab wounds, as if the killer struck all of them repeatedly before they died. So how come there were no defensive wounds on anyone's hands? No one lets you use them for knife practice without fighting back."

Steve was silent, thinking about it. "So the first wound killed and the others were just inflicted to suggest an amateur?" He thought a little more. "And possibly a rich, crazy, angry man could wipe out an entire family and frame some poor throwaway kid for the murder of his own wife to make it look like a completely different kind of killing?"

Det. Billings listened, a small smirk playing around the corners of his mouth. "Too bad you weren't my partner back then."

"But you never went any further with this?"

"The case was closed. I was told to let it go. But it always kind of stuck in my craw. So tell me, why are you looking into it?"

"A few reasons." Steve was just getting started when Cassie interrupted.

"But the entire family *wasn't* killed," she said suddenly. "Right?"

Det. Billings fixed her with a cool stare. “Why do you say that?”

“I just realized that maybe it’s the only explanation for everything.” She turned to Steve. “You told me you were adopted, right? It was one of the things you and Gus had in common?”

“Yes.” Steve was puzzled.

She was still working it through. “‘Find’ and ‘tell.’ Those were the messages I kept getting. Find and tell. He meant you–” Cassie stopped abruptly, realizing that the room was going away. “Oh, no, no,” she whispered.

“What is it? Cassie? Hey, Cass?”

She heard Steve’s voice from a distance. She looked at him, was able to see the worry on his face for just a half-second, and then she disconnected from the here and now completely.

*...She was at her front porch, watching as two shadowy figures led, perhaps dragged, a third figure up to the door. “Please don’t,” the third figure said. The voice was anguished, but something in the tone also suggested resignation. “Please don’t,” he whispered again.*

*It was Jeremy Mott. Cassie watched as the two larger figures, both men, both with guns, pulled him to the house and up to the door. One of them grabbed Jeremy’s wrist hard enough to make the youth cry out and forced him to wipe his fingers on the door jamb, leaving a dark smear. Then they entered the house and all moved into the living room, Cassie included. They stood looking down at the couch. Sprawled half on it was the body of Mary Velasco, bloody and torn.*

***...I felt so bad I knew they were all dead...***

*Cassie wanted to turn away but she forced herself to look just as Jeremy was being forced to look. Again one of the men, his face in shadow, grasped Jeremy’s wrist and thrust him forward, pressing his hand into a pool of blood.*

***...there was so much blood I had to put a hand in it...***

*He cried out once more but the man took no notice. Instead he maneuvered Jeremy's hand to smear blood across his jacket.*

*Then they pulled the unwilling youth up to the second floor, their combined steps making slow, heavy footfalls on the stairs. Cassie followed them silently, first into the master bedroom where Jeremy began to sob quietly when he saw Jane Norridge. Again he was forced to dip his hand into the blood and apply it to his jacket, this time on the sleeve.*

*Still weeping, still being led unwillingly, Jeremy at last arrived at Cassie's room. The men stood him outside the door. "Open it," one of the men rasped out.*

*Jeremy didn't move, remaining at a standstill just outside the door.*

*"Open it."*

*Again Jeremy didn't move. It wasn't until one of them shoved him forcibly at the shoulder that he actually placed his hand on the knob. Still, he didn't move. The man who had pushed him opened the door. "I don't want to do this," Jeremy whispered, still balking. "Please don't make me do this," he pleaded even as he was being forced through the door.*

*Then Cassie was inside her room as it had been thirty years ago when Martin, Jr. and little Robbie slept there. There were bunk beds against one wall, both of them empty, although the bottom one was nearly covered with toys, picture books, and a large stuffed giraffe.*

*Martin, Jr. lay on the floor before the closet, his small body curled up almost into a ball, one bare foot covered with his own blood.*

*Jeremy entered the room alone.*

*"You know what to do," a voice said from the hall.*

*Jeremy looked at the small boy on the carpet. Tears spilled down his face, streaking the dirt and some of the blood that was smeared on his chin. He knelt down in front of Martin and touched the boy gently.*

*"The blood," the voice called out to him.*

*Sniffling, Jeremy put a finger in Martin's blood and wiped a little of it onto his sleeve. He looked into the closet and Cassie saw him freeze, eyes widening with wonder, and then with fear. She looked past him into the closet but could see nothing. Jeremy leaned forward a little, over the sad little body, pretending to dip his hand again into the blood, but instead he whispered, "Stay alive. Get in the back and hide. Stay alive." And he shook his head just a little.*

*"Hey!" The voice from outside the room was harsh. "What are you doing? Who you talking to?"*

*Jeremy got up immediately, wiping his hand against his jacket. "No one. I just said I was sorry." His voice broke.*

*"Yeah, yeah, let's go."*

*They grabbed him by the arms and began to pull him back down the hall, toward the stairs.*

Cassie opened her eyes and was lying on her back in a room she didn't quite recognize. She blinked, trying to get clear of the last images she had just seen, her own darkened house, Jeremy being led to his death…

"How are you?" Steve sat in a straight-backed chair beside her. Det. Billings was in his easy chair, staring at her thoughtfully.

"I'm not sure." She didn't quite know where to begin.

"You went under pretty quick," Steve said.

"I'll get you some water." Det. Billings rose and disappeared down the short hall.

"You want to tell me what happened?" Steve asked gently.

"I had a dream. Or a vision," she corrected, trying to pull it together in her head. "Jeremy didn't kill anyone. They were all dead when he got to the house. When he was brought to the house, that is."

Steve nodded. "He wanted you to know."

"There's more," Cassie said. "Robbie Norridge wasn't killed with the rest of the family."

He frowned. "But all the newspapers reported–"

"Some things were omitted." Det. Billings stood in the doorway with Cassie's glass of water. "We found Robbie Norridge hiding in the closet."

## ~ CHAPTER THIRTY-THREE ~

There was a moment of silence and Cassie realized they were both waiting for Steve to work through the man's simple statements. "Robbie Norridge wasn't killed?"

"No." The detective came back into the room and handed Cassie the water. "He was hiding in the back of the closet behind the coats and the winter clothes. We didn't know he was there until they came to take his brother's body away. Then we heard him moving around. He said that Martin told him to hide, to stay hidden until his mom came for him."

Until his mom came for him. ...*Have you seen my little boy?* Cassie thought about the pretty woman in the jogging suit, then thought about the voice that she had heard in her own room, the single word "Hide." Martin had saved his brother's life. And so had Jeremy.

"So what happened to him?" Steve asked.

"He was adopted," Cassie answered slowly. "He was adopted by one of the police officers who was there that day." She stared at him, willing him to make the connection, nodding when at last she saw comprehension beginning to cross his face.

"He *was* adopted," Det. Billings agreed, looking at her keenly. "He was never fostered out, and he never went to an orphanage. He went home with one of the officers at the scene and eventually was adopted by that officer."

"Lieutenant William Crawford?" Steve asked in a hollow voice.

"Officer, at the time," Det. Billings replied.

"Officer Crawford who changed my name from Robert

Steven Norridge to Steven Robert Crawford?"

The other man nodded.

Steve frowned. "But why wasn't that in any of the papers? Withholding that suggest—"

"Suggests that we thought the killer might still be out there and come looking for you?" Det. Billings gave him a lopsided smile. "There may have been more than one of us who thought that at first, although even if the killer was still on the loose, he didn't seem to know there were two kids in that room, or both of them would have died. The lower bunk, Robbie's, *yours*, was so covered with toys it almost looked like it was just storage space. The cops didn't know to look for another kid. The killer certainly didn't.

"Still, it did leak out that a child had been found alive in that house. The department did a song and dance about not traumatizing that child any further. Back then, the local press was more accommodating that way. We even managed to keep you out of the national news when the story was covered for a few days."

"And how was I kept out of foster care? Or an orphanage?"

"Hey, this was over thirty years ago. There was a county department that handled orphans and homeless kids, any sort of domestic or family situation, and they had a staff of two and a half people to do it all. The entire county. What happened with you when Bill Crawford took you home solved their problem for them. They were thrilled to have nothing but some paperwork to take care of."

"I had no other family, then? Grandparents? Someone out of state?"

"Guess not. The county looked, but Bill and Natalie kept you."

Steve appeared shocked. "All my parents ever told me was that my whole family died when I was young. They just told me it was very sad and that someday I would get the whole story. Eventually, I stopped asking them." He paused a moment. "But I guess I'm going to get the whole story now."

Det. Billings nodded. "It's good to know how that little boy turned out. I lost track of you when I got reassigned. Give my regards to your father when you talk to him. Arizona, isn't it?"

"Close to Tucson," Steve said. "And you better believe I'll be giving him your regards just as soon as I get home today."

"And you," Det. Billings turned to Cassie. "You're a psychic?"

Cassie, struggling to sit up, shook her head. "I wouldn't call myself that."

"Neither would your dad." He grinned at her expression. "I knew about him, even met him a couple of times. I should have known right away when I heard your name but sometimes the brain is a little slow to make the connection these days. You look like him, both of you dark as gypsies." He turned to Steve. "Bet you didn't expect all this to come from your questions, did you?"

Steve looked back at him. "You must have known my whole story the first time I met you. Why didn't you say anything?"

"You didn't come to me as a Norridge asking about your family. You came to me as a Crawford, ex-cop, asking about an old case. I figured if your dad hadn't told you the whole story, it sure wasn't my place to do it."

"I guess you're right," Steve agreed slowly. "I guess now I talk to the old man. And a few other people besides."

Cassie had people she needed to talk to herself. She filled everyone in on the story, with Steve's permission, gratified that for once her mother listened to what she had to say in complete silence. At one point, Mrs. Valentine slipped her hand, the new engagement ring glittering on her finger, into Richard's hand. "Steve was a baby in this house?" she asked. "And it was his family that was killed here?"

Cassie nodded, silent now that the story was finished.

"How awful," she murmured. "That's just dreadful."

Richard cleared his throat. "That's a very powerful story," he said. "Will it ever be written, do you think?"

"I don't know." Cassie shook her head. "I don't think any of this will ever be written unless Steve does it himself. But in the end, both he and Det. Billings reminded me that if what I've seen is correct, this is an unsolved murder and the killer is probably still out there somewhere. Mary's husband. They don't want to take any chance of the story coming out if there's a possibility this case could be officially reopened."

"Does Steve want that? To reopen the case?" her mother asked, and she looked genuinely concerned.

"He isn't sure. He's been really different at work, Mom. He's a lot quieter and a lot more serious. Sometimes I feel like I did something terrible, bringing all this back out into the open."

"It wasn't you, Cass." Richard spoke first. "You didn't kill anyone. But Steve has to readjust his whole frame of reference with what's come to light. He always knew his family had died, that he was adopted. But to find out they were all murdered and that he survived only because both his older brother and the last unfortunate victim of these evil men unwittingly conspired to hide him? To find out that a thirty-year old haunting is because of something that happened to his immediate family? That had to be some kind of shock." He shook his head. "You tell him if there's anything we can do…" He let his voice trail off and Mrs. Valentine nodded in solemn agreement. "Anything at all."

Cassie was touched and nodded back. "I'll tell him."

At work even Nick grew quieter around Steve after hearing the whole story. Fredo, family man, was furious. "His whole family?" he said. "If that murdering son of a bitch is still out there, I hope Steve and this Det. Billings find him. I'll help them. I'll nail him to the wall myself." He followed this up with a surprising string of language that left both Nick and Michael blinking.

"Fredo never talks like that," Nick said after the man had gone back to receiving.

"Yeah, well, I'll just make sure he never talks to *me* like that," said Michael. "Ever scc him work with a crowbar?"

* * *

Home life became different for Cassie. There was a change in the house that even Eloise noted. "It's quiet," she said. "I don't mean it was ever noisy, either. It just *feels* quiet. Like something was turned off or taken away." She was there more often, staying past dark, even without Nick or Michael present. Life was like it had been back in the Valentine apartment, when Eloise would spend the night and she and Cassie and Mrs. Valentine would sit for hours at the kitchen table talking, painting their nails, laughing about Nick, and now Michael and Richard as well. Just being the girls. Cassie had almost forgotten what those evenings had been like and when they started happening again she realized how much had been missing.

She and her mother finally had their heart-to-heart one night when Richard was out of town and Cassie came home from work to find Mrs. Valentine waiting for her in the kitchen. She took in the mug of coffee, the partially eaten bowl of vegetable soup and beside it, on a small plate, a buttered croissant. Her mother's comfort food. "We need to talk, don't we?" Cassie asked, and her mother nodded. Cassie sat down on a chair and waited.

"I hate this," Mrs. Valentine began without preamble. "I absolutely hate this." She held up a finger for silence when Cassie began to reply. "Let me finish. Back during the party, Steve asked me if I had never seen your father 'trance out,' as they used to call it. Disconnect. Whatever the term for it would be. The answer is yes, I did. Just once. It was enough."

She looked away for a moment, straightening out her thoughts. "When you were four years old, I came home from the hospital late one night after working second shift. Your father had already bathed you and put you to bed and he was drying the dishes when I came in. He looked tired, but happy. He always loved his time with you, Cass."

She reached across the table and tugged gently on a strand of her daughter's dark hair, and Cassie felt her eyes sting with sudden tears. "He used to call you 'Junior.' Did I ever tell you that? I didn't know that he probably meant something by it. I suppose I didn't want to know." She swallowed.

"That night after he put the dishes away, we went into the living room to catch up before going to bed. It was our little bit of time together, those late nights after you were already asleep and I had just gotten home. We would sit on the couch with just one light on, no TV, no music, and chat. That night, we only talked for a little bit before he got so quiet I thought he had gone to sleep. I looked at him and when I moved, he looked back at me.

"Cassie, whoever was with me on that couch, it wasn't your father. He patted me on the top of my head and called me 'Lorelei.' My grandfather used to do that, pat me on the head and call me by my full name. No one else ever did that. But my grandfather died when I was twelve." Her voice was growing shaky. "So there I was, totally bewildered when your father did that. And then he said, 'Be strong. You will be strong enough to do this. And you will be happy again. Don't ask yourself the questions. Do not doubt. It was meant to be this way.'

"I took your father's arm when he stopped talking and shook it, hard. He blinked a few times and then asked me what was wrong, what did I want. He said he must have dozed off. I didn't understand what had just happened. I didn't tell him anything about it. We just went to bed as always."

She swallowed again. "Three nights later we ran out of milk and I sent your father out to get more. It was raining that night." She stopped, then said in a quiet voice, "He never came home." Then she looked at Cassie with frightened, haunted eyes. "Oh, Cassie, if I had told him, maybe – Should I have told him? And why did I ask him to go out for milk that night? It was so stormy, so ugly. Why did I do that? It could have waited." She started crying quietly, her hands against her eyes in sudden anguish.

"Mom." Cassie rose and went to put her arms around her. "Why didn't you ever tell me any of this?"

"Because I thought you would blame me. Because I blame myself. Maybe if–"

"Don't do that. Remember? 'Don't ask yourself the questions. Don't doubt yourself.' They tried to tell you. Both Gus and your grandfather. They wanted you to be okay."

Her mother found a tissue and blew her nose. "It all scares me. The trances. The *seeing*. Your father was like you, just like you. He would tell me what he could see, every time we went somewhere new, whether it was someone's house, an apartment building, even a restaurant or a hotel. I would just listen and nod. I never understood it, even when Steve used to tease your dad about his 'secret weapon' on the job. But after that one night, and then after he died…" She looked at Cassie sadly. "And then you started doing it, too. I was so afraid of being alone. And when Steve started coming over that summer, with his pictures of missing children–"

"It's okay, Mom," Cassie said again. "I understand now, I really do. And it's all right."

Mrs. Valentine looked at her. "You couldn't just stop, could you?" she asked hopefully.

Cassie shook her head apologetically. "I don't think it works like that."

Her mother sighed. “And now with this house… I’ve grown so fond of it, but I understand that we should probably move, now that we know. That poor family. Poor Steve. And here we are.”

“Here we are because we’re supposed to be.” Cassie smiled. “There’s nothing to be afraid of anymore.”

After that, Mrs. Valentine began to talk about Gus openly. She gave Cassie a framed picture of the three of them, Cassie in her father’s arms, her mother hugging both of them. They were beside a lake on vacation in Wisconsin, Mrs. Valentine said, and they all looked outdoorsy and happy, laughing as the picture was taken. Mother and daughter looked at the picture together and both of them cried, but Cassie felt as if something that had been missing from inside of her was slowly being filled.

She studied the picture for hours, trying to remember Gus, and sometimes was able to get just a bit of him, the feel of his arms when he held her, the smell of him after he came home from work, took a shower, and then picked her up in a damp hug. She learned the smile lines in his face, the strong curve of his jaw, the wave in the locks of hair that forever fell across his forehead, as they did in the picture and as her mother told her they did in life.

And now when Cassie looked in the mirror, she realized how much she did take after her father and she no longer minded, as she had when she was younger, that she didn’t have her mother’s blue eyes and straight dark-blond hair. “I look like Gus,” she would whisper to herself, and the thought brought her a joy she never would have imagined.

Sometimes Cassie and Mrs. Valentine sat up into the night and talked about wedding plans for her mother and Richard, always starting with practicalities such as chapels and restaurant venues for the reception, but eventually branching out to wedding cruises and sunset ceremonies in Tahiti. They laughed a lot and Cassie thought that perhaps they had never been happier. Even on the night they talked about both Gus and Daniel in one conversation.

The house itself remained still. There were no more rustlings through the room, no more breezes, no more footsteps or shifting furniture. It seemed as if it had been vacated and there was a feeling of emptiness although everything within was still the same. Even the cold spots had faded away. Cassie appreciated the new-found peace but couldn't help feeling a sense of sadness. She wondered about Jeremy Mott, how he had come to be a lost, thrown-away kid with no one to look after him, so isolated that he would be an easy victim.

## ~ CHAPTER THIRTY-FOUR ~

"So Jeremy Mott was a sensitive?" Michael said when she told him what was on her mind. "Or psychic? Whatever you want to call it?"

They were standing on the bank of Emerson Creek, one of Cassie's favorite places to go and think and one she decided to share with Michael. The trees that lined the creek bank were past the peak of autumn color, but there were occasional yellow and scarlet leaves still clinging to the branches, bright patches of color against the bark and the remaining brown, shriveled leaves that hung lifeless from brittle stems. Michael was staring down into the murky water, sometimes kicking a small stone off the bank with the toe of his shoe.

"Doesn't that make sense?" Cassie asked. "It's why he could write all those things through me, show me things, even speak through me."

"It's like he was waiting for you. All those years, waiting for someone to learn he hadn't killed his only friends."

The breeze was chilly and Cassie shivered. "It's more like he found me. At the house, but even at Bridgeton Park Cemetery." She caught his quizzical glance. "I went to visit Daniel once. You know, before you told me about your family. I just wanted to talk to him, I guess. I don't go there very often, but that afternoon it felt right. And then—" She hesitated a moment. "And then after a while it was like I wasn't alone there, or even alone with Daniel. It was like someone else, well, had come up to us. I could feel it."

"You never told me about that," Michael said. He made it

sound like an accusation.

"There was really nothing to tell. It was just a feeling. Still, I had been working on my List when that happened. I wondered sometimes if that's why Jeremy chose to reach out to me that way. On Daniel's list."

He looked at her. "Did you ever find out? Was Jeremy Mott buried in Bridgeton Park Cemetery?"

"No. May told me that he was never claimed by his family and so he was buried in one of the potter's fields at the edge of the county. "

"So if he wasn't buried in Bridgeton Park and he found you there…"

"I know. He really was haunting me, not just the house."

She saw that Michael was thinking it over and a sudden gust of wind, coupled with her thoughts, made her shiver again. The dead leaves that spiraled past her didn't help. It wouldn't be long before the creek was silent under a layer of ice and the banks themselves were shrouded in snow. She tossed the hair out of her face and glanced up at her companion. "Ask you a question?"

He was still gazing thoughtfully down into the water, but he turned to her and shrugged. "Sure. What?"

"You know that first night you came to the bookstore? When you got stuck telling the ghost story because you were the new guy?"

He nodded.

"So why did you tell the one you did? About us?"

He stared at her a moment longer, and then his eyes slid away from hers. "No reason."

"Okay. Let's try that again. Why that story? About us?"

He looked back at her, a smirk on his face. "God, you're pushy."

She smiled at him but didn't relent. "Come on, Penfield. If

this is a need to know kind of thing, I need to know. For a while there, I thought maybe you were sending me secret messages."

He laughed. "You mean like with invisible ink or something?"

"No. Just hidden in the choice of story." She tilted her head at him. "Were you? Trying to tell me something?"

"I don't know." He thought it over for a long moment. "Maybe it was just a reaction to seeing you there. I wasn't expecting you to be at my new job. It brought back a lot of memories when I saw your face. I'd been trying to come up with some kind of ghost story after Steve told me about Thursday nights when he hired me. I had a couple in mind but when I saw you I decided to tell that story instead."

"It was a weird one," she said softly. "Didn't it bother you that I could describe a ghost that you were seeing?"

"Hell, yeah. You're pretty scary, Valentine."

"I know," she agreed quietly. "I scared myself sometimes. It's been good to find all that out about Gus. Makes me feel…" She paused. "I guess I can't say it makes me feel normal, because I'm not sure this is. But it makes me feel less alone. But what about you?"

"What about me?"

"Mr. Sees Dead People."

He shrugged again. "I don't always. And half the time I see them, I don't know they're dead until way after. So it doesn't ever really freak me out."

She thought that over for a moment. "I was right about you, back when we were kids."

"What?"

"You *are* weird."

He smiled at her and went back to studying the water.

They were both silent for a while. "How does Steve seem to you?" Cassie asked.

"Pretty much the same. Quiet. Thoughtful. He's coming around a bit, though. Nick even got him to laugh this afternoon. But I think it won't be quite right for him until he feels like he's done something about his family."

"I absolutely agree."

Michael looked at her, and the serious expression on his face caught her attention. "You know, I think Steve is going to be asking you to do a few things for him."

"Around the bookstore?"

Michael gave her a look of annoyance. "Now, what do you think?"

"Oh. You mean the little investigative process he and Det. Billings are starting? I don't know what else I can help them with, but if he asks I can't turn him down."

"I figured you would say that."

"Does it bother you? Why?"

"Cassie, that guy is probably still out there."

"Oh, and how is he going to know about me? It's not like we're putting this on the national news."

"No, but you're in the house."

"So? I'm not the last person in a family that guy tried to obliterate. I think Steve's potentially at higher risk than I am."

"Maybe."

"You know, you're really cute when you worry about me."

"Shut up." But he turned toward her and grinned when he said it and his eye crinkled into his scar and he looked at her in the way that always made her stomach drop.

* * *

Fredo ran the bookstore as much as Steve did for a time, as Det. Billings helped get as much information together as he could. The retired detective dug up his old notebooks, tracked down police officers who had worked the case, went online and looked for all the information he could find, sharing everything with Steve and Cassie.

"Turns out Ms. Velasco had filed for divorce in Massachusetts," he reported at one point. "About a week before she was killed. There were some papers still on file from back then, and it's only luck they weren't destroyed since her death made it a moot point. And I think it's possible her mother still lives out East. I'm looking into it."

"Her mother?" Cassie asked Steve when the older man had gone.

Steve nodded when he looked at her. "Her mother would be one person who'd know what kind of trouble Mary Velasco was having with her estranged husband. Maybe there's a reason she came to the Norridge house instead of going home to her mother." He looked sad as he said it.

Cassie gave his arm a quick squeeze. "If your mom and dad gave Mary Velasco a place to go when she had nowhere else, then you really are just like your parents. You'd do the same thing, wouldn't you? To help out a friend?"

"I suppose." He looked at her. "I know she didn't think she was placing her friend and the entire family at risk. Still…"

"I know." After a moment of silence, she turned to leave his office but he called her name to stop her. She looked at him. "What do you need?"

"I guess this will sound really stupid, but Cass, what was my mother like? You saw her, right? That one night?"

The question surprised Cassie, although she realized it made sense that he would ask. "She came and rang the doorbell. That was the first night I heard the entire haunting, pretty much. The front door opening and closing, those heavy steps coming up the stairs." She had goose bumps from the memory. "But right after all that, I heard Martin." She smiled at him. "I did hear your brother, Steve. Telling you to hide. He sounded like he was used to keeping you in line."

He looked wistful. "I can barely remember. I keep trying, but sometimes I think I'm just making up stuff in my own head so I can have some kind of memory."

"Your mom had your coloring," Cassie said softly. "When the porch light hit her hair, it looked like gold, just like Abby's does. She was wearing a jogging suit. And she was looking for her son." She paused a moment, remembering. "She must have been looking for you. She said her boy was about this tall–" She indicated the height with her hand the same way Jane Norridge had all those weeks ago. "–and she said he was wearing gray sweat pants, a gray sweatshirt, and Superman shoes."

A sudden light came to Steve's face. "Superman shoes," he repeated. "For just a second I remembered that. They were red and blue with a big yellow *S* over the top of the toes. I do remember those."

"She also said that her son liked to hide."

"I liked to hide?"

Cassie nodded at him. "Maybe it was her way of trying to tell me about you. Hiding saved your life, Steve."

"Martin saved my life. So did Jeremy." The bleak expression on his face turned suddenly cold. "If he's still out there, we're going to nail him."

"I bet you will," Cassie said.

## ~ CHAPTER THIRTY-FIVE ~

Store business continued as usual even as Steve and Det. Billings made their forays into an old, closed murder investigation. The holidays were approaching and Nick put turkeys and cornucopias filled with books in the windows. Eloise started turning up at the store with organic pumpkin squares. Steve stocked the break room with apple cider as well as hot chocolate. And Michael stopped Cassie one afternoon to invite her to dinner with him and his grandfather. Finally.

She rang the doorbell of the McCormick-Penfield house at six o'clock on the dot on the agreed-upon evening, and when Michael answered, thrust a huge bouquet of flowers at him.

"Thanks," Michael said, taking the florist-wrapped bundle as gingerly as several sticks of dynamite. "Uhhh–"

"It's a hostess present, silly," she said. "Or host's present, in your case. I was brought up never to go to someone's house for a sit-down meal without bringing something."

"Oh. Thanks. I guess." He still seemed completely bewildered. Then he looked at her with a pleased grin. "I cooked. Guess what's for dinner?"

"You cooked? Is it cold cereal or is it a frozen pizza?" The smug expression on his face was too much for her and she couldn't ignore the perfect set-up. She saw Grandpa Henry coming around the corner and waved at him. "Oh, wait. Let me see…" She closed her eyes and thought for a moment, putting her hand to her forehead to heighten the drama. "You made broiled marinated steak and asparagus and a fruit compote, got Grandpa Henry to do his famous twice-baked potatoes, and there's apple pie for dessert." She opened her eyes and looked at him. "Am I close?"

Michael looked as if she had struck him. "Dammit, Cassie, how did you do that?" Then he eyed her suspiciously. "Have you always been able to do that?"

She laughed, then, unable to keep up the pretense any longer. "I could never do any of that. I'm no mind reader, Michael. Grandpa Henry stopped in the store the other day and told me the menu."

Michael turned around and glared accusingly at the old man. "I thought the point of this was to get her here so we could all have some time together. If I knew you were just going to visit her at the store–"

"Now, Mikey," he said. "I had to make sure you actually invited her. I was afraid if I left everything to you I'd be meeting her after I was already in my grave. So let's just make our guest comfortable. I'll tell you what. You finish putting everything on the table, and I'll bring Cassie to the dining room and help her settle in. Now, go on, before all the food gets cold. There's a good lad." And he offered Cassie his arm and left his grandson at the front door holding a bouquet of flowers and muttering under his breath.

The meal was excellent, from the cheddar-richness of the potatoes to the tender snap of the asparagus, from the fleeting taste of summer in the fruit compote, the savory tang of the grilled steak, to the tart and sweet of the apple pie. Cassie dabbed her mouth on the paper napkin one more time and sighed. "I can't eat another bite," she said.

"Don't worry, Cassie. Nothing in this house ever goes to waste." Grandpa Henry smiled at her and then at his grandson who was on another serving of pie. "Do you drink coffee?"

"Oh, no, thank you. I am very content. But thank you."

"Well, I'll get some for myself, then. Please, just relax. I'll be back in a moment." He got up and went into the kitchen, and they could hear him pouring out the hot beverage and adding cream. He returned with a mug of coffee, the spoon sticking up over the top of it. "Now we can talk," he said.

Michael looked at Cassie and raised his eyebrows, reflecting her own curiosity. "Talk?" he echoed.

"I hear you tell ghost stories down at the bookstore on Thursday nights," Grandpa Henry said.

Cassie nodded. "Steve loves ghost stories. I don't know how long they've been doing it, but I think Nick said he can't remember a time when they didn't, and he's been there for a couple of years."

"Steve's right. Ghost stories are fascinating. And now both of you have one to share that's quite amazing."

Michael's expression was between amused and annoyed but he was silent.

Grandpa Henry looked at the two of them. "Think it's okay if I tell Dale Cotton what transpired at Cassie's house?"

Cassie nodded, but Michael said, "Only Mr. Cotton. We don't want this going all over the place in case the investigation gets reopened."

"Son, we can both keep a secret."

Michael snorted in disbelief. "If you need to tell Mr. Cotton, apparently not. By the time that crowd is done, the whole story will have spread to both coasts."

"I'm sure it will be fine." Cassie grinned at Michael.

"That's because you've never sat at a card table with that lot. Well, if it's just you and Mr. Cotton it should be okay," he said to his grandfather.

Grandpa Henry nodded. "Good."

"Speaking of which, don't you have a card game to get to?"

"I can be a little late."

"No need," Michael said cheerfully. "I can clean up."

Grandpa Henry smiled at Cassie. "The boy is not very subtle, is he?"

Cassie laughed and Michael turned slightly pink and fidgeted with his silverware.

The old man looked at his grandson and winked. "But before I go to my card game, I do have something I need to tell you. And I think it's fine that Cassie is here to listen as well." He took a sip of coffee and was silent for a moment. Then he turned to Cassie and said, "Michael has never heard this story before, either."

He cleared his throat. "One morning, I got a phone call from my daughter, Michael's mother. It was an August morning. I remember that, because it was already too blamed hot and humid and it was only going to get worse. I was working out in the garden but gave it up and came inside for some iced tea. And then the phone rang."

Cassie glanced at Michael's face and saw that he was sitting absolutely still. She looked from him to Grandpa Henry, and saw that they were staring at each other, Michael with an intensity she didn't understand, Grandpa Henry with his brows slightly raised, demanding his grandson's full attention.

"I picked up the receiver and there was my beloved Amanda on the phone. You need to know, Cassie, Amanda was a godsend to her mother and to me. We never thought we would have a child. Michael's grandmother was sickly and though we had tried for years with no success, we finally decided that given her health situation, it was for the best. So when our Amanda was born after we had given up all hope, we were both over the moon.

"And what a miracle she was to us. When she married Michael's father, a wonderful man, and then blessed us with two grandsons, we couldn't have been happier. Michael's grandmother died much too soon, but at least she died knowing her daughter had a loving and happy family of her own." He stopped for a moment.

Cassie's heart went out to him. She knew the story could only get sadder.

"Now where was I? Oh, yes. The phone rang that August morning and when I picked up the receiver, there was Amanda on the other end. I barely had a chance to greet her properly before she interrupted me. 'Dad?' she said. 'I don't have a lot of time but I need to tell you something. I need to tell you that I'm going to be sending you the most precious thing I have and I need you to take care of him for me.'

"Well, that was quite a riddle. Of course I started asking questions, but I could hear Michael's father saying that they needed to go, that Benny was calling for them. She interrupted me once more and said, 'I love you dad. Take care of him for me, okay?' And then she was gone."

There was another silence. Cassie felt Michael's hand groping for hers under the table, and she laced her fingers through his. He gripped her hand so tightly she nearly jumped, and she wiggled her fingers in protest. He loosened his grasp, but not by much.

Grandpa Henry was still staring at his grandson. "You know the rest, don't you boy?"

Michael opened his mouth, but closed it again without saying anything.

"I got the phone call from the hospital within minutes of her call, telling me that my grandson had been brought to the ER after a serious car accident and that I needed to get there as soon as possible because they were taking him into surgery immediately. When I arrived they told me about his mother, his father, and his younger brother, that they were all gone."

Michael's mouth worked several times before he found his voice. "She called you even though…" he began, and then faltered.

"She did." Grandpa Henry looked at Cassie. "We all have a ghost story, don't we?" he said. "It was high time Michael heard mine." He turned back to his grandson. "I never doubted what you told me about them all when you were in the hospital, son. Your mother loved you very much. And if anyone could find a way to take care of her child one last time, it was my Amanda."

There was silence at the table. Grandpa Henry finished his coffee and rose. Michael rose with him, cornered the table in a flash, and pulled the old man into a hug. His grandfather patted him on the back several times and then pushed him away to look up into his face. "Don't ever forget how much they loved you, boy." He smiled at Cassie and then placed his chair neatly back at the table. "And now I must go to my card game. Dale Cotton owes me some serious money."

They walked him to his car, watched him drive away, and Cassie took Michael's hand after they reentered the house and closed the door.

"Are you okay?" she asked.

He looked at her, his eyes a little too bright, and managed, "My mom…"

Cassie hugged him. "I'm so sorry, Michael."

He hugged her back. "It's okay. I'm okay. But Grandpa." He looked down at her and could only shake his head in wonder. "That sly old devil," he said. "He never once hinted. Not ever."

# ~ CHAPTER THIRTY-SIX ~

The days grew colder and shorter. Life was so routine at work and at home that Cassie could almost have forgotten about the events at her house just weeks earlier. Almost.

But there was no denying the change in Steve. He remained quieter than usual, more serious, frequently preoccupied. One late afternoon he came to Cassie. "I finally need your help," he said, no hesitation on his part. They had just closed the store and she was wiping down the coffee nook, cleaning up spilled sugar and cookie crumbs, plastic coffee stirrers and tea bag wrappers. "Would you be willing to help me?"

Michael, on his way to the break room to grab his flannel shirt, paused with his hand on the door.

Cassie nodded. "Sure, Steve. Anything I can do."

Steve looked at Michael. "You're a witness. I didn't coerce her, did I?"

"No, sir," Michael said.

"Don't be silly," Cassie said. "My mother's gotten a lot better. She'll understand, too. And if she doesn't, Richard will help explain it to her."

"Good." Steve began patting down his pockets in the familiar routine that made both Cassie and Michael grin, at last drawing a folded index card from his back pocket. "Det. Billings has gotten us a time tomorrow to go over some of the files at the police station. I know you're not scheduled to work in the morning, so can you meet me there? Just sign in at the front desk and tell them that Mark Hemmler told you to arrive at ten-thirty.

Mark is working with us on this. He pulled the file and will let us look at that, as well as a few other things he was able to get together. I wrote all the information down, though I imagine you'll remember."

Cassie took the card. "I'll be there."

Steve sighed, then leaned over and kissed the top of her head. "Thanks."

She shrugged at him and smiled gently. "Gus would have done it, too."

Michael walked her to her car and kissed her, but he was quiet and remote, and Cassie didn't push at him. She had an idea what was bothering him, but didn't want to nag.

At close to ten-thirty that night she finished brushing her teeth, switched off the bathroom light and went to her room, marveling again at how still and calm the house felt. She was just pulling up her sheets, determined to have an early night, when her cell phone chimed. It was Michael. She answered with a simple "Hey. What's up?"

"Can I come in?"

Cassie blinked. "Can you come in? Where are you?"

"On your front porch. If you were asleep, or whatever, I'm sorry. I just wanted to talk a minute."

"Sure. Hang on, I'll be right down." She threw back her sheets and pulled on a pair of sweatpants and a heavy sweatshirt, slipped into her flip-flops, and went downstairs. Her mother and Richard had gone to dinner and a movie, and she wasn't expecting them back for a while.

Michael was sitting on the porch rocker. She could see the top of his hair through the side window even when she was still on the staircase. She put the hall lights on and opened the door. "What's up? Come on in, it's fricking freezing out here."

He seemed edgy, awkward, and didn't quite look at her when he entered. She took his hand and led him into the living room, turning on the row of track lights over the book case, but leaving the rest of the room dark. He was making her nervous. "Talk to me," she said.

He looked at her then. "This thing you're doing for Steve tomorrow," he began. "Are you sure it's okay?"

"Why wouldn't it be?"

"Cassie, if they're right and this guy is still alive out there somewhere… I mean…" He couldn't finish.

"Are you still worried about this being dangerous?" She was incredulous.

And he looked embarrassed. "I know it sounds stupid. I know you think it's stupid. I just can't help thinking that you might get hurt."

She shook her head. "Michael, he doesn't even know I exist. He's never going to find out I exist. And I'm working with one cop and two ex-cops. How much safer can I get?"

He looked away from her, staring at his knees.

She tried waiting him out and realized that would go nowhere, and fast. Michael could be as unexpressive as the Rock of Gibraltar, and she knew that from past experience. Still, she had never seen him in a mood quite like this. "Hey," she said softly.

He didn't look at her.

"Hey," she said again. "Steve's like my family. How could I not do this?"

"Steve's like my family, too," he mumbled. "You all are. I wasn't expecting that when I took the job. It was just a job in a bookstore. But since I started, Steve and Fredo and Nick, even Eloise, they're all like family. And then you—" He broke off helplessly.

"That's how it is at the bookstore. You're part of it, too."

There was another silence. Then he said, "Family can be taken away." His voice was small and quiet.

And it pierced her when she finally realized what he was trying to say. She thought of the first time she had seen him at the store, the night he told their ghost story. Yes, there had been some anger, but she knew him well enough now to understand how much of that had been self-protection, reticence, even fear.

She took his hand and held it tightly. "I'm not going away, Michael. I'm not going anywhere." He looked at her then, and she could see the shadow in his eyes, of doubt, of pain. "All I'm doing tomorrow is looking at files. That's all. I'm not leaving town. I'm not meeting anyone besides Steve and Mark and Det. Billings. It's just us. That's it. That's not so scary, is it?"

"I know it shouldn't be," he said. He stared at her wordlessly for a moment. "I don't want to go back, Cass," he added, his voice trailing off into a whisper. "I was in hell, before. I don't ever want to go back."

"I know," she whispered. "Me, too." She put her arms around him then and hugged him. "So we won't let either of us go back." They held each other a long while before both of them were ready to let go. "Are we okay?" she asked at last.

He shrugged and then nodded. "Yeah. I guess." He looked at her straight on and the pull of the scar at his eye, his mouth, made him appear both somber and resigned. "I know it's what you have to do," he said. "I know Gus would have done it, too."

She smiled at him. "I'll tell you what. Why not meet me at work and walk me over to the police station? And you can meet me again when we're through. Actually, I think I'd like that."

"I can do that." He nodded. "I'll meet you there at ten-fifteen."

"Ten-fifteen it is."

She walked him to the door and he stopped just under the porch light and mouthed something at her, then disappeared into the night. *I love you.* She understood him even though he hadn't said it aloud. It was a bit of a shock. *Michael loves me*, she thought. And she was troubled by how she felt about that, by her own feelings for him.

When she got back up to her room, still thinking about what had just happened with Michael, she found that her computer had been switched on. *Déjà vu.* Cassie felt cold, a little sick, when she saw the light emanating from the monitor. Jeremy had moved on weeks ago. Hadn't he? She was afraid to approach her desk but she forced herself to walk over and take a look. On the screen she saw the final page of The List: Item 98. *He was the most beautiful guy I ever knew.* Item 99. *I will never forget him.* And then with widening eyes she saw that the last space was now filled in. Item 100. *And he will never forget you. Now get on with it, Valentine.*

* * *

The next morning was cold and bright. Cassie shivered in her jacket, the November wind slipping easily through the ends of her sleeves, finding its way through her collar. Inside, though, she was still warmed by what she had read on her computer screen the night before. There was no question of a trance: she knew she hadn't typed that herself and the thought filled her with a secret joy.

Michael waited for her at the entrance to the store in a soccer shirt and a windbreaker, unperturbed by the wind. He took her hand in silence and walked her to the steps of the municipal building where the police department took up most of the first floor and the entire basement.

"Are you sure?" he asked her again for perhaps the twentieth time. It was the only thing he had said to her during the course of their walk together.

And as she had done all nineteen times before, Cassie smiled up at him. "I'm sure, Michael. I have to do this."

"Okay." He sounded resigned. "You know you can call me if you need me. I'll just be over at the store. Fredo and Nick won't mind."

"I know."

"Okay," he said again. He turned to her and took her face very gently in his hands. "Be careful." He kissed her forehead, but before he released her she caught his hands and mouthed back to him his three-word message from the previous night. The shock of pure elation in his eyes, on his face even as he turned to leave, warmed her, warmed her the same way as Daniel's final message.

Fortified with both memories, she let herself into the police department, signed in at the front desk, told them she was looking for Det. Mark Hemmler. After waiting a few minutes, Mark came to get her. "Hey, Cassie. Come on back this way."

She followed him past the front desk, through a locked door that he opened with the swipe of a plastic card, and down a short flight of stairs. It was cold and the whole area smelled of disinfectant. "Steve's already here, but Det. Billings said he was running late and we should go ahead."

She followed him down another tiled corridor and he led her into a room with a closed door that had a window in it. "I'll be right back," he said.

"Thanks, Mark." She entered the room, trying not to feel nervous.

Steve looked up at her entrance. "Thanks," he said simply. He was sitting at a table with an assortment of folders, papers, and reports spread out in front of him.

She sat down across from him.

"You need to look at these." He offered her a handful of photographs.

Cassie took the pictures and looked at them carefully, feeling a sadness growing inside her. "Your parents," she said softly, gazing at a young couple smiling at the camera, posed in front of the church steps on their wedding day. They were squinting into the sun, and though the wedding gown and tuxedo both looked dated, there was no questioning the happiness on their young faces.

"Martin." The boy in the second picture could not have been older than seven, if that. He was freckled and green-eyed, with dark hair that fell across his brows in irregular bangs. His grin showed several gaps where some teeth were missing. She put the first two pictures aside.

"This is *her*," she said of the next one, studying a dark-haired woman, perhaps in her thirties, who had been gazing at something past the photographer when the picture was taken. Even with the makeup and fashion of yesteryear, Cassie could see that she had been a stunningly beautiful woman with mischievous lights in her dark blue eyes and a small, full mouth. She was the sort of woman that would pull attention to herself just by entering a room. And Cassie understood how a possessive, abusive husband would be loathe to let her go.

"Mary Velasco herself," Steve said.

Cassie stared at the picture a moment longer, then put it aside and looked at the last photograph that she held. It was a school picture, high school she guessed, and the boy in the picture looked tousled and serious but his expression gave no hint of the trouble that would begin in such a short time. "Jeremy Mott," she said.

"Sophomore year."

She studied the face, comparing it in her mind's eye to the scared, blood-streaked young man she had seen in her house. The thought saddened her enormously and she hoped that he had at last found some sort of peace.

There was a noise outside the door, and Mark Hemmler came in carrying a tray with cups, a coffee pot, and a Coke for

Cassie. "Never too early for caffeine," he winked.

Det. Billings entered while Mark was distributing the beverages. "I have something just for Cassie," he said mysteriously. He took off his coat and tossed it onto the back of a chair, then sat down at the table. "Steve told us about the pictures and the missing children all those years ago. See what you make of this, Ms. Valentine."

He took an envelope from his pocket and produced a picture.

"Is that–" Mark began, but the older man shushed him.

"Just let Cassie have a stab at it."

Mark leaned back in his chair and folded his arms. "You know I don't believe in any of this stuff."

"You always say that, and yet you always stay," Steve said with a small smile. "What do you think, Cass?"

She had barely been paying any attention to them. "This is Mary Velasco with her family, isn't it?" she said. She put the picture down on the table and studied it. Mary Velasco stood next to a good-looking man with dark hair parted on the side and combed back from his forehead, deep brown eyes beneath straight brows, a well-formed mouth, and a slight cleft in his chin. But there was just the hint of a cruel twist at the corner of his mouth, or so Cassie imagined. She thought about Det. Billings' and Steve's theory, that he was capable of killing an entire family and framing a defenseless, troubled boy for the murder just to get revenge on his soon-to-be ex-wife. She shuddered and looked at Mrs. Velasco, Mary's mother, instead.

Mrs. Velasco looked tired and worn in the picture, a small, bowed-shoulder woman who had once been as pretty as her daughter but now appeared simply resigned. She had looked at the camera without a smile and Cassie wondered if the whole family had always been so serious, so grave. Had Mary and her mother ever shared laughter or teasing when she, Mary, had been a girl? Did they whisper together and giggle as she had so often seen Audrey do with Emma and Abby? It seemed an impossible thought, looking at this picture.

And how had the news of her daughter's death affected her? Such a violent, bloody end to a life she had brought forth, nurtured, protected, raised. She looked so frail in the picture. Had the murder been too much for her?

But Cassie was hedging and she knew it. She took a deep breath and looked up, saw Steve's hopeful expression, saw the curiosity on Det. Billings' face, saw the studied neutrality that Mark affected, even as he sat with his arms still firmly folded across his chest. This was it.

After a moment's hesitation she traced her finger slowly down the face of the older woman in the picture. Nothing happened. For a moment she didn't understand. And then she remembered. She looked at Steve, almost shocked by what she had to say. "She's alive," she whispered.

Mark opened his mouth to say something and Steve leaned forward to take the picture, but Cassie stopped them both with one upheld hand, tracing her finger down the man's face as well. This time she knew exactly what she felt. She looked up at the three of them. "And so is he," she said.

Steve nodded as if he had been waiting for Cassie's corroboration, the hope on his face shifting to something cold and grim. He gathered them all with a glance. "So now our work can begin," he said.

* * *

# ~ABOUT THE AUTHOR~

I grew up in a haunted house on the north side of Chicago and still live in Illinois. I am fascinated by all things paranormal. I believe everyone has a ghost story so I'll listen to anyone who wants to tell me a tale. If you ever meet me, we can swap a story or two.

My website is www.opheliajulien.com. Write to me there, I'll answer!

I am on Twitter and FaceBook, and also have a weekly blog (I try!) called *Ubiquitous Ghosts* on BlogSpot.

24183074R00152

Made in the USA
Lexington, KY
09 July 2013